JARMEN'S JANE DOE

S.E. SMITH

ACKNOWLEDGMENTS

I would like to thank my husband, Steve, for believing in me and being proud enough of me to give me the courage to follow my dream. I would also like to give a special thank you to my sister and best friend, Linda, who not only encouraged me to write, but who also read the manuscript. Also, to my other friends who believe in me: Julie, Jackie, Christel, Sally, Jolanda, Lisa, Laurelle, Debbie, and Narelle. The girls that keep me going!

And a special thanks to Paul Heitsch, David Brenin, Samantha Cook, Suzanne Elise Freeman, PJ Ochlan, Vincent Fallow, L. Sophie Helbig, Allison River, Bethanne Reid, and Hope Newhouse—the outstanding voices behind my audiobooks!

– S. E. Smith

Science Fiction Romance
JARMEN'S JANE DOE: LORDS OF KASSIS BOOK 6
Copyright © 2023 by S. E. Smith
First E-Book Published April 2023
Cover Design by Melody Simmons

Summary: A genetically altered man must do the impossible to save
the human woman he loves.

ISBN: 9781959584339 (Paperback):
ISBN: 9781959584322 (eBook):

Romance (love, explicit sexual content) | Science Fiction | Paranormal
| Multicultural | Action/Adventure | Suspense | Thriller | Saga |
Destined Love

Published by Montana Publishing, LLC
& SE Smith of Florida Inc. www.sesmithfl.com

CONTENTS

SYNOPSIS

He is a monster who discovers he had a heart; she is a woman who wants to remain unknown…

Jarmen D'ju has no memories of his previous life. They were stolen in the lab that changed him into a monster. Though he was rescued, he knows he will never truly have the life he wants. As a being of half organic material and half cybernetic engineering, Jarmen will always need to hide. Finding a partner is not an option, for who could ever love a monster?

Jane Doe awakes aboard an alien spaceship with haunting memories of her former life—a life filled with tragedy that almost killed her. Rescued and protected by her new circus family, she knows she has been given a second chance at life—but chances are fleeting and happiness is nothing more than an illusion where she came from. She thinks it will be the same here until she meets an alien who is more machine than he is man.

In the most unlikely of places, Jarmen discovers he has a heart and Jane finds the only man in the galaxy who can take away her nightmares. A single moment in time changes their lives forever and forces Jarmen to make a decision that could change the history of the universe.

With the help of some unusual friends, can Jarmen defy time? Or will a cheated death refuse to be denied?

PROLOGUE

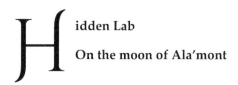

H idden Lab

On the moon of Ala'mont

"Destroy everything," General Cerberus Teivel ordered in a loud, commanding voice above the sound of laser fire and alarms.

Jarmen D'ju was conscious enough to sense the deep wave of panic sweeping through the room even before Cerberus came charging into the laboratory. The cold rage in the Draka Commander's voice jerked him out of the haze of pain clouding his mind. The Draka seldom showed emotion, but when he did, it was anger... and usually directed at Jarmen.

"What about the subjects?" a harried scientist asked.

"The General said *everything* must be destroyed. No survivors," another scientist replied in a terse voice.

Strapped to a metal frame in the center of the room, Jarmen kept his head lowered and eyes closed so the men would not notice that he was

conscious and aware of their conversation. The two subjects next to
him did not react either, but Jarmen was certain this was because they
were not conscious. They were newer units, not yet completed, and
still retained a portion of their memories and emotions, making them
unpredictable.

The distant sound of laser fire could barely be heard above the frenzied
destruction in the room. Jarmen turned his head to watch Cerberus
walk past the line of men sealed in cryo-cylinders to the emergency
control box.

The scientists called him Commander Sama'el, the Angel of Death.
Jarmen simply referred to him by his species name—Draka, adding
enough derision when he said it to make it sound like an insult. It was
a small act of defiance, but knowing that the man detested it gave him
satisfaction.

The expansive complex had been constructed where a meteor
impacted a millennium ago. The full lab and surgical center contained
a multitude of computers and medical equipment. There were
currently less than a dozen test subjects left in the complex. The failed
specimens were disposed of as quickly as possible in another section of
the lab.

Smoke filled the room as more and more equipment was hastily
destroyed. Jarmen dispassionately watched Cerberus pull open the
protective clear lid on the small metal box attached to the wall and
press the red button inside. Every cryo-cylinder began filling with a
dark red acid.

When their flesh began to dissolve, the men in the cylinders woke and
struggled against their restraints. Their organic casing disappeared,
revealing the adamantium frame beneath, which continued to move.

Their brains, semi-protected by their skulls, kept their basic systems
operational—until Cerberus shut off their access to electricity. One by
one, Jarmen documented the light fading from their eyes.

In the chaos, a lab tech ran into a nearby scientist, knocking him against Jarmen. The man recoiled from the contact, but not before Jarmen stole the key card attached to his jacket.

Connecting with the mainframe through the key card access chip, Jarmen downloaded as much information as he could before it shut down. His eyes glowed as he processed the data.

The sound of laser fire was growing closer. Scientists began rushing through the emergency exit at the far end of the room behind him.

There was no need for Jarmen to turn his head now. The room's vidcom system recorded them, which meant Jarmen saw everything that was happening on the base... including what... or he should say who... had sent everyone into a panic.

He did turn his head to monitor Cerberus as he approached with a laser short-sword in his hand. Cerberus paused in front of the unit next to Jarmen and raised the glowing sword. Both units were awake now, and they desperately struggled against their restraints.

"Please, let us go!" Unit 558 begged.

"I think not," Cerberus coolly replied.

"No!" Unit 558 screamed.

The smell of burning flesh made nearby scientists gag. One turned away with a look of horror as Unit 558's head hit the stone floor and rolled under a nearby console.

Unit 624 struggled more frantically. Guttural curses and promises of retribution filled the air.

Jarmen could have informed Unit 624 that threats, struggling, and begging would not result in a different outcome. The order was 'no survivors', none—including the scientists who thought they were escaping through the long tunnel behind him.

The other end of that tunnel had already been sealed. Once inside, the scientists would be trapped, and a series of lasers would terminate their lives. Already, he could hear panicked cries for someone to open the door at the other end.

Cerberus dispatched Unit 624 with a clean slice, severing the man's head from the rest of his body. Unit 624's head hadn't even hit the floor before Cerberus turned his pale gray eyes to sweep over Jarmen with a grim promise. He was given a brief reprieve from death, however, when Cerberus's attention was caught by the last scientist entering the tunnel. The Draka General's lips curved into a sadistic sneer as he lifted the laser pistol in his other hand and focused his attention on the control panel of the tunnel's door.

Cerberus fired a single shot, a direct hit. The tunnel's thick steel door rapidly closed. Now there was just Cerberus, Jarmen, and the invading forces remaining on the moon base.

Jarmen twisted his stolen key card between his fingers. He slid the card down until he was holding it by the edge and extended the key as far as he could. The sensor embedded in the card chimed, unlocking his wrist restraints. The faint alert was masked by the noise of the steel door closing and the sounds of battle just outside the room.

Cerberus, unaware of Jarmen's sudden freedom, faced him again. The Draka's lips curled with anticipated satisfaction.

"I'm going to enjoy killing you."

A grim contentment filtered through Jarmen. Cerberus was about to encounter the monster he had created.

The Draka swung his sword, only to freeze in shock when his assault was halted in midair. Jarmen gripped the man's wrist, the movement tearing wires out of his left arm. The sword's swing was halted inches from Jarmen's neck.

"No... you will not," Jarmen said.

Cerberus paused in surprise. The hesitation was a mistake the Draka would regret. Jarmen snapped his captor's wrist with a powerful twist of his hand. He caught the short laser sword as it fell from Cerberus's limp fingers.

"You are a monster who must be destroyed," Cerberus hissed, his face contorted with pain.

"Not by you," he stated in an unemotional voice.

Cerberus raised his pistol. Jarmen slashed the sword, slicing through the flesh and bone of Cerberus's forearm before he could fire. The Draka General's face paled until it was the same color as his ash-white dreadlocks, and he sank to his knees.

Jarmen swung the sword again, detaching Cerberus's head from his body the same way the man had dispatched the two Units next to him. Seconds later, the first of the facility raiders entered the lab.

Jarmen did not look up. His life was about to be terminated, and he accepted this outcome. Already, he could feel his body shutting down.

"Lord Jazin! There is still one alive," a man shouted.

Jarmen looked dispassionately at the cables still attached to his other arm, legs, and back. The sound of boots against the stone floor were of no interest to him.

When a pair of boots stopped in front of him, Jarmen felt faintly curious about the man who would kill him. He slowly looked up into a pair of brilliant silver eyes that conveyed horror and compassion. The horror was something Jarmen understood, but the compassion....

Jarmen offered his sword to the man.

"You may dispatch me now. I... will not resist," he said, his voice slurring on the last few words.

Jazin slowly reached out and took the sword. He then turned the sword's power off and set it aside. Jarmen frowned.

"Do you have a name?" Jazin asked.

Jarmen tilted his head. "I... call myself... Jarmen D'ju."

"The same as the Jarmen D'ju from *Tales of Two Galaxies*?"

"Yes."

"That is one of my favorite books," Jazin stated, stepping closer.

Jarmen watched in puzzlement as Jazin disconnected him. His legs gave out when the strap holding him to the metal frame was removed.

Jazin wound his arm around Jarmen and lowered him to the floor. Another man hurried over and knelt next to them.

"This is Shavic. He is a healer," Jazin explained.

Shavic did not resemble the healers Jarmen was familiar with. His hands were gentle, and his eyes were kind.

Jarmen gripped Jazin's wrist, turning his head to look at him. "It would… be best for you… to terminate me now."

Jazin smiled sadly and shook his head. "I didn't come all this way to kill you, my friend."

Confusion once again poured through Jarmen, and he frowned. Shavic murmured that it was imperative that they transport him to the warship.

Jarmen needed to shut down. His mind and body were damaged from the experiments the scientists had been conducting and he needed time to repair—but there was a question he needed answered first.

"Jarmen… was… a monster—but… your… favorite?" he asked, forcing his eyes open.

Jazin gripped his hand and shook his head. "Jarmen was a hero who saved the galaxy."

Jarmen processed this. "People feared… him," he challenged.

"Suzanne loved him," Jazin gently pointed out.

Jarmen thought about that for a moment before he pulled his gaze away and stared up at the ceiling.

"It… is a good… story," he replied before closing his eyes and shutting down.

Ten hours later he woke with the strange sensation of feeling... refreshed. He took a few seconds to assess his surroundings. The first thing he noticed was that the room was dimly lit.

There was no bright light bouncing off every surface as there had been in the lab on Ala'mont. The light here was a comfortable and faintly warm color. The walls and ceiling were a non-reflective gray.

The platform beneath him was soft. Everything felt... foreign. Curling his fingers, he assessed the material covering him. He was loosely enfolded in fabric, one flat beneath him, and one flat above him. They were not binding him. He slowly sat up, marveling that he was unrestricted.

He immediately accessed the computer system to ascertain what he was up against. The information he received was surprising. This was not a research ship. It was a warship.

Jazin was the third son of Ajaska Ja Kel Coradon. Ajaska had passed control of his House to his eldest son, Torak. Information about the House of Kassis and their position within the Alliance flowed through Jarmen's mind as fast as the computer could upload it.

He found no immediate threat. What he did find was an emotion: confusion. Why would a member of the Kassis royal family expend so many resources to free him?

The chime of the door alerted him that he was no longer alone. The healer from earlier stepped around the partition and paused, looking at him with a quiet, assessing expression. Jarmen tensed, his mind documenting every detail of the man's life contained in the ship's database. There was nothing in the man's past—at least according to the information stored in the ship's computer—to cause alarm. He studied the items the healer was holding.

"I see you are finally awake. It is good that you were able to get some rest," Shavic greeted.

Jarmen kept his eyes on the healer as he slowly approached. Shavic held out the pile of folded clothing, along with a pair of black boots. Jarmen reached out and accepted the unexpected gift.

"These are for you," the healer said.

His mind processed the information he received from the sensors embedded in his fingertips. In one hand: organic material, dye, pre-washed—the purpose of which was to make them soft.

In the other hand: supple, strong organic material that was sewn, constructed and laced—the purpose of which was protection and comfort.

He curled his fingers in the fabric. It had been a long time since he had been permitted to wear clothing. None of the Units had been allowed such a luxury. It only impeded the scientists' experiments.

"I'll wait for you in the other room while you dress. Lord Jazin would like to see you," Shavic stated.

Jarmen nodded. He heard the healer pause, and then leave, the door sliding shut behind him.

It was quiet. The absence of speaking, screaming, and beeping was disorienting. The unfamiliar silence was only highlighted by the faint hum of the ship.

He placed the clothing on the bed and carefully dressed. He took his time, enjoying the sensation of the soft material against his skin. Picking up the long-sleeve shirt, he slid his arms into the sleeves and fastened it before pulling on the black matching undergarments and trousers. The clothing was a perfect fit.

Next, he pulled on a pair of socks. He stared at his feet, wiggling his toes that were concealed under the thick, soft material. He couldn't recall the last time he had worn shoes, much less socks. He bent and slid the boots on. He rocked back and forth from heel to toe, testing the fit and comfort. It was as if the boots had been made specifically for his feet.

Straightening, he glanced around the room again. It was clearly a part of the medical wing, but there was nothing here that felt threatening. He returned his attention to the door by which Shavic had entered and exited. The faint noise of a boot heel against the floor caused him to look down. This time, the sound came from him!

He adjusted his gait and took several practice steps, walking around the room until he felt confident that he made no sound when he moved. Satisfied, he exited the room.

Shavic gave him a critical once-over, and then smiled. Jarmen did not mimic this facial expression, and the healer's smile slowly faded.

"Yes, well, let's get you to the officers' room," Shavic said.

Jarmen followed Shavic out of the medical unit. They turned left and walked along a wide, brightly lit corridor. He ignored the curious gazes of the Kassisan crewmembers as they walked.

They paused and waited for the lift. The doors opened to reveal several crew members. Their laughter faded when they saw him and their expressions became guarded. Shavic waved them out with a growl before he stepped inside and turned.

"What is he?" one of the men muttered, looking over his shoulder.

"Did you see the way his eyes glowed?" another whispered.

The closing doors cut off the rest of their comments.

"Ignore them," Shavic said.

Jarmen focused on the changing lights. They were going to Level 5 where the bridge was located. He pulled up the ship's map in his mind.

"This way," Shavic stated when the doors opened.

Jarmen was already turning to the right as Shavic spoke. Crew members stepped aside as they passed.

A scene from *Tales of Two Galaxies* flickered through his mind.

I stare into the eyes of the men and women who watch me walk by and I see the horror, fear, and pity in their eyes. I can live with the horror. I can relish their fear. It is the pity that I find abhorrent and wish I could erase from my memory....

Shavic motioned for him to enter another room. Jarmen stepped through the doorway and paused, uncertain of what was expected of him.

"Jarmen, come in."

Jazin's voice held a note of warmth. Shavic's voice could be characterized similarly, which was something Jarmen had not processed until now. The categorization of 'healer' had added a delay.

Jarmen remained where he was, wondering if this was a new test that his captors had created. He looked at the table. The aroma of food tantalized his senses. Hunger gnawed at his stomach. He placed his hand on his stomach when he felt it growl. It was—an unusual discomfort.

Jazin handed him a translucent crystal goblet filled with a golden liquid. Jarmen accepted it, and they stood staring at each other for several seconds before Jazin smiled and lifted his drink.

"A toast to freedom," Jazin said.

Jarmen mirrored Jazin's movement, and Jazin tapped their goblets gently before taking a sip and turning away. Jarmen pulled his attention from the man's back and studied his own raised glass.

The Kassisans were most famous for a specific crystal that was abundant on their planet. Many of their creations were made from it, including this goblet. The Kassisan Crystal provided not only building material but energy, and this vast resource gave the Kassisans an edge in technological advancement.

Slowly, analyzing each move, Jarmen lifted the goblet to his lips and drank the liquid it contained. Soothing heat filled his mouth and rushed down his throat to his growling stomach. A myriad of flavors washed over his enhanced taste buds. Savory bits of fruit and grain. It was Kassisan liquor, fermented and aged.

"Why are you... doing this? Why am I here?" Jarmen asked, lowering the goblet, and walking across the room to stand next to Jazin.

Jazin turned away from the view of space and gently rested his hand on Jarmen's shoulder. "Do you remember Keff?" he asked.

Jarmen nodded. "Keff saw Jarmen D'ju... as a man, not a monster. He was a friend to Jarmen in *Tales of Two Galaxies*, the only one Jarmen trusted besides Suzanne. But, your name is not Keff. You are Jazin Ja Kel Coradon, third son of Ajaska Ja Kel Coradon, and ruler of the Third House of Kassis."

Jazin laughed. "Yes, that is who I am—and I'm also your friend."

Jarmen frowned as he processed what Jazin was telling him. He looked down at the glass in his hand, then touched the clothes he was wearing before he looked back at the man who was waiting for him to respond.

"You... are my Keff," he finally replied.

Jazin nodded. "Yes... I am your Keff," he agreed.

CHAPTER 1

K assis:

Present Day

Amidst the chaos of the circus performers practicing in the big tent, Jarmen studied the petite young woman from a distance. Her straight, shoulder-length brown hair framed her face, and her honey-brown eyes twinkled with delight at the antics of her companions. She was wearing a dark blue blouse again today. He knew that dark blue was her favorite color because she wore it almost daily.

He watched the robots who were *supposed* to be gathering information for him. IQ was the irritating one. The smaller bot rolled alongside Jane. IQ could not possibly be listening to anything Jane said because he chatted nonstop. The larger robot lumbering behind the pair was called Numbnuts—or Num, in deference to the kids who were running around the tents and Jane's outrage that anyone would name the sweet robot something so offensive.

"You are talking too much," he informed IQ through the communicator.

A stunning trapeze performance by Alan and Tami Strauss caught Jane's attention just as IQ rotated on his frame to face Jarmen. IQ lifted both hands and extended his middle fingers.

The laughter from the nearly empty stands told Jarmen that the two Frenchmen, Luc and Jon Paul, had noticed the small robot's insulting gesture.

As IQ swiveled around again, Jarmen resisted the urge to reprogram the annoying bot. He had tried it once before, but Luc and Jon Paul had threatened to make his life even more miserable than they already were if he didn't change IQ back. They informed him that Jane liked IQ and Num just the way they were. Given the affectionate greetings everyone called out to the bots, it appeared everyone else in the circus did as well. Jarmen was still trying to process why.

"Hi, Jarmen," Jazin's human mate cheerfully greeted as she came to stand beside him.

Jarmen reluctantly turned to the aerial performer who was even smaller than Jane. Star and Jane were of a similar age: twenty Earth-years. He forced a smile to his lips. It was a motion that he was still working on. The amusement in Star's light blue eyes told him that she was aware smiling was not a natural gesture for him.

"Good day to you, Star," he replied.

Star's white blonde hair was a beacon among the numerous performers, even tied back in a ponytail, but Jarmen's eyes strayed back to Jane. Star Strauss lifted an eyebrow and followed his gaze. She smiled and looped her arm through his.

"You know, you can talk to Jane. She won't bite you," Star teased.

He flashed a confused look at Star before his focus invariably went back to Jane. "Why would she want to bite me?"

Star chuckled lightly. "It's a figure of speech. Why don't you talk to her? You've been following her around for months."

He stiffened. "I wish only to monitor the robots. They can be quite irritating," he replied.

She gave him a disbelieving look before she slid her arm from his and stepped away. "Well, if that is the case, I'll see if Jane can bring them over to you to assess," she said.

Before he could stop her, she walked away. For a moment, Jarmen was rooted to the spot, but then he did what any rational cybernetic man would do—he bolted.

"Somewhere in the stars, I'll follow you forever…"

Jane fought back a laugh at the bot's off-key singing. Several of her circus family members turned and grinned at the odd trio. She blushed in response, bowed her head, and silently hoped that her hair hid her rosy cheeks.

"Jane," Star called from behind her.

She stopped and waited for Star to catch up. She was finally used to her new name—Jane Doe. It was given to her months ago when she woke in a medical unit aboard a starship. She had decided to keep it.

A new name for a new world and a new me, she thought with pleasure.

"Hey," Star greeted.

Jane smiled with affection and curiosity.

"Um, Jarmen was wondering if you'd like to bring IQ and Num over to get checked out," Star said.

"More like he wants to check Jane out," IQ chortled.

Jane's cheeks heated again, and she glanced over at Jarmen—but he was no longer standing near the bleachers. She didn't see him anywhere nearby. She frowned and looked at Star.

Star sighed loudly and shook her head. "He was there a second ago," she muttered.

"He is afraid," Num calmly stated.

Jane turned and looked up at Num with wide, questioning eyes. The idea that anyone would be afraid of her was almost funny, but Num was a perceptive robot. He was smarter than everyone realized. Num was sweet and contemplative, unlike the more boisterous IQ. When combined, the two bots balanced each other perfectly, just like Jon Paul and Luc.

The two French Canadian men had become father figures to Jane, something she had never truly had before. Her life before—

Jane slammed the door on her memories. She was no longer that person. She was Jane now.

"Hey, are you okay?" Star asked.

She nodded, her throat moving up and down as she tried to force the words out. She still wasn't used to talking.

"Yes. I… have to go," she said.

Star nodded and gave a compassionate smile. "Would you like to come to dinner tonight at my parents' house? They've invited Jazin and me over and I think several others."

Jane shook her head. "No… I… no, thank you."

She smiled politely and backed up, turning away before Star could say anything else. She needed fresh air. Glancing over her shoulder, she saw that Jon Paul and Luc had risen from their seats and were following her.

She sighed with both relief and frustration. She was not alone in this new life. She had so many shadows, including—

Jarmen, she thought, rolling his name along her tongue like a candy that she wanted to savor. He haunted her dreams.

She hurried toward the exit of the big tent, pushed the heavy canvas flap aside, and stepped out into the late afternoon sunlight. There was a park nearby where a winding path followed the river. She loved going there.

"My batteries are running low," IQ informed them. "I knew I should have gone on the charger sooner last night. Well, I knew and then I forgot because I was distracted. I think maybe I need an upgrade."

"You and Num can go back to the trailer," she offered. "Jon Paul and Luc will be with me."

"Jarmen said one or both of us must be with you at all times or he will deactivate us," Num replied.

Jane stopped and placed her hand on Num's metallic arm. "He would never deactivate you," she said with confidence.

"Well, he'll reprogram us. It isn't like he hasn't done that before!" IQ moaned.

"And then he programmed you right back. He learned his lesson," she replied, trying to ease the bots' doubts. "Go on. I'll be fine. Num, perhaps you can make dinner for me while IQ charges. I won't be out long. I just want to see the sunset."

"I could use a good dose of oil, too. I think I have a squeak," IQ said.

Num briefly swept twin lasers over IQ, his eyes glowed, and he nodded.

"You have rust on your left wheel hub," Num said.

"Rust! I have rust? I'm getting old. Jarmen will decommission me if he finds out! Jon Paul will say I'm getting senile and won't let me pilot anymore," IQ wailed with dismay.

Jane knelt and cupped IQ's round head between her palms. She waited until his body stopped spinning in a circle before she spoke. IQ's eyes opened and closed in an opposing sequence.

"You are not getting old, Jon Paul loves the way you pilot, Jarmen is not going to decommission you, and you are not senile. You have the latest memory chip, remember? All you need is an update, an oil bath, and to recharge. You'll be back better than new," she promised.

IQ blinked again, this time both eyelids coming down at the same time. "Are you sure?" he asked.

"I'm positive." Jane kissed his round head before she stood up. "Num, please make sure IQ's oil is heated to the correct temperature."

Num emitted a sigh sound effect, and she couldn't help the smile that curved her lips. Num tapped IQ on the head, and Jane's expression froze.

The ting-ting of metal-on-metal sent a shiver down her spine. She wrapped her arms around her waist as the two bots changed direction and headed to their travel trailer.

The Land Yacht trailer looked nothing like it had before Num and IQ came to live with her. The contoured aluminum outer shell had been cut down the middle to make it more spacious. The ceiling had been raised a few feet to keep Num from putting a permanent dent in his head or putting a hole in the roof every time he swatted it like a fly.

Jane liked the new look of the trailer better. It was both a Frankenstein monster and a perfect jigsaw puzzle. It was home.

Once the two bots disappeared from view, she turned and followed the narrow trail that led to the Riverwalk, the main trail between the temporary Cirque de Magik village and the Crystal City. The path to the Riverwalk was empty, but the one along the river had several pedestrians out enjoying an early evening stroll.

She turned to the right and walked away from the more congested part of the trail that was closer to the Crystal City. She was soon far enough away that she had the trail to herself—besides Jon Paul and

Luc who continued to follow her at a distance, casually strolling arm in arm.

She drew solace from the quiet and the security of knowing help was near if she should need it. The only sounds were those of the river, her footsteps, and a few birds in the distance. Her surroundings could almost be somewhere on Earth, if not for the unusual flora and fauna, as well as the flying air ships crisscrossing the sky on an unseen highway.

There were so many different species and habitable worlds in the vast universe. Jane became lost in thought, remembering all that she had learned in the past few months. In many ways, she really was a new person. Her perspective was completely different, and so was her life.

Ten minutes into her walk, she looked over her shoulder to make sure her bumbling godfathers were doing okay. She stopped and turned when she realized they were no longer behind her. Worry for them made her bite her lip and ponder if she should go find them.

"I told them that I would walk with you," Walter Bailey stated in his deep voice.

Jane gasped, her hand flying to her throat in alarm, but her expression softened when she looked lower and saw the owner of Cirque de Magik, the man who had saved her life, standing before her. Walter's head barely reached her chest, but the man was as broad as the Kassis Lords, and Jane always thought of him as larger than life.

"Would you like to sit for a bit?" Walter asked.

Jane smiled and nodded. "Of course," she replied.

They walked to one of the many benches lining the path, and Walter smoothly boosted himself onto the seat next to her, his feet dangling once he was settled. They looked out over the river, the silence between them comfortable.

She didn't pull back when Walter gently held her hand. It took a few seconds before she could convince her fingers to wrap around his, but she was proud when she accomplished that difficult task.

"How are you settling in?" he asked.

Jane pulled her hand free and clasped her hands together in her lap. "We're doing fine," she replied.

"Are you sure you don't want a bigger house here? Torak said to let him know if anyone needs anything."

Walter was referring to the official leader of the Kassisan. Torak's father, Ajaska, was still alive, but Ajaska devoted a lot of time to the Alliance council, representing Kassis in galactic matters. Torak was mated to one of the circus performers, River Knight.

Jane shook her head. "We're fine," she replied.

She waited, wondering if Walter was going to tell her the real reason he was here.

"Shavic is worried about you," Walter finally stated.

Jane glanced at him in surprise before she frowned. "Why? He said I was… healed. At least, as much as he could heal me," she said, turning her focus back to the river.

"He's worried about your mental health," Walter said softly.

She lifted her chin. "I don't know why he said that or why he should be telling you or anyone else that," she retorted before she bit her lip at the sharpness in her tone.

When Walter slowly reached for her hand again, Jane flinched and stood, wrapping her arms around her waist. "We're fine…. I'm fine," she corrected.

She had gotten into the habit of saying 'we'—as in herself, IQ, and Num. It was as if they were an extension of who she was and she wasn't whole unless she included them. Breathing deeply, she tried to smile at Walter.

"I'm fine, Walter. You can tell Shavic that I am getting better mentally. It-It is just going to take a little while," she replied.

"Do you remember anything about your past?" Walter gently asked.

"No."

She shook her head, ignoring how uncomfortable it made her to lie to Walter. It felt like pressure on her chest.

"From what… what you and Shavic have told me, perhaps it is best if I don't. I like being Jane. It feels right," she said.

Walter slid off the bench, holding onto the edge to slow his descent until his feet hit the ground. He stepped close to her and didn't try to touch her this time. She kept her expression serene and returned his steady gaze.

"We just want you to be happy, honey," Walter said kindly. After a moment, he continued in a rueful voice. "I promised Nema that I would talk to you. She said if I didn't, I'd be sleeping on the couch!"

Jane smirked with suppressed mirth.

"She also wanted me to ask if you'd like to come over for dinner. She doesn't think you are eating right," he added in a gruff undertone.

Jane smiled. "Num is cooking me dinner. He would be heartbroken if I told him I didn't want it. I'll try to stop by tomorrow and spend some time with Nema."

Walter's expression relaxed and he nodded. "That would be great! I'll let her know. Ever since Ricki married that… _Ristéard_, Nema has been like a hen searching for a new chick," he said with a sigh.

Given that Ricki was the circus bookkeeper, Jane knew that Ricki was likely in contact all the time, but she understood that Ricki living away from them would be a difficult adjustment for her parents—especially when she was on a different planet, but Elpidios wasn't that far away given the speed of the spaceships available to them.

"I thought you two were going to visit her," she replied.

"We are, but not until this weekend," Walter said.

Jane nodded. "I promise to come by before you leave," she assured him, looking up at the sky. The sun was close to the horizon now.

Walter's gaze followed hers. "I'd better get back. I need to have a talk with Marvin and Martin," he said with a grimace.

Jane nodded and smiled. As Walter hurried away, her smile faded until all traces of it were gone. She watched him until she couldn't see him anymore.

When she was truly alone, a surge of fear and anguish crashed over her. She gave a tortured cry and sprinted down the path, trying to outrun the feelings that threatened to drown her.

CHAPTER 2

Moving like a ghostly apparition in the shadows of the forest, Jarmen crept closer to Walter and Jane. He stopped behind a large tree and scanned their surroundings.

Before dawn tomorrow IQ was going to have a new powerpack installed and whatever other servicing he needed to be fully optimized. Jarmen would not risk either robot failing and leaving Jane undefended.

His fingers tightened in the wood of the tree, digging through the rough bark when he heard Walter ask Jane how she was adjusting.

He had already accessed Jane's records. After his first glimpse of her, he had felt intensely... worried. He felt compelled to protect her. His chest tightened in an unfamiliar way, and he analyzed his strange reaction.

Fear. He recognized the unpleasant emotion, and also that it resulted from his concern for Jane.

This section of the riverside path was clear of threats to her. He was about to scout ahead when he realized that Walter was leaving.

He waited for Jon Paul and Luc to resume their protective duty, but before they could, Jane's distraught cry tore through him.

The sound of her distress triggered Jarmen's defense mode, and he dropped his hand to the laser pistol strapped to his thigh. He searched the surrounding area again. The scan showed no threats, but Jane sprinted down the path, her scent conveying fear.

Jarmen left the concealment of the trees. Realizing that Jon Paul and Luc would not be able to keep up with her, he did the only thing a man could do for the woman he loved. He ran after her.

~

Jane stood on a crystal bridge, facing away from him. Her shoulders were shaking, and she lifted a hand to her face.

"I know you are there," she said, not turning around.

Jarmen paused at the foot of the bridge and swallowed. In all the months that he had been following her, this was the first time that she had spoken to him. He… did not know what to say.

"Do you need assistance?" he finally asked.

She gave a strangled laugh and shook her head before she sighed. The sounds would have been lost beneath the noise of the water rushing under the bridge if it had been a human standing with her, but Jarmen's hearing had been enhanced by his tormentors.

"No… I don't need assistance… at least not in the way you mean," she said.

Jarmen stood motionless, undecided about what he should do next. He wanted to make sure that she was safe. At the same time, he did not want to frighten her. The decision was taken out of his hands when she turned to face him.

"Will— Would you…?" She beckoned to him.

Jarmen bowed his head and stepped onto the bridge. He approached her slowly, trying to copy Jazin's mannerisms. He stopped several feet from her.

"Thank you for your help with IQ and Num. The maintenance to keep them working well, it... means a lot to me," she said, not looking directly at him.

"I could make IQ less irritating," he offered.

She looked up with a startled expression. "NO! I mean, no, no, you don't have to change him. I like him just the way he is," she assured him.

He frowned. "Jon Paul and Luc said you did. I can't imagine why. IQ talks too much."

Jane's soft laugh caused a strange reaction in his body. He analyzed his reaction and decided he liked it. The corners of his mouth lifted into an uncharacteristic smile.

"You have a nice smile," she said before she turned away from him.

He stepped closer and studied her averted face. "Your face is warmer. You are hot?"

Jane giggled, lifted a hand to her rosy cheeks, and shook her head. "No."

He frowned. She was smiling, so he did not think she was ill. He decided to refrain from inquiring further. If she wished to tell him, she would have done so.

He stayed by her side, resting his hands on the railing of the bridge, and studied the surrounding area. Staring down at the water, he noted that the crystals scattered amongst the rocks gave the water a faint purplish tint. The crystal bridge glowed with a soft blue, releasing some of the energy it had absorbed during the day. The trees surrounding the water were old and graceful, their leaves a wide range of size in shades of green, reds, orange, and yellows.

"It is peaceful here," he observed.

"Yes," she replied.

"It is not unlike my home. At least where I live now."

She peered at him under her eyelashes. "Jon Paul and Luc said you don't live on Kassis."

"They talk too much—like IQ. I can't reprogram them," he said.

"Jon Paul and Luc are like—"

He frowned when she stopped in mid-sentence. "They are like?"

She shook her head and didn't answer him. Frustration burned inside him. There was so much that he didn't know about her. The only information he had was what he downloaded from her medical records, what he had observed, and the little information that the two Frenchman and the robots would relay. There were gaping holes he could not fill.

"You were gravely injured when you were brought aboard Manota Ja Kel Coradon's warship. Your medical records state the cause is unknown. Will you tell me what happened?"

She stiffened beside him. He noticed her hands clenching the rail before she tucked them in the pockets of her coat. Her expression did not convey distress anymore, but her elevated blood pressure and increased heartbeat indicated that she still felt it.

"I don't remember," she stated, turning, and walking away from him.

He followed her as she exited the bridge the way she had come. They walked in silence. He wondered if he should apologize.

"I—" they said at the same time.

"You speak first," he quietly requested.

She stopped and faced him. "How did you know about my injuries?"

"I accessed the medical records server," he answered with an inquisitive tilt to his head.

Her expression was incredulous for a moment before it softened. She shook her head. "That is wrong. It's supposed to be confidential."

"I did not share it with anyone else," he promised.

She gave a small laugh and shook her head again. "'Confidential' in this context is supposed to mean that only the doctor and the patient know. You should not be accessing information that has nothing to do with you."

Jarmen was perplexed. "But… it does have something to do with me," he said.

"How would my medical records have anything to do with you?" she asked with exasperation.

His expression cleared. This was a question that he knew the answer to. He smiled. "Because I—"

"Jane, *ma chère fille!* There you are! We were worried about you," Luc called out from down the path.

Jane watched with dismay as Jarmen murmured his goodbye and disappeared into the woods. Her eyes followed his departure with longing. She reluctantly faced her adopted godfathers with a sigh of resignation.

So much for watching the sunset in peace—or with Jarmen, she thought.

"Jon Paul and I feared the worst!" Luc breathlessly explained.

"I told you she would be fine," Jon Paul said.

Luc scowled at his husband and wagged a finger at him. "No, you did not. You wanted to go back for a search party," he scoffed.

"I did not! I said it was getting dark and that we may need help if we could not find her."

Jane interrupted their argument by touching their arms. The relieved expressions on their faces made it impossible for her to be upset. They cared enough to be relieved that she was safe, and that was a gift to be treasured.

"I'm fine, really, I am. I think I can handle going for a walk without being chaperoned," she gently insisted.

They shook their heads. "No, no, no. Have you seen the men here? They collect…. Their houses…. The things we've heard would make a Frenchman blush," Jon Paul said.

"We know because *we* are Frenchmen!" Luc added.

Jane bit her lip to keep from laughing. "I think I already figured that out, Luc," she replied.

Jon Paul lightly tapped Luc on the arm and shook his head. "She is not an idiot. She can tell we are Frenchmen," he growled.

Jane sighed when the two men began arguing in French. She started walking home. It didn't take long for them to finish their argument, make up, and catch up with her. The walk back was quieter, punctuated only by the gossip the men shared.

She veered through the ensemble of travel trailers that many of the circus performers kept as their homes after coming to Kassis. Their evening rituals were soothing, and once again she marveled that she had been found by Walter and Nema and given safe harbor with their large, unusual family.

"Jane, before you go, Luc and I would like to talk to you about something," Jon Paul said.

She slowed near the front steps of her trailer and faced the two men. Luc was looking at her with an expectant, hopeful expression. Jon Paul was slightly uneasy.

"Jon Paul pulled the short straw," Luc added.

"Are you going away again? Do you need IQ and Num to go with you?" she asked.

"No, no, we are not going anywhere. This is more personal. This is about Jarmen, *ma chérie*," Jon Paul said, gently grasping her hands.

"Jarmen?" she repeated, confused.

"He cares for you, Jane," Luc said in a rush before Jon Paul could.

"He— Well, I know he…. Oh…. You mean he….?" She looked back and forth between the two men with wide eyes.

Luc was vigorously nodding while Jon Paul looked at her with a softer expression.

"Jarmen is taking forever to tell you, so we thought we would help him," Jon Paul said.

"Something tells me he wouldn't be happy with you telling me this," she lightly responded.

Luc waved her comment away with a dismissive hand. "Of course he would not be happy, eh. He is never happy unless he is with you! Jon Paul and I have been coaching him on the ways of love, but the man thinks too much with his head instead of his heart," he scoffed, patting his hand over his heart as he spoke.

Jon Paul frowned at his partner. "Of course he thinks with his head. That is what he is supposed to do. We are trying to get him to *act* with his heart, Luc. This is why the poor man is confused!"

"I have to go," Jane hastily interrupted. "I'll think about what you've said."

She opened the door and disappeared inside, shutting out the sound of the two men arguing again. She stood in the doorway, her hand pressed against her pounding heart and a silly grin on her face. Across from her, Num turned and tilted his head.

"You had a good walk tonight, Jane?" he inquired.

Jane looked back at her metal housemate and nodded. "Yes, I did, Num," she murmured.

Num gave her a brief nod of satisfaction. "Good. Perhaps you would like to share it with me while you eat," he said.

Jane nodded and sat down on the bench seat of the table. Num retrieved the plate of mixed vegetables and pasta from the replicator and placed it in front of her. He wiped his hands on his apron, sat down on the re-enforced bench seat across from her, and folded his large metal hands.

"Num, what do you know about Jarmen?" she asked, leaning forward.

Num's eyes glowed with delight. "I thought you would never ask, Jane," he said.

CHAPTER 3

J ane sat on the end of her bed and slowly brushed her hair. Her
mind was swirling with thoughts of Jarmen. Lowering her brush
to the bed, she studied her hand. She flexed her fingers, remembering the pain from before.

He understands what the pain feels like, she thought, turning her hand
back and forth and curling her fingers.

Her abuse hadn't come from strangers. It came from someone who was
supposed to protect her. She rose to her feet, using the movement to
push the memories away.

Knowing that she wouldn't be able to sleep, she quietly changed
clothes and slipped out of her bedroom. Num and IQ were in their
'bedrooms'—not rooms at all, but two distinct sides of a former
wardrobe where they had installed their charging ports and decorated
each compartment with personal trinkets.

Their eyes were closed. A thin line of red lights running along their
chests showed that they would be in charge-mode for another couple
of hours.

She tiptoed past them, thankful that she no longer had to stop and step over the thin beam of light that triggered their internal alarm. She had finally convinced the two bots that the beam was a bad idea because every time she got up to get a drink she would trigger it.

She pulled her sweater off the nearby hook and unlocked the door. The click made her wince and she glanced over her shoulder to make sure that it hadn't alerted the bots. With a sigh of relief, she quietly exited the trailer, leaving the door partially ajar.

Jane breathed deeply and looked up at the stars. It was a magnificent view. Unlike back home, there was very little light pollution here. She stepped away from the trailer, turning in a circle as she continued to stare upward.

"Careful," said a deep voice from the shadows.

She whirled with a squeak of alarm. Her hand flew to her mouth to stifle the cry while her other hand flew to her wildly beating heart. Jarmen stepped closer.

"You would have tripped," he said, waving a hand toward the ground.

Jane followed the movement of his hand and grimaced. She had forgotten about the potted plants that she had set outside to get some sun. She lowered her hands and pulled the front of her sweater closed.

"Thank you," she murmured.

"I did not want you to get hurt," he explained.

She smiled and nodded. "What are you doing here?" she asked.

His expression was so fleeting that it was difficult to tell what it had expressed. Most people, she could tell what they were thinking by the look in their eyes. His eyes were different, though. While they were brown like hers, there was a ring around his pupils that glowed with a faint red light that reminded her of Num and IQ.

Jarmen lowered his eyelids and turned partially away from her. She reached out, afraid he would disappear again. For once, she didn't want to be alone.

"Please… don't go," she said in a soft voice.

He looked at her and nodded. "Would you… like to go for a walk?" he asked.

Warmth filled her, and she eagerly nodded. "Yes, I would like that very much."

Neither one of them were aware that they were being observed by not just one set of prying eyes, but three as they walked into the dark distance and disappeared. Luc placed his warm hand on Jon Paul's shoulder and sighed. Jon Paul covered Luc's hand with his own.

"Do you think he will kill us when he finds out that we told her even after he told us not to?" Jon Paul asked.

"He will want to, but he won't," Luc said with a confident grin.

"How can you know?" Jon Paul asked.

"Because he has a heart now, and Jane loves us." Luc smiled.

Jon Paul chuckled softly and rose to his feet when Luc pulled on his hand. "You are a devious matchmaker, *mon amour*," he said, kissing Luc.

"Who everyone but you underestimates, eh?" Luc replied, wrapping his arm around Jon Paul's waist. "Something tells me that life is about to get very interesting."

Jarmen walked beside Jane in silence. He was mentally running through the courting tutorials that Luc and Jon Paul had given him. He also pulled up the additional information he had collected through observation. Human rituals were not documented in any database that he could access, but he'd had some time with the Cirque de Magik humans. The information was disorganized and cluttered with unfamiliar phrases and strange customs that he didn't yet understand. Emotions, he was discovering, were complicated and messy.

They walked through the Cirque de Magik housing complex. Many of the residents had retired for the night, but there were still a few who had their lights on. The complex sat on one-hundred acres of land outside the Crystal City, and it was next to the palace grounds. A tributary of the main river flowed through the center of the complex and continued before emptying into the Ja Kel Coradon river.

They followed the path until they reached the Riverwalk, the trail they had been on earlier. Two moons cast shadows on the path, and the Spaceport glowed brightly above the planet.

A small catch in Jane's breathing caused him to search for what had alarmed her in the sky. She placed her hand on his arm.

"Look! It is so beautiful," she breathed.

The aurora borealis filled the sky with dancing lights of green and silver. He had never really looked at it before with appreciation.

"The lights are caused by solar storms on our star's surface," he explained. "They release huge clouds of electrically charged particles—"

Jane gently placed her fingers against his lips. He pulled his focus on the sky to her face. She had a small smile on her lips.

"It's made of magic," she said.

She leaned toward him. Jarmen stiffened but didn't pull away. Their eyes remained locked on each other as she kissed him.

The first touch of their lips sent a shock of awareness through his body. The analytical part of his brain collected data, permanently preserving this memory, while the organic part of his brain wanted to lose himself in the moment.

He was conscious of her hands sliding up his arms to his shoulders. She trembled and swayed, so he wound his arms around her waist to steady her. Her fingers threaded through his dark brown hair.

His lips parted under the pressure of hers, and as pure pleasure coursed through him, his body relaxed—at least, most of it did. One part of his body was growing very hard, very quickly.

Breaking their kiss, he took a deep breath.

"Jane...."

Even with a wealth of information available in his working memory, he couldn't find the correct words to articulate what he wanted to say.

She pressed her fingers against his lips again and smiled. "Let's walk," she said, pulling out of his arms.

He resisted—or at least his arms did—before he forced his body to listen. He dropped his arms, and he had moved his foot to step back when she entwined her fingers with his, keeping him close to her. They turned and began walking again.

"You asked me earlier if I remembered what happened to me," she said.

He nodded and glanced at her. "You said that you do not remember. That is not uncommon after a traumatic injury," he replied.

She drew in a deep breath and released it. "I lied," she said in a barely audible voice.

He paused, and she released his hand. He studied her as she continued walking. She had wrapped her arms around her waist again. He realized that she did that when she was feeling vulnerable. He strode forward, catching up with her.

"Why did you lie?" he asked.

She released a strained laugh and lifted her hand to brush her cheek. The moonlight turned her tears silvery white. His fingers twitched as he resisted the urge to stop her so that he could wipe them away. He remembered Jon Paul's words, and he was determined to follow his advice.

If she starts to tell you about herself, let her. You can comfort her afterwards, but let her share her pain with you. Only then can she heal.

Her voice trembled when she replied, "Because… lying meant I didn't have to admit it was real."

She wiped her cheek again. "I want to tell you. Out of everyone here— out of everyone in the universe—I think you might understand."

He held out his hand. Her breath shuddered as she reached out and took it. Their pace slowed as she began speaking.

"I should have been taken away from him—my father. He should never have been allowed near children. I barely remember my mother. He said that she left when I was four. I don't think she did."

"What do you think happened to her?" Jarmen asked.

Jane stared straight ahead. "I think he killed her. I remember them fighting. I remember the yelling and the screaming. Then… I remember the silence. Our house was never quiet, but it was after that night. My da—"

She shook her head.

"He came into my room that night, and we left. I remember flames. It turned the sky yellow and orange," she whispered.

"After that, it seemed like there were endless days and nights in a truck. There were breaks where we lived in a building, but it wasn't a new home. Sometimes we would stay in one place for a few weeks, other times a few months, but we always returned to the truck—until the last place."

Jarmen silently listened and hoped that holding his hand gave her some measure of comfort.

"He refused to let me go to school. We were never in any one place long enough for anyone to care. It was as if I had died that night with my mother. I no longer existed to the world. No one noticed the girl in the dirty dress with a black eye and a busted lip. They looked the other way," she said, a hint of fury beneath her words.

"There was no trip to the hospital when he broke my arm for some minor misdeed that I don't even remember now. No one heard my cries when he broke my fingers after he found out I had stolen some books from the library. He didn't mess with my face as much after we were in town and some little old lady asked me how I got the big bruise on my face," she said, lifting her hand to touch her cheek.

"You could not leave? Was there no one to help you?" he asked.

She shook her head. "No one that I trusted. *He* made sure of that. He swore that he would never let me go. That if I tried, I would regret it and so would anyone who tried to help me," she said in a wobbly voice.

"But you did escape. Walter and Nema—"

"…. Saved my life. He was working odd shifts. I was on my way to the store when I saw the Cirque de Magik drive by and set up near where we were staying. I had never seen anything so magical in my life. They were going to be there for five wondrous days and nights.

"I took advantage of every single minute I could, sneaking in between the travel trailers to watch the shows. For one week I wanted to dream of the impossible, and I did, until…."

She bit her lip and bowed her head.

"… Until he caught me. He came home early. He was fired for roughing up the boss's son at a construction site. I had stayed too long, but I didn't want to leave."

She stopped and looked up at the sky again. When she began to shake, Jarmen wrapped his arms around her. She stiffened at first before relaxing.

"He accused me of sneaking out to see someone. It didn't matter what I said. His fists… I tried to escape but I couldn't. He kept calling me by my mother's name, said that he had warned me of what would happen if I ever tried to leave him," she said with a shuddering breath.

Rage surged through Jarmen. He wished that he could face this man.

"How did you get away?" he asked, making sure he kept his voice calm and soothing.

"He passed out, drunk. I guess he thought I wouldn't be able to get up. I knew that if I didn't, he would kill me. I don't know why I went back to the circus. I knew he would come looking for me there. I was drawn by the lights, by the laughter, and most of all by fam-families who loved each other."

She looked up at him with dark, haunted eyes.

"I wanted to touch the magic one last time before I died."

Jarmen caressed her cheek. "I will never let another hurt you again," he vowed.

The trust in Jane's eyes as she looked into his sealed the pact, and she met his lips in a tender kiss filled with hope and longing.

CHAPTER 4

Early the next evening, Jarmen's expression was mutinous as he studied the heinous blue sequined jacket that Luc was holding up. It had blue rhinestones down the front of it that shimmered in the light. Wherever Luc had found the jacket, he could return it.

"I am *not* wearing that," Jarmen said, his jaw hurting from clenching it.

"What is wrong with it, eh? All women love shiny things," Luc argued.

"Let him wear his boring brown jacket, Luc. Jane doesn't want flashy," Jon Paul grunted with a dismissive hand.

Jarmen tilted his head. "How do you know that Jane doesn't want flashy? Luc said all women like flashy."

Jon Paul shrugged. "If you want to be plain Jarmen, then you will be plain, *boring* Jarmen. I'm sure that Jane will see you for who you are and love you anyway," he said in a reassuring tone.

Jarmen's eyes narrowed as he studied the two men staring back at him with expectant expressions. With a growl, he took the coat Luc was still holding out and slid it on. It was tight in the shoulders, but he ignored the discomfort. Straightening it, he glared at the two men once more before exiting down the ramp of his ship.

He was thankful it was dark. The jacket reminded him of the clothing that Marcus the Magnificent or worse—Walter—often wore. Striding over to the air bike, he mounted it and sped away from the royal airbase.

He preferred to stay in his sleek starship rather than at the palace. After his years of imprisonment, he valued his peace and solitude— well, as much as he could get when Jon Paul, Luc, and the two robots weren't driving him crazy. For some reason, they believed he needed them.

Tonight, he had a date with Jane. He had been busy working all day with Jazin and Manota. Fortunately for him, he could process many levels of information simultaneously, much of which had been analyzing the resources he would need to hunt down Jane's father and extract retribution for his crimes.

He had the location of Jane's planet, her last known location, and the date of the Cirque de Magik's departure from Earth. What he didn't have was a name or description of Jane's father. Jane had refused to share either.

He wove through traffic on his way to the Cirque de Magik village. He generally avoided the larger population when he could. Vehicles traveled both along the ground and flew above in designated lanes illuminated by thin laser lines. Pedestrians filled the sidewalks.

He passed the entrance to the palace and the guards standing at attention. After Grif Tai Tek had attacked the royal family through a traitorous council member, and a rebel group of Tearnats, and Crutheran assassins, security had been enhanced. There was still concern that not all the traitors had been ferreted out. The recent arrival of additional humans also justified more protective measures than there were before.

Jarmen followed the road along the river and then turned right onto a long winding road. He slowed to a stop when he reached the gated entrance of the Cirque de Magik village. The guard who came to the security window did a double-take before motioning for Jarmen to continue. As Jarmen passed, he overheard the guard asking, "Did you see what he was wearing?"

The second guard's response was lost as he sped up. Doubt was beginning to build about Luc and Jon Paul's knowledge of clothing customs. As he pulled up in front of Jane's travel trailer, he wondered what other misinformation the two men may have given him.

"Hi, Jarmen! What a fantastic jacket!" Suzy called as she and her husband, Curly, walked by.

"That looks like one of Marcus's old coats," Curly said with a grin before he grunted.

Jarmen wasn't sure if Suzy meant to elbow her mate, but his gaze followed them suspiciously as they continued their stroll. When they were out of sight, he walked over to the travel trailer and knocked. Stepping back, he rolled his shoulders, wishing the jacket had been a touch larger. The door swung open.

"Whoa! It looks like someone went dumpster-diving at the local thrift store and found the rejects," IQ said in a loud, drawling voice.

Jarmen scowled at the little bot and resisted the urge to short-circuit him.

"Jane, Lover-Boy is here! Wait until you see him! You're gonna need to dig out your sunglasses for what he's got on," IQ continued.

Jarmen raised his lip in a silent snarl when Num stuck his head out the door. "Luc and Jon Paul helped you, didn't they?" Num politely inquired.

"Yes," he replied in a tight voice.

He was in the process of removing the too-small jacket when Jane appeared in the doorway behind IQ. She shooed the two bots back so she could exit. He grunted with irritation when his arms caught in the sleeves. With a jerk, the fabric ripped down the middle, leaving him with the bunched-up material dangling from each arm.

Jane's stifled giggle made heat rise in his cheeks. He yanked on the material, feeling the sequins catch on his shirt-sleeve.

Tonight was a mistake. He should never have come.

"Here, let me help you," Jane said, gently untangling the rolled material so she could pull it off.

"I should never have listened to those two. They know nothing of dating or courting or whatever it is called," he muttered.

She giggled, knowing exactly who he was talking about. He stared, horrified, at the glittering pile of ruined fabric hanging from her hands. It was even worse than he remembered.

Jane's giggle turned to laughter. Jarmen relaxed at the sight of her glowing cheeks, the mirth in her eyes, and the sheer happiness in her demeanor. A strange wave of emotion filled him, and he found his body reacting to it. The low rumble from within him took him by surprise, and he realized that he was laughing!

"Their hearts are-are in the ri-right place," she said between breathless gasps of delight.

He ruefully took the damaged jacket from her and tossed the pieces onto a patio chair. Stepping forward, he cupped her cheeks, and kissed her. There was no logic involved, just a strong impulse to feel her lips against his. She wound her arms around his neck, and their kiss became more heated.

From within the trailer, they heard IQ say, "Well, I'll be damned. Those two loco Frenchmen's dress-up plan actually worked!"

"Mind your manners, IQ. They are kissing," Num admonished.

Jane giggled and pulled away to bury her face against Jarmen's chest. She bit her lip as she peered up at him with eyes filled with mirth. Jarmen decided he would wear whatever heinous outfit Jon Paul and Luc gave him if this was the result.

"Hi," she shyly greeted.

"Hello," he replied before he reluctantly released her. "Are you ready for our evening?"

Jane nodded. "I just need to get my purse," she said.

Jane felt as if she was floating on air as she hurried back into the travel trailer. She smiled at Num when he held out the small pocketbook she liked to carry. Nema had given it to her. It was the first one she had ever owned and she prized the colorful patterns stitched into the fabric. She didn't carry much in it: a comb for her hair, a barrette, a hairband, some lip gloss, and the crystal card Ricki had given her. People here didn't use dollars the way they did back home. They used credits.

Walter had given her a job as a courier for the circus. She ran errands, delivered messages, and basically helped in any way that she could. She had no idea how many credits she had—or even earned.

"Now, you two behave yourself while I'm gone," she said, pointing a finger at IQ.

"Why do you always look at me when you say that? I've been good!"

Jane laughed and kissed the top of IQ's head. "Yes, you have, but sometimes you let your battery run down too low. I don't want you getting stranded."

"No worries, mate," IQ retorted in an Aussie impression. "We're watching Dundee tonight, aren't we, mate?"

Num nodded. "I downloaded a movie from Stan's collection," he said in a low, rumbling voice.

"Well, you two have fun," she replied, trying not to laugh as IQ wiggled onto the couch and turned on the TV with glee while Num delicately settled his giant frame on a cushion.

"Don't forget to be home by midnight!" IQ hollered. "Jarmen turns into a pumpkin if you don't!"

Jane shook her head and exited the trailer. Jarmen held his hand out to her, and she smiled as she placed her hand in his. There was a dark red glow around his pupils tonight.

She was learning his tells. Light red meant he was interacting normally with people. Medium red meant he was processing information. Dark red meant he was feeling a deeper emotion, like anger… or passion.

"Where are we going?" she asked.

"I am taking you to dinner," he replied, guiding her to his air bike with his hand on her lower back.

She paused, glad that she was wearing a pair of jeans, soft ankle boots, a silky white camisole, and a royal blue jacket—sans rhinestones. She held Jarmen's hand as he helped her onto the air bike. He climbed on and she wound her arms around his waist.

"Is this alright?" she asked.

He pressed his hand over hers and nodded. "Hold on tight."

She grinned and wondered if he said that because he wanted to make sure she wouldn't fall off the air bike or because he wanted to feel her arms squeezing him. She hoped it was the latter. Scooting forward a bit more, she pressed her chest to his back, her thighs to his, and held him very tight.

"I… like your grip," he stated.

"Good, because I enjoy holding you," she replied.

Exhilaration filled her when the big bike lifted off the ground. She tightened her arms even more when the bike continued to gain altitude. She didn't realize the bike could go so far off the ground.

"This is… is amazing!" she laughed.

"There is more," he promised.

Jane's breath caught as they soared over the treetops. They flew over the complex, passing by the big top that was erected in the center of the compound. Sydney and Myrtle, along with their newborn calf, lifted their trunks as if to wave. Jane was tempted to wave back at Tony's elephants, but was afraid to loosen her hold.

She rested her cheek against Jarmen's back, marveling that she was here on this wonderful, alien world, holding a man who was unlike any man she had ever seen. Joy, hope, and a strangely breathless feeling filled her until she thought she would burst. She wanted to release all her pent-up emotion in a shout to the world.

"There's the Crystal City," he pointed out.

"Everything seems to have a slight glow, so they don't need street-lights," she observed.

"Yes. The crystal gathers energy from the sun, wind, pressure, and movement," he explained.

She peered down below them. The sidewalks were teeming with pedestrians, backlit by the light blue sheen of the street and sidewalk. Her lips parted in wonder as she saw the colorfully dressed women and tall, dark-haired men out for the evening.

A vehicle that looked like a rectangular box with no roof passed them. The driver looked at her with an assessing expression before his lips curved, his eyes conveying appreciation for her appearance. She tightened her arms instinctively and pressed harder against Jarmen, lowering her chin against his back. He sensed her unease and turned to stare at the man.

The man jerked the wheel and slowed.

She pressed her face against Jarmen's back and nuzzled between his shoulders to show him her gratitude. He left the lane and headed south, descending as they went until they were on a winding road that led to the top of the mountain. She could see the silhouette of a dome at the top.

"Where are we going?" she asked.

"It is a surprise. Luc and Jon Paul said women like surprises," he said.

She smiled against his back and wondered if he could feel it. She wanted to tell him that the biggest surprise for her was that he wanted to be with her at all—plain, boring Jane! He was like a mythical god with his strength, smarts, and glowing eyes. He made her feel as if he could see beneath the scared woman to the person she wanted to be.

He made her dream of things she never thought would be possible. His kisses were… well, they made her want to know what other kinds of feelings he could ignite in her. She didn't bother hiding the silly grin on her face as he pulled up in front of the dome.

He dismounted the air bike and turned to help her dismount. Her lips parted when he lifted her up, taking her full weight with just his hands holding her waist. She held onto his shoulders, staring down at him with an astonished expression. She knew he was strong, but not this strong!

He brought her closer to his body, and she slid down his chest until her feet lightly touched the ground. He wasn't as tall as Jazin and the other Kassisans. In fact, he wasn't much taller than Stan and Marcus, but his strength reminded her of some superheroes that she had read about in books.

"Come, I wish to show you something," he said.

She mutely nodded, released his shoulders, and stepped back. He grasped her hand in his, and she followed him into the building.

Like many things on Kassis, the building was made of crystal. The walls and floors were polished to a shine so bright, she could see her reflection in them. They emitted a soft glow of blue light.

The building was circular. Twin staircases led upward to a clear dome ceiling. Through the glass, she could see the aurora and a million stars. The stars shone down through the ceiling, and when she looked at the floor, she could see a reflection of the night sky. It felt like she was walking among the stars instead of merely staring up at them.

"This is incredible. I've never seen anything like this before," she breathed, pulling away from him to turn in a circle.

"This is an old training center for young star pilots. I read about it in one of the archived manuals. Not much remains of the original site. This was part of the main library," he explained.

"Look! What is that?" she asked, excited.

"Star charts. The red star is Helma. That is Darmona, and at the top of the triangle is Gamma T'mer," he said, walking along the lines that connected the three bright points. "Look up and you will see them."

She looked up and laughed. Through the clear glass, she could see the triangle of stars above. Her breath caught when Jarmen wrapped his arms around her waist and pulled her back against his body. She relaxed against him as soft music began to play.

"Jon Paul and Luc said that women like shiny things. I thought you might like this," he said.

She turned in his arms and slowly moved her hands up his chest to wrap her arms around his neck. His eyes glowed with a soft, red light that reminded her of Herma. She rose, wanting to kiss him again.

"The only shiny thing I love is your eyes when you look at me," she confessed. "I have from the first time I saw you."

CHAPTER 5

"**I** *see not a monster standing before me, but the man I knew I could one day love with all my heart...*"

The line from *Tales of Two Galaxies* flashed through Jarmen's mind, and his throat tightened. Was it possible for fiction to become reality? He wanted to believe it was true—that Jane was his Suzanne.

The sound of someone clearing their throat pulled their attention away from each other. They both looked over to the staircase. Jon Paul stood on the second from the bottom step, dressed handsomely in a black tuxedo and white gloves.

"Dinner is served on the upper terrace," Jon Paul announced with a bow.

Jane giggled and looked up at Jarmen with eyes that shone with delight. Her lips were parted and her face flushed with excitement. Out of the corner of his eye, he saw Jon Paul lift his arm to his side, elbow out, and wave his other hand to indicate that Jarmen should mimic the move.

He frowned but bent his elbow. Jane immediately slid her arm through his. Jarmen smiled with surprised delight. He guided Jane across the glowing floor to the staircase.

"A dinner fit for a princess," Jon Paul murmured as they passed him.

An unfamiliar twitch at the corner of Jarmen's lips made him realize he was smiling again, this time at the two Frenchmen's interference. He had asked them to have a basket of food delivered to the observatory. He would never have expected them to create such an elaborate feast. At the top of the stairs, Num stood by a cloth-draped round table set for two. The large bot was holding a chair out for Jane.

"I thought you and IQ were watching a movie tonight!" she exclaimed.

Num tilted his head. "Jon Paul and Luc said this was to be a surprise. It would not have been a surprise if we had told you," he replied.

Jarmen escorted Jane to her chair. She murmured her thanks to Num when the big bot pushed her chair in and rewarded Num with a stunning smile. Jarmen walked around the table and sat down across from her.

A trio of short candles flickered in the center of the table. IQ whizzed out of hiding, stopped in front of Jane, and handed her a delicate red flower. She grinned at the little bot before she accepted the bloom.

"Thank you, IQ," she said, kissing the top of IQ's head.

"The food is safe to eat. Luc and Jon Paul wouldn't let Num near it tonight," IQ informed her in an overly loud whisper.

Jon Paul cleared his throat. "IQ," he admonished with a stern look.

IQ mumbled a series of beeps, his way of cursing when he wasn't supposed to curse, took the cloth napkin next to Jane's plate, shook it out, and placed it on her lap.

"I hope you enjoy your meal," IQ said before he twirled on his single wheel and disappeared behind a partition.

Jarmen looked up, startled, when Jon Paul shook out his napkin and gave him a wink. Jarmen took the napkin before the man could place it in his lap.

Jon Paul straightened and smiled. "Tonight, the magnificent Chef Luc has prepared a brilliant appetizer of fruit prepared in the lightest of pastries that will melt in your mouth with a selection of gourmet cheeses and bread with fresh-churned butter, followed by chilled squash soup. The main course is fresh fettucine pasta in a light garlic, parmesan cream sauce served with fresh vegetables for the lady and roasted sea trout glazed with a delicate lemon sauce for the gentleman. Dessert is a Honey Roasted Panna Cotta with Blood Orange Sauce. May I offer you each a glass of wine?" Jon Paul asked.

Jarmen nodded. "Yes... please," he said.

Jane held up her glass to Jon Paul. "This is amazing, Jon Paul. Thank you for doing this," she said.

"It is our pleasure, *ma chérie*," Jon Paul responded with a bow before he smoothly left them alone.

Romantic music played softly in the background. The stars glittered above their heads. The candlelight danced, casting shadows across Jane's face and lighting up her eyes. He lifted his glass to her.

"There is no woman in the universe more beautiful than she who sits across from me," he quietly said, quoting a line from *Tales of Two Galaxies*.

Jane blushed and lifted her glass to touch his. "There is no man in the universe who makes me feel more beautiful," she responded.

Jarmen sipped the fine wine. His mind processed the ingredients in the fermented fruit liquid, but he was also processing something else—the way his heart beat a little faster and the warmth that filled his mind and body. He felt—like a man. Even more, he felt whole when he was with Jane.

"Tell me about yourself," Jane suggested, leaning forward to hold his hand.

"There is not much to tell. I was held in a lab run by the Draka. Jazin explained that he heard about the lab from a drunken guard. If not for him, I would still be there or I would be dead," he said.

"Oh, Jarmen, that is terrible. Do you know why they did that to you?" Jane asked, tears glittering in her eyes.

"They were experimenting with a new military prototype. There is very little known about it. The Draka ordered the destruction of the equipment. As far as I have been able to discern, no data survived except what I downloaded before everything was destroyed. I have not given up. If the Draka believe their research to be viable, someone will build another lab. However, they did kill all the scientists involved. I do not believe that plan was well thought out," he mused.

She squeezed his hand. "No, I don't suppose it was," she commented.

They both sat back when IQ and Jon Paul returned with their meal. Jarmen had never thought of food as something to be enjoyed. He ate to survive, and because of the modifications to his body, he could survive on very little if needed. The meal tonight tantalized his enhanced senses, and his stomach rumbled with pleasure. Each course made him ponder if murdering the two Frenchmen might be a travesty to the universe. From the mouthwatering appetizers to the main course, he found each one more fascinating than the previous course. The combinations of flavors and textures in a great meal was a science, he decided.

"You do not want any of the sea trout?" he asked.

Jane shook her head. "I don't eat meat," she responded with a smile.

He looked down at his plate with a frown. "Does this mean I should not eat it?" he asked with a hint of dismay in his voice.

She laughed. "No, it just means I don't care to eat meat. You can eat all you want. It took many years for me to realize that every time I ate meat that I felt sick afterwards. When I went to the library, I found a book that talked about different food reactions. I wrote down what I ate after that and discovered that it was every kind of meat causing me this problem. I don't remember the details, but basically, my body can't handle digesting it," she explained.

He looked down at his plate again and sighed. "I am happy to say I do not have this issue."

She laughed again. "So am I because that does look delicious. Would you like to try some of my pasta?" she asked.

He looked at her plate and shook his head. "No. That reminds me of Luthgorium flatworms. They are disgusting to eat."

Jane's peal of laughter made him smile.

The rest of their meal passed quickly. Jane shared stories from the Cirque de Magik complex and Jarmen described his work with Ristéard Roald, the Grand Ruler of Elpidios.

"Everyone was terrified when Ristéard kidnapped Ricki. I'm glad everything turned out well," she said.

"The Elpidiosians are an interesting species—Ristéard more than the rest," he acknowledged.

Jarmen drank in Jane's shining eyes and her flushed cheeks. The night might have started out with him having doubts, but they all melted away by the end of their meal.

"You're staring at me. Do I have whipped cream on my face?" she teased.

He shook his head. "No, I was just thinking about how beautiful you are."

Jane seemed to glow with happiness. She placed her napkin on the table and rose from her seat. Unsure of the reason, he slid his chair back and stood as well. She held out her hand, and he enfolded it in his own, allowing her to lead him to a small area away from the table.

When she stepped closer to him, he wound his arms around her. She released his hand and slid both of hers along his arms to his shoulders.

Following her lead, they moved back and forth. It took a second for him to realize that she was moving in time to the music.

A flash of panic hit him when he realized that he had never down-loaded information on dancing. He looked up and saw Jon Paul and Luc peeking out at them. He widened his eyes and mouthed 'How do I do this?'

The two men mimicked him and Jane. Luc dropped his head against Jon Paul's shoulder, and the couple moved as one. Jarmen pulled Jane closer, and she turned her face into his neck. The men chuckled, blew him a kiss, and disappeared.

He felt his body relax as he picked up the rhythm of the music and the way their bodies moved in unison. Resting his cheek against the top of her hair, he breathed in the floral scent of her shampoo and marveled at the exquisite feel of her in his arms. He never wanted the night to end.

In the kitchen, Luc handed Jon Paul a glass of wine, and they moved to a small table in the adjoining recreation room to enjoy the meal that Luc had prepared for them. Jon Paul smiled and tapped his wine glass against Luc's.

"You did magnifique tonight, Luc," Jon Paul complimented.

"When it comes to love, I had the best teacher," he responded with an affectionate grin.

"Is it me, or is it getting hot in here?" IQ muttered, looking up at Num who was washing dishes.

Num paused and tilted his head. "No, I think it is rather pleasant myself," he answered.

CHAPTER 6

"Y ou are glowing! I take it last night went well," Nema teased.

Jane blushed and nodded. It was hard to contain her happiness. Last night had been like a scene out of a fairy tale.

"I think we might need to tie a rope around her ankles to keep her from floating away," Suzy remarked with a laugh.

"Oh! Do tell! We miss all the great stuff being at the palace, don't we, Jo?" Star said, looking over at her sister.

"Trust me, there is enough gossip going on there to keep me entertained," Jo replied with a snort.

Nema clucked and motioned with her hands. "Come on, we need Gossiping Catch-up Time," she announced with the same flair as if she were introducing an act.

Jane bit her lip to keep from smiling. Star and Jo set down their performance ropes. Suzy twisted a chair around and sat down with her arms folded along the back of it with gleeful anticipation.

Excitement built inside Jane because she knew what was about to happen. Walter might be the Master of the Big Top, but Nema was the master when it came to gathering information. She now understood where Ricki learned her skills.

"I knew I shouldn't have said anything," Jo groaned as she plopped down on an oversized bean bag chair.

"Scoot over," Star ordered, sinking down next to her sister.

Jo grumbled and the two sisters started picking on each other. Their giggles made her laugh. Nema's teasing mutters didn't help, and soon they were all laughing. No one had even gotten to the gossip yet, and it was all so funny.

Between one breath and the next, a melancholy pall fell over Jane, and the air left her lungs. She fervently wished she could recapture the bubbly emotion she had just been feeling. She didn't want to notice how new and rare that feeling was. She didn't want to mourn what had been missing all her life. She just wanted to stay in this wonderful moment. Nema reached out her hand in concern.

"What is it, Jane?" Nema asked.

Emotion threatened to choke her at the quiet, compassionate note in Nema's voice. She lifted a hand to her cheek to make sure the tears burning her eyes hadn't overflowed.

"This—" she said with a wave of her hand. "I can't tell you how much being a part of this means to me. It is like I have sisters… a real family."

"Are you getting your memory back?" Suzy asked.

Jane swallowed and shook her head. She couldn't—wouldn't—lie to them, but she also didn't want to bring up her past. She was terrified that if she shared it, somehow, someway, she would break the magic. Sharing it with Jarmen had been different.

"It doesn't matter, love. What matters is that you are with us now," Nema said with a gentle smile.

Jane clasped Nema's hand. "Thank you," she murmured, her throat tight with heartfelt emotion.

"So, how did your dinner date with Jarmen go last night?" Star asked.

Jane gave her a startled look. "How did you—?" she began before she looked at Suzy.

Suzy shrugged. "I didn't say anything—yet. It must have been Curly," she replied, lifting her hands up.

Jane blushed again and smiled. "It was… magical," she confessed, rising out of her chair, and twirling in a circle as if dancing. "He took me to a beautiful observatory and we had music and dinner and we danced under the stars," she said with a breathless laugh.

"If I didn't know any better, I'd say our Jane Doe is falling in love with a cyborg," Jo commented with a smile.

Jane froze halfway in a turn and looked back at the expectant eyes staring at her. Her lips parted into a big smile. They knew—because they were all in love too.

"Yes… yes, I am," she laughed. "I love Jarmen!"

Nema reached down into the basket next to her and pulled out five shot glasses before she pulled out a large bottle of bourbon. She plunked it in the center of the table. Star and Jo rose from their comfy seat and pulled up two rickety chairs.

"I think this calls for a celebration," Nema announced.

"Oh, hell yeah! A Nema-bration!" Suzy crowed with delight, grabbing the bottle, and opening it.

Jane slid back onto her seat and grinned as Suzy poured her a shot glass full of bourbon and set it in front of her. She had never had hard liquor before. She picked up the glass and sniffed it.

"A Cirque de Magik tradition when we find our soul mates," Jo explained.

"To soul mates!" Nema shouted, standing on her chair, and lifting her glass.

"To soul mates!" Jo, Star, and Suzy echoed, standing, and holding out their glasses.

Jane lifted her glass to touch the others. "To soul mates!" she shouted before downing the glass in one gulp.

Her eyes watered as the bourbon burned a path down her throat to her stomach. She covered her mouth with the back of her hand and coughed. Laughter burst from all the women and they collapsed back in their chairs. Well, all except Suzy who took the time to refill their glasses first.

"Now, we'll *savor* this, otherwise we're all going to need our mates' help to get home," Nema cautioned.

Jane grinned. "Gossip time," she laughed, sitting back in her chair.

When Jazin walked into the room with Walter, Jarmen did not look up from the diagram of the new shield he and Jazin were designing—at least until the uncomfortable sensation of having twin gazes burning a hole through his back broke his concentration. He rotated on the bench seat and returned their stares with one of his own.

"Is there something that you need?" he politely inquired.

"Yes," they both responded at the same time.

Jazin cleared his throat. "Walter wanted to speak with you. I, uh, have something I need to attend to. I'll leave you two to talk."

Jarmen frowned when Jazin turned on his heel and exited the room. He turned his attention to Walter. The man's piercing glare was a worrying result to an unknown cause. Jarmen's cheeks heated slightly with a suspicion of what this was about, but more data was needed to understand. He motioned to a table with several chairs around it.

"Would you care to sit down?" he asked.

Walter looked at the chairs and sighed. "This world is made for giants," he grumbled.

Jarmen's lips curved in understanding. "Follow me. I believe I know of a place that may be more comfortable for you," he said.

They walked through the sliding glass door into a large room filled with equipment. As the door slid closed behind them, Jarmen crossed to his air bike. Next to the bike was a workbench with several red and black mechanics' seats. The low-backed seats hugged the ground and had wheels for ease of moving while working on equipment low to the ground. He pulled two out, raising them as far as they would go.

"Thanks," Walter gruffly replied, sitting down with a sigh.

Jarmen sat down and adjusted his seat so that he and Walter were practically at the same height. He knew how it felt to be at a disadvantage. He respected Walter and didn't want him to feel uncomfortable.

Resting his arms on his knees, he waited for Walter to speak. Walter cleared his throat and folded his hands in front of him.

"As you know, Nema and I have taken Jane under our wing. She is like another daughter to us," Walter began.

Walter ran a finger along the collar of his pristine black shirt. Jarmen's mind was already listing all the outcomes, and none of them boded well for his continued courtship of Jane. Why would a man of Walter's prestige think that a cyborg with a stolen past would be an appropriate match for his daughter?

"I can understand your misgivings, Walter. I mean no disrespect to you or Nema. My... attraction to Jane—" He stopped and pursed his lips.

Walter scowled. "I certainly hope it is more than attraction you are feeling for that girl," he growled before continuing. "Jane deserves someone who can love her and treat her like a—well, who can treat her like a woman should be treated. My Nema is the most precious woman in the world to me. She is my partner, my friend, my lover, and I couldn't be prouder that she chose me to be the one to stand by her side," he declared.

Jarmen replayed Walter's words. A deep frown of confusion creased his brow. Was Walter telling him that he *wanted* him to court Jane?

He looked at Walter, seeking clarification. "You and Nema... do not mind that I wish to take Jane as my mate? If she wishes that as well," he quickly added.

"Are you kidding? I've been watching you two for months wondering if I was going to have to step in and do something! You two were made for each other," Walter said, slumping back in his chair with relief.

Jarmen continued to stare at Walter in disbelief. "But... I am... different. I am not like Jazin or Curly or Stan," he said.

Walter's bark of laughter echoed loudly in the cavernous work bay. "Son, if you haven't noticed, all of us are a bit different. I think that is what makes you so perfect for our Jane. She doesn't need a normal human. She needs a man who can love her, and Nema and I... well, we just want one who can protect her—and treat her right," he said, returning to the stern expression he began this conversation with.

"I can do that," Jarmen promised.

Jazin stood watching the exchange on the vidcom. He folded his arms and smiled when he heard Jarmen's response. Walter had wanted to talk to Jarmen alone. Jazin had agreed, but that didn't mean he wouldn't listen in.

"How did it go?"

Jazin turned and smiled at his father. "Good. Better than I expected. Walter handled this much better than he did Ristéard," he commented.

Ajaska crossed from the door to the monitor and studied the screen. As Jarmen asked Walter what he knew about Jane's past, Jazin frowned with concern.

"I would love for the man who hurt Jane to have to answer to Jarmen," Ajaska muttered.

"You and me both," Jazin agreed.

"Do you think he can feel emotions?" Ajaska suddenly asked, looking at his youngest son. "I mean… real emotions like love."

Jazin studied Jarmen's face and thought about the man he had saved nearly ten years ago. There had been times when he thought he glimpsed emotion in Jarmen's eyes. How deeply and what kind of emotions, though, he didn't really know. One thing he did know was that he had never seen Jarmen act this way about anyone before.

"He never gave up on me. I know he can feel protective of another, but can he feel love? That is a question only he and Jane can know for sure," he replied.

Ajaska rested his hand on his shoulder. "As long as he makes that girl happy—and keeps those two robots and the Frenchmen out from under our feet—I'll be satisfied," he said with a nod before he turned and left.

Jazin's gaze returned to the screen. "I hope you can feel love, my friend. It is one of the most powerful and rewarding emotions that a man can experience," he murmured before he reached down and turned off the screen.

CHAPTER 7

G eylur Prime I

"General Namla, the information you requested," Second Lieutenant Hast said with a formal bow.

General Palatine Namla took the crystal disk as he walked by Hast and continued along the maze of corridors. His mind was churning with thoughts about his predecessors' failures.

Years of research were lost when the lab on the Ala'mont moon was destroyed ten years ago. Commander Teivel's orders to wipe everything clean had resulted in a tremendous setback to their research. On top of losing the lab, the sudden appearance of the three prophesied warrior women from another world had shattered his superiors' plans to bring down the three Houses of Kassis.

Palatine's predecessors had wasted precious energy and credits on the Kassisan Councilman Tai Tek and others. Tai Tek had made promises he failed to keep. Instead of driving a rift between the different worlds, the conflict, and subsequent revelations of Draka involvement, had instead united them.

All the time and energy spent cultivating an alliance with governments who wanted to break free from the Alliance and the influence of the Kassisans had ended in failure.

Palatine had been promoted and handed the task of achieving what everyone before him had failed to accomplish—bring down the Alliance and find a way for the Draka to take control of this section of the galaxy. He idly rotated the crystal disk with his fingers. If the information on the disk was what he hoped, there might still be a way to change the course of history.

Palatine entered the room he had taken as his office and crossed to the computer. Pulling the chair out, he sat down and slipped the disk into the reader. He sat back, waiting for the static on the vidcom to clear.

"General, I found something you may find interesting. A Red Crystal ship has been found on Elpidios. It is under high security," his informant stated.

A map, pinpointing the location, and a blurred image of the security buildings protecting the site were included. The information was bare bones, but it could be priceless. He touched the communicator at his lapel.

"Lieutenant Hast, escort Dr. Labyrinth to my office," he ordered.

"Yes, sir," Lieutenant Hast replied.

"Computer, search for 'Red Crystal ship'," he ordered.

"Red Crystal ships are mythical starships said to have belonged to the Ancient Gods: Zephren, the God of War, his two sons, and his three daughters. Red Crystal ships are classified as living vessels capable of traversing through time and space. No evidence of Red Crystal ships has ever been found. There are currently three theories pertaining to the ships.

"Kassisan legend states that thousands of years ago, Kassis was attacked by an unknown alien species from another galaxy. Some retellings state the creatures came from a parallel world and traveled through time/space. All Kassis retellings agree that the attack happened during the alignment of the twin moons of Kassis. This alignment occurs once every two thousand years. A storm raged over the entire planet, and a Red Crystal ship appeared above each of the five remaining Kassisan cities. Each ship was commanded by a God or Goddess, and they saved Kassis.

"A similar legend has been recorded in the archives of Elpidios with significant variations: the planet's atmosphere was non-viable for the attacking creatures, and they retreated. Elpidios cave paintings show a single Red Crystal ship landing in the planet's only mountain range. In the Usoleum sol year 9034, Andric Ikera, a Usoleum explorer and scientist, reported his observation of mountain natives using red crystals as a healing tool. This report has remained unsubstantiated, as no other research has been done. End of available data," the computer responded.

"A living ship that can traverse space and time," Palatine repeated in a low voice.

"Computer, list the known dangers of the Red Crystal that these ships were named for," he requested.

"Insufficient data available to answer this request," the computer replied.

He rose from his chair and walked over to the long, narrow, rectangular window that looked out over the vast oceans of Geylur Prime I.

Where Geylur Prime II was a desert planet, her twin sister was one of mostly water. Fifty-foot waves crashed against the structure, spraying the window with frigid water.

Palatine turned when the door chimed and his Second Lieutenant entered, followed by a woman wearing a black coat with the red blaze insignia of the Draka across her left breast. They were almost the same height at just over six foot. Doctor Seanna Labyrinth's ash-white dreadlocks were twisted together and bound by a thick, black ribbon. Her pale gray eyes were outlined by thick white lashes.

"You wished to see me, General Namla?" Seanna asked.

He motioned to the seat across from his desk. Seanna crossed from the door and gracefully sat down. She was beautiful, smart, and completely devoid of emotion. The last two characteristics were why he had personally requested her for this assignment.

"That will be all, Lieutenant," he said.

"Yes, sir," Lieutenant Hast replied with a bow and exited the room.

"I see you have trained him well. I wonder how long he will last," Seanna commented.

"Until he makes his first mistake," Palatine replied, relaxing in his chair. "How are your new experiments going?"

Seanna raised an eyebrow. "Poorly, which is to be expected since I'm starting from scratch," she said pointedly with a disdainful expression.

"Commander Teivel believed it was imperative that the data not fall into Kassisan hands. The only way to ensure that was to destroy everything and everyone involved," he said.

Seanna stared back at him with cold, empty eyes. "Fortunately, my father failed at that as well," she replied.

Palatine sat forward and rested his forearms on his desk. "You've had some success?" he asked.

Seanna nodded. "Some. The specimen delivered to me is—less than perfect. I've had moderate success in reprogramming it. With the injections, its body repairs itself. Unfortunately, the medication also makes the unit more volatile. If only—" She stopped and pursed her dark gray lips.

"If only…?" he asked.

"There has been a report of another who survived," she said.

"The one that Jazin Ja Kel Coradon is said to have rescued," Palatine replied.

Seanna nodded. "Unit 482. He is the only successfully functioning unit that did not require additional medications to survive. The few reports my father conveyed to me were remarkable. The scientists could not replicate their success. There were a few that were close, like the Unit your men retrieved, but the results are not the same. The Unit I have requires medication to function without severe deterioration," she said.

"But your Unit *is* functional?" he pressed.

She lifted an eyebrow. "Almost. Do you have a mission?"

Palatine nodded and relaxed again. "Yes. What do you know about the mythical Red Crystal starships?"

$\sim$

Kassis

Jarmen stared into the small, oval mirror Jon Paul had given him and debated whether he should remove his facial hair or leave it. If he removed it, he would be late for his date with Jane. Deciding he would leave it, he turned away from his image.

"Jane has not complained about the hair on my face before," he reasoned as he strode through his spaceship.

The back platform opened with a thought. He blinked with surprise when he saw Jane standing at the bottom of the platform. She bit her lip as she looked up at him with a shy, expectant expression. She held up her basket, her slender limbs showing signs of significant strain as she lifted the weight.

"I thought I would surprise you tonight. I know you've been working a lot. It didn't dawn on me until I got here that a spaceship probably doesn't come with a doorbell," she said with a self-conscious laugh.

"No, but I could install one. My sensors should have detected you. I hope you have not been waiting long," he said, striding down the platform.

He stopped in front of her and gently took the basket from her. He held it in one hand, barely noticing the weight.

"I've only been here a few minutes. I hope you don't mind. Num didn't think you would," she responded.

"I am glad you came. I…. Would you like to come aboard?" he asked.

She nodded and smiled. "Yes, I've been dying to see where you've been staying. Num was the one who told me you've been living here, on your ship," she said.

He looked up the platform into his ship. "Yes, I can work in peace here. I do not require a lot of rest and there are times when being around others—" He paused. "I prefer solitude."

She slipped her hand into his.

"I can be quiet," she promised.

He shook his head. "The only thing I prefer more than my solitude is being with you. You never have to be quiet around me. I could listen to your voice forever."

His senses spiraled when she slid her free hand against his nape and pulled his head down for a kiss. He could feel her lips part, and she swept her tongue across the crease of his lips, demanding entrance. He eagerly complied.

His body hardened in response to the passion in her kiss. He wanted to drop the basket and pull her into his arms, but he didn't want to spill whatever she had brought. His heart raced when she lifted their entwined hands and slid them between her breasts. She reluctantly broke their kiss and stared up at him with luminous eyes filled with desire.

"Jarmen, I was hoping… I hoped that maybe I could… stay the night with you tonight," she said.

"You wish… to—" He looked up at his ship, then back at her. "I would like that very much."

She smiled at his response. *No, she glowed,* he corrected with a sense of pleasure.

He kissed her again before turning to guide her up the platform. Once inside, he ordered the platform door to close and double-checked his security systems to make sure they were functioning properly. His steps slowed when she looked around them.

"This is so—futuristic," she said with a laugh.

He studied the inside of his ship. Jazin had given him the ship shortly after his rescue. Over the last ten years, he had made some significant design changes and was pleased with the results.

"The changes were no easy feat," he commented.

"I can imagine! I wouldn't even know where to start," she confessed.

"It was not the starting that was difficult. It was the not killing Jon Paul and Luc or dismantling the two bots that was the problem. Since they were discovered a few years ago, the four of them have insisted on being my constant companions," he said with a shake of his head. "I thought I had been tortured enough."

Jane stifled a snort of laughter. "They love you. That's why they want to be with you. You are their family, just like I am now," she informed him.

"Family…," he said thoughtfully. "I do not remember ever having a family before. Jazin is my friend. I now have many of those."

She squeezed his hand. "Friends and family are very important."

He stopped and faced her. Pulling his hand free, he caressed her cheek. She leaned her face into his hand and rubbed it against his palm.

"You and I will be a family when you become my mate."

She nodded. "I would like that very much," she softly replied.

"I cooked a meal tonight that I think you will enjoy. No worms," she promised with a laugh.

"I would eat them if they were prepared by you," he reluctantly confessed.

She paused in unloading the basket and scrunched her nose with a look of amusement. "I would never make you worms," she stated before turning to finish her task.

"I have a good old-fashioned meatloaf with mashed potatoes, green beans, and dinner rolls," she said, placing each item on the table in front of him. "A word of warning: the meatloaf is made with plant-based meat, but I think you'll like it. I've been experimenting with Jon Paul and Luc."

"Plant-based?" he asked with a skeptical expression.

She leaned over and kissed the tip of his nose. "It's really good—much better than worms. It's made from a combination of pea protein, spices, vegetables, and natural flavors. Suzy grew most of the vegetables," she explained.

"I will trust you," he responded.

His senses had already processed all the ingredients, and his mouth watered from the tantalizing aroma. He watched as she dished up two plates before she sat down across from him. He waited for her to take the first bite before he began eating. A low moan of pleasure slipped from him.

"This is very good," he said.

She laughed and waved her fork at him. "I told you."

"How did you get here? I am surprised that Num and IQ are not with you. I programmed them so they never leave you alone," he said between mouthfuls.

Jane gave him a pointed look. "I know. I had Stan look at their programming. He found the code you inserted," she stated.

He frowned. "The human Stan? He found the code?"

Jane nodded. "Yes. Stan is brilliant. Oh, and the next time you decide to mess with the bots' programming, please warn me. I don't enjoy having them surprise me when I'm about to get in the shower. Thank goodness I was still wearing my robe!"

A crooked grin curved his lips. "I should have written certain exceptions into the code," he acknowledged.

"Yes, you should have. When I screamed, Num tore the bathroom door off the hinges. That is what the four of them are working on tonight. I wanted something a little more private than a bed sheet to replace the door," she dryly commented.

"Did one of them drop you off here?" he asked.

She shook her head. "Nope! River showed me months ago how to drive a mini air bike. It isn't as powerful or fancy as yours, but it gets me from point A to point B. It reminds me of the scooters and electric bikes back on Earth. I've been using one to pick up and deliver items that Walter and Nema need. It made my job so much easier," she explained.

"Job? They allow you to go on an air bike alone?" he repeated, placing his fork next to his empty plate.

She gave him another pointed look. "Yes, I have a job, and no, they didn't 'allow' me to go alone on the air bike. I'm old enough to make my own decisions," she said in a firm tone.

Jarmen swallowed the protest building in his throat. He understood that she felt defensive, and he would not do anything to make her feel more threatened.

"If you like, I can show you how to operate the larger air bike," he offered.

Her eyes widened, and she smiled. "Oh, Jarmen, that would be wonderful," she laughed.

"I'll give you your first lesson tomorrow," he promised.

"Thank you."

Warmth filled him again. "Can I have some more of your plant-based meatloaf?" he requested.

"Of course!" she replied, filling his plate again.

CHAPTER 8

S everal hours later, the galley was clean, the dishes placed back in the basket, and a tour of his ship was completed. They sat in the cockpit, staring out the front viewport at the twinkling lights of the city. The tension inside him built as darkness descended and Jane's words from earlier played like a loop in his head.

… I could stay the night with you. I could stay the night with you….

He tried to remember the various facts about pleasuring a woman that he had learned from vidcoms, but for once, his mind was blank. He turned to Jane when she slid her hand in his. She kept her eyes focused on the view in front of them.

"Do you want me to stay?"

"Yes," he replied, his voice reflecting his growing panic. "Yes, I would like for you to stay."

She swiveled in the co-pilot seat to face him. "What's wrong? I can… I feel like… This is my first time," she blurted out.

"Mine as well," he confessed.

She stared at him for several seconds before she blinked. Then, she blinked again. A small crease puckered between her eyes.

"Are you saying that... you've never been with a woman before?" she asked in a hesitant voice.

"No. Yes. I mean, I do not remember ever making love before, so yes, that is what I am saying," he replied.

"I don't think it's going to be too difficult to learn," she mused.

She rose to her feet, pulling him up with her. The shy smile on her lips and the excited desire in her eyes made him want to strip her naked and explore every inch of her. His body hummed with anticipation.

He followed her to his sleeping quarters. The dim lighting revealed a room devoid of any decorations. It contained only the bare-essentials: his bed, the built-in wardrobe for his clothing, and a small cleansing unit.

It was hardly a romantic setting, but when she turned to face him and began to unbutton his shirt, his dismal thoughts of not giving Jane a more romantic setting for their first joining disappeared. He flexed his fingers as she moved down the line of buttons with slow precision, silently cursing Luc for insisting that he wear the shirt with the tiny torture fastenings.

"I could remove this faster if you would like," he suggested through clenched teeth.

The soft breath of her chuckle caressed his hot skin. She looked up at him with mischievous eyes. It was then that he realized that she was aware of her effect on him. His shy, gentle Jane had an impish side to her.

"We have all night," she teased.

He closed his eyes and breathed deeply through his nose. The delicate scent of the floral lotion and shampoo she used washed through him. He wanted to see if her skin tasted of that hint of vanilla. His head lowered to her neck as his hands traced the neckline of her bodice.

When he felt her lips touch his chest, the sound of material ripping and buttons bouncing across the floor caused him to grimace. He peeked one eye open and looked at her astonished face. A crooked, apologetic grin curved his lips.

"Oops," he said, using a word that he heard IQ use frequently.

"You are so naughty," she chided, putting her hands on her hips to allow the inner curves of her breasts and her flat stomach to be seen through the gap in her ripped shirt.

"Nema won't be happy." She inched the fabric off her shoulders. "She just bought this blouse." She revealed her nipples and let the fabric fall to the ground.

"Sweet galaxies, Jane," he breathed, staring at her small, firm breasts.

"I don't always wear a bra," she said, stepping close enough that her nipples touched his chest.

He cupped her twin globes. Rubbing his thumbs across the taut buds, he was rewarded by her hissing moan. She wrapped her hands around his wrists, holding him to her.

Their lips met in a frantic kiss. The months of sexy dreams and dancing at a distance with just their eyes was finally being released in a torrent of passion. He guided her backward to his bed.

Their lips tore from each other and their eyes locked as the back of her legs touched the bed and she laid back. They had all night, but they were only focused on this moment.

He reached down and removed her shoes and socks. Her hands moved to the fastening of her trousers, and she undid them as he removed his boots, pants, and shirt faster than humanly possible. He slowed his movements when he tugged off her trousers, and he paused to look at her when she was lying gloriously naked on his bed.

"I have envisioned this moment since the first time I saw you," he confessed.

Her passion-filled eyes greedily roamed his naked form as well. Thin scars lined his body, a reminder of his time in the Draka lab. He let her look for as long as she wanted to, his body hard and his heart thumping heavily as the seconds expanded.

Jane scooted back until her head was near the headboard and held her hands out to him. He knelt on the bed, sliding his hand up her smooth calf to the inside of her thigh. Her legs parted and her eyes widened when he crawled up between her legs and lifted her hips far enough for his mouth to capture the vulnerable bud hidden by dark brown curls.

"Jarmen!" she cried out, her hands dropping to clench the covers.

Jarmen held her hips still when she tried to buck. He parted her soft labia with his fingers and lavished the hidden nub with the tip of his tongue until it swelled under his passionate caress. Delicate flavors of her desire flowed over his taste buds, and his body reacted to the aphrodisiac.

His cock lengthened, becoming harder and throbbing until it was painful. He wanted more—the taste of Jane's orgasm on his lips and tongue, the feel of her wrapped around his throbbing cock, the ability to share his joy with her.

Sliding his finger along her slick lips, he penetrated her. Soft, warm flesh wrapped around his finger, squeezing him. Her vaginal channel was tight, and images of his cock slowly impaling her, her wrapping around him and squeezing, made him moan.

Her soft whimpers and pleas for more urged him on. He rose to his knees to relieve the painful constriction of his full cock trapped between his body and the bed. Turning his head slightly, he sucked hard on her engorged nub while he pressed another finger deep inside her. Her loud cries and panting breaths told him that she was enjoying his passionate attention.

She dug her heels into the bed, lifting her hips higher while her legs spread so that she was completely exposed. He began pumping his fingers as he sucked. His tongue lashed at her nub, teasing it, pulling and nipping, until she released a loud scream and froze. Her body arched as she came. Warmth flooded his mouth, and he knew he would never forget the taste of his sweet, beautiful Jane's first orgasm.

When her body began to relax, he released the nub he still held clasped between his lips. Her shuddering cry of protest showed him that she was still locked in her release. He slid up her body, pressing hot, open-mouthed kisses along her stomach, up to her breasts. He suckled on each taut nipple until they were as hard as pebbles.

Rubbing them against his chest, he captured her lips as he aligned his cock with her pulsing core and slowly penetrated her. The slickness of her orgasm smoothed the way, and her tight channel wrapped around him like a fist. He rocked his hips when he felt a thin barrier against the head of his cock and deepened his kiss before he pushed through the barrier, burying his cock to the hilt.

Jane stiffened in his arms for an instant before she relaxed and lifted her legs to wrap them around the back of his thighs. Her hands slid down his sides to cup his buttocks, and she squeezed. A shudder ran through his body. He wrapped his arms around her and held her as he began to rock in a rhythm as old as time.

"Ah, sweet Jane," he murmured, his eyes closed as he processed every sensitive movement.

The friction of his cock sliding along her pulsing feminine depths caressed his entire length, stretching her and allowing him to sink deeper until he swore he was touching her womb. Her nipples brushed along his chest, tangling with the wiry hair. Over and over, the combination of sensations tortured him until the strange, deep tingling sensation that had been growing inside him burst outward through his body.

"Jane!"

His hoarse cry shocked him, as did the hot intensity of his release. The pressure inside him snapped, sending him into a spiraling freefall. Time stood still, and for that fraction of a second, there was no one in the galaxy except Jarmen and Jane. He stared down at her. Her face was suffused with the afterglow of her second orgasm.

I love her.

He loved her. It was more than their coming together physically. Their physical connection was intensely pleasurable, but it was deeper than that. Love meant vulnerability, fear, courage, passion, hope, and never feeling alone.

It means being whole.

The sensation of the galaxy shifting on its axis swept through him. Jane's eyelashes fluttered and she stared up at him with a soft, dazed expression. Her eyes were as hot and enticing as melted chocolate. A tender smile curved her lips.

"I love you, Jarmen," she said, sliding her arms up his back.

Her lips captured his before he could respond. His heart thundered, feeling as if it had grown three sizes as he poured his newfound love for Jane into his kiss and fervently voiced that love between kisses. He may not have much of a past, but he had a future—a future with Jane. He would tell her that he loved her every day for the rest of their lives.

Jarmen woke from a deep sleep with a frown. Jane lay in his arms. His body spooned hers. His arm was wrapped tightly around her waist. He pressed his face against her hair and breathed deeply to calm his racing heart. He seldom dreamed, and when he did, it was always about his time in the lab.

Tonight's dream had been different. This dream— He closed his eyes and focused, replaying the scene detail-by-detail as he tried to decipher its meaning.

The image, as clear as any vidcom, formed in his mind. He saw a large tent. There was a long rectangular table filled with equipment. He was sitting at it with a group of friends and laughing—

His eyes popped open. *I had friends!*

His eyes burned as he fought to remember other scenes from the dream. He was on a planet that was being inducted into the Alliance.

He ran his tongue along his teeth. They felt different from what he remembered. They were smoother. There was an explosion, and the woman in the dream yelled out a name. The name was on the tip of his tongue, but he couldn't quite grasp it. It danced along the rim of his memory. Lonnie. She had called out the name Lonnie, but it wasn't directed at him. She had called him something else. He closed his eyes, trying desperately to remember what she said—

"I can't carry him, Buzz, you'll have to do it. Go!"

Buzz, his name…. The woman with hair the same color as Star's had called him Buzz.

Jarmen stared up at the ceiling. He'd had a life before the Draka lab. He hadn't been cloned as he'd originally thought. He had been like the guards who had tried to escape.

No, not like them.

Frustration burned through him at not being able to retrieve more of the memory. Jane must have sensed his unease because she grasped his hand and murmured in her sleep.

He kissed her shoulder and forced his body to relax.

Perhaps if I fall asleep, the dreams will return and I'll remember more.

CHAPTER 9

Days turned to weeks, and Jane felt like she was floating on air. They spent every moment they could together, dividing their time between her home and his spaceship when they weren't working. This evening, they were meeting at her trailer.

She opened the screen door to her home, grinning when she noticed Jarmen in the narrow kitchen; an apron tied with a perfect bow around his waist. He was concentrating so hard on the recipe Nema had given him, he didn't hear her sneak up behind him—or so she thought.

She was tiptoeing closer with exaggerated menace, her lungs filling with enough air to huff and puff like a big, bad wolf when he asked, "Did you have a good day at work?"

She blew all her air out, comically deflating, before she surged up on her tiptoes again to give him a quick kiss.

"Yes. What are you making?" she asked, leaning against his side.

"A mess."

His unexpected response made her laugh. "It looks like it. Why didn't you just use the food replicator?"

"You deserve food that tastes like Jon Paul and Luc made it, not Num. Luc said cooking is a science and an art. I understand the science of the measurements. It is the art I am struggling with," he grumbled, looking at the picture and then at the plates he had prepared.

Jane giggled. The vegetable lasagna didn't look... too bad. The top layer was sliding off, the vegetables were sticking out in long thin slices instead of being cut into smaller bites, and the ricotta was oozing onto the plate. The side salad was large enough for a dozen people to eat and looked like it had everything, including the kitchen sink, in it.

"It looks wonderful."

He raised a disbelieving eyebrow at her. "This is my third attempt."

Her eyes widened. "Your third?" She looked around the cozy kitchen for his other creations. "Where are the others?"

He grunted and picked up the plates. "I asked Num and IQ to feed them to Jon Paul and Luc."

She touched his arm. He looked so disheartened that her heart was melting. Rising up onto her tiptoes, she cupped his jaw and kissed him again. All he could do was stand there as both hands were full.

"Thank you," she said.

He looked at the cloth-covered table where a candle flickered in the center. She followed his gaze, noticing the red rose next to her plate.

"Today is the six-week anniversary of when you first kissed me. I wanted it to be special," he said.

Jane felt her heart melt all over again at his quiet confession. She caressed his cheek, loving him all the more.

"Every day is special when I'm with you," she breathed.

He glanced down at the plates in his hands before looking at her with a slight grin.

"How hungry are you?"

It took her a second to realize what he meant. Pleasure, excitement, and a slight feeling of naughtiness swept through her. She took one of the plates from him and placed it on the table with a wiggle of her nose.

"Very... for you," she teased.

Her laughter turned to a gasp when he placed the other plate on the table, turned, and scooped her up in his arms. She rested her head against his shoulder as she placed little kisses against his neck. The glow in his eyes warned her that they would be using the food replicator later... much, much later.

The next day, Jane hummed as she finished her shopping. She was lost in thought, thinking of Jarmen and their night together. Her face heated when several pedestrians paused to stare at her. A brief glance in the reflective glass of the storefront showed that she had a silly grin on her face.

Yes. Last night was that good! she thought with amusement.

Who was she kidding? Every night in Jarmen's arms was that good. Shoot! Just being with him was. She loved their chats, their walks, the way he looked puzzled by the antics of the circus members, everything!

"Jane, wait up!" River called.

She turned on the downtown sidewalk and waved when she saw River standing near an outdoor café. A moment later, Star and Jo joined River.

Jane looked both ways before crossing the street. A smile lit her face when she saw the three toddlers sitting in matching air strollers. Ajaska Ja Kel Coradon, Jr., aka AJ, giggled when she made a face at him.

"I wish we had known you were going shopping. We would have invited you to go with us," River said with a smile.

Jane shook her head. "I didn't plan on it. I had some errands to run and it was close to town so I thought I would stop by a shop that Suzy told me about."

"It looks like you found something," Jo remarked.

Jane blushed and nodded. "Several things," she admitted, thinking of the new lingerie tucked in her bag.

"We were about to order some food. Would you like to join us?" Star asked.

Jane shook her head. "No, thank you. I've already taken more time than I planned. Walter is probably wondering what's taking me so long," she replied, biting her lip.

"I'm sure Walter won't mind if you take a little break. Besides, we haven't seen you in weeks. We're dying to know how things are going between you and Jarmen," Star said, wrapping her arm through Jane's.

Jane resisted the urge to fan her face when she blushed again. The last few weeks had been incredible. There were no other words to describe them.

"Well, maybe just for a quick drink," she conceded as Star ushered her through to the open patio.

A hostess rushed over, clearly delighted that the legendary warrior women who had saved the House of Kassis were dining at her establishment. Jane slid into a seat while the other three women settled their toddlers down for a nap.

"These strollers are awesome. I would love to have an adult size one," Jo said with a grin.

Star nodded. "GPS tracking so they follow you all day long, no rough patches to jostle the babies, gentle rock mode to put them to sleep, and climate controlled so you don't have to worry about them getting too hot or cold," she sighed with delight.

River laughed. "All it needs is an expresso maker," she said, relaxing back in her seat.

"Now that we have you to ourselves, how's it going with Jarmen?" Star asked, leaning forward to rest her chin in the palms of her hands.

Jane laughed. "It is going very well. That's one of the reasons I came to town. I wanted to buy a new dress to wear tonight," she confessed.

"Oh! I'm a master at designs. If you ever want anything, let me know," Star said, sitting up.

River snorted. "Star should add a disclaimer to her 'master of designs'. She's a master at hiding every weapon known to man in her creations," she clarified.

Jane nodded. "I've seen some of your costumes. They are incredible. I can't believe how many knives appear as if by magic during your performances."

"Where are you going on your date?" Star asked.

"We're having dinner and going for a walk along the river," she replied.

"I'm so happy that you two found each other," Star said.

"I love him so much," Jane confessed with a happy sigh. "He is sweet and gentle and smart... and he is a fantastic lover," she added with a blush.

River laughed. "That helps," she said with a nod.

The topic turned to their men and Jane listened as they each described how they met their mates—and the challenges they had faced. It wasn't until she looked down at the time that she realized how late it was getting. She rose and gave the women an apologetic smile.

"I need to go. I'm making dinner," she said.

"I'll walk you out," Star offered, starting to rise from her chair.

"That's okay. I'm just parked over there," Jane replied with a wave of her hand.

"We'll see you later," Star replied.

Jane smiled and waved a hand before exiting the café. She paused on the curb and looked back and forth. The light to cross changed, and she started across. She was almost to the other side when the sound of an air bike revving caught her attention.

"Jane!" Star screamed.

Jane jumped out of the way, but the bike swerved and followed her. Pain exploded in her abdomen when the biker struck her and sent her flying. She rolled several feet before she came to a stop. She lifted a shaky hand and pressed it against her stomach. Warm liquid slid between her trembling fingers.

A crowd quickly gathered around her. She felt frantic hands touching her. Tears blurred her vision, and one slid down from the corner of her eye. A chill washed through her. Fortunately, shock was numbing any pain.

"Jane, hold on. Help is coming," River urgently said in a far-away voice.

"River, she's been stabbed," Star exclaimed with horror.

Jane licked her lips and tilted her head slightly toward Star. "Tell—"

"Hush, the medics will be here any minute," Star said.

It was hard to breathe, and dark spots danced in front of her eyes. She could hear people talking, the sounds of sirens, but it was hard to keep her eyes open.

"Star," she whispered.

"I'm here," Star said in a soothing voice.

"Tell-tell Jarmen— Tell Jarmen I... love... him," she forced out.

"You will tell Jarmen that, Jane. You just need to hang on for another minute," Star said in a determined voice.

"I'm… sorry," she whispered, suddenly feeling at peace.

"Jane, don't! Jane, Jarmen needs you!" River said in a sharp voice.

Jane didn't hear River and Star's frantic calls to the medics that arrived. Everything had faded, and she no longer heard the murmur of voices or felt pain. She couldn't escape the dark hand of Death this time.

The figure dressed in black watched from the shadows between two buildings. The glowing red eyes behind the face shield narrowed on the limp body being placed on the med skid. Lifting a gloved hand, Unit 626 connected the secure line.

"Mission A complete," Unit 626's emotionless voice relayed.

"Prepare for Mission B," Seanna ordered.

"Affirmative," Unit 626 replied.

Unit 626 replaced the communicator in the utility belt and turned the bike down the alley. Weeks of monitoring had finally paid off. The Unit who called himself Jarmen D'ju cared for the human woman, and after all this time watching, 626 was certain the Unit would do *anything* to save her. There was only one way now—and 626 would join him when he tried.

"Stand down!" Jazin ordered his men. "Jarmen, I know you are hurting, but killing Shavic will not bring Jane back."

Jarmen stared at the group of men standing between himself and the room where Jane was lying. Jazin reached down and helped Shavic up off the floor. The healer touched his bloody lip and grimaced. Jarmen's eyes flashed to the sedative that Shavic had been holding. It was still on the floor.

"Move out of my way," he snarled.

Fury and grief battled for supremacy. His body shook as he fought to keep from killing the man who he considered a friend. He whirled when he felt a hand on his shoulder. Gripping the man by his throat, he lifted him off his feet.

"Killing poor Luc will not bring our beloved Jane back either, Jarmen. Come, let us go see her together," Jon Paul said in a calm, soothing tone heavily laced with sorrow.

Luc clawed at Jarmen's wrist, struggling to breathe. Jarmen slowly lowered the human to his feet and released him. Num wrapped his arm around Luc's waist when his knees buckled.

Jarmen looked at Jon Paul. The tears in the man's eyes broke through his haze of rage—leaving behind heartbreaking sorrow and pain.

He gasped as the intense feeling of loss hit him. He staggered back, and Jazin reached for him. The overwhelming grief tore through him with more precision than the scalpels the scientists had used to slice him open. Jon Paul reached out and grabbed his other shoulder, steadying him.

"She cannot be gone," Jarmen hoarsely denied.

His voice was filled with confusion, pain, and an emotion he could not name. He shook his head, trying to clear his chaotic thoughts. They had just celebrated their six-week anniversary. Jane was going to teach him the art of cooking tonight. She couldn't be gone. They… had made plans.

Looking up, he stared into Jazin's eyes.

"Shavic can heal her," Jarmen said.

Jazin's eyes filled with compassion and grief. "There are some wounds even our technology cannot heal."

"Come, Jarmen. Do not let her go without saying goodbye," Jon Paul said, motioning for the men standing in front of the doors to move.

Jarmen stumbled forward, shaking off Jazin and Jon Paul's hands. He paused as the doors opened before he entered the surgery where Jane lay. The doors closed behind him. It took a moment for him to realize that Jazin and Jon Paul had stayed in the other room. They were giving him time alone to say goodbye.

The low hum of equipment surrounded him. He frantically focused on Jane's pale, peaceful face. A soft gray sheet was tucked around her. She looked as if she was sleeping. He stopped next to the surgical bed.

He lifted his hand and tenderly caressed the scrape along her temple before sliding his fingers down her bruised cheek. Bending, he slid his arms around her and cradled her. He buried his face along the curve of her neck, his shoulders shaking with grief. Low, gasping sobs shook his body.

He was supposed to protect her. She was his everything, and he was supposed to protect her. He tangled his fingers in her hair and held her tightly against him as he gasped for breath.

"Please, Goddess. Please...," he moaned, rocking back and forth.

He didn't know how long he held her. Time had no relevance to him. It wasn't until he felt a warm hand on his shoulder that he knew it was time to let her go.

"I want to know everything that happened," he demanded in a raw voice.

"Shavic completed a detailed report. River, Star, and Jo saw what happened. There was also video of the incident. I've already sent everything to you," Jazin said.

Jarmen tenderly laid Jane back against the cushion. He brushed her hair back from her face before running his fingers along her cheek. He analyzed her blood. Adjusting his eyes, he scanned her body, pausing on the deep puncture wound to her lower abdomen.

"I will find who did this and kill them," he warned, continuing to caress her cheek.

"I would do no less," Jazin answered.

He nodded. Bending, he kissed Jane's lips. Pain seared through him, turning his heart to ice.

I love you, Jane, he silently told her one last time.

Straightening, he turned and walked out of the room. He saw Jon Paul and Luc sitting in the corner. Jon Paul looked up at him with sad eyes. Luc's cheeks were damp from his tears. Num turned and followed behind him in silence.

CHAPTER 10

"How is he?" Torak asked.

Jazin shook his head. "He hasn't changed. He works all the time, seldom eats, and never sleeps," he replied.

Jarmen stepped into the room. Resentment that they were discussing him coursed through him. He walked over to his friends and held out the crystal disk.

"Here is the information Ristéard requested on the golden cylinder. There isn't much to go on. It would have helped having the actual item at hand. My analysis is based on the information he sent and the vidcom image. You can also tell him the next time he needs information, to ask me directly," he added, not concealing the resentment in his voice.

"Ristéard was reluctant to disturb you at this time because he knows that you are grieving. I was the one who suggested he involve you in this. You have been working closely on this project since the beginning, and I thought it... might help... if you were kept busy."

Jazin's expression conveyed the helplessness and compassion that Jarmen was now accustomed to seeing. He did not respond to this latest instance. There was nothing anyone could say or do to make it better.

Jazin quickly continued. "His own scientists were unable to give him any concrete answers, and you know Ristéard, patience isn't one of his strengths. I figured it was better to ask you and save a few scientists' lives than... well, you know what I mean," Jazin explained with a hesitant expression.

Jarmen knew exactly what he meant. He had much in common with Ristéard these days. In the month since Jane's death, he had thrown himself into his work and into his search to find the person responsible for her death. It was the only way he could survive the pain ripping him apart.

He had banned Jon Paul and Luc from his ship. Their promises that the pain would lessen with time angered him, and he was afraid he might hurt them. Jazin, Star, Walter, and Nema had come by a few times, but they left when he did not acknowledge them. He could not deal with their grief and his own.

"From the data given to me, I have concluded that the material is a foreign element, not found on any of the known planets within the Alliance. There is a high probability that it came from the same place as the red crystal," he added before turning to leave.

"Jarmen," Jazin called.

He continued walking. It would be daylight soon and he wanted to retreat to the isolation of his starship before the world woke. Darkness was his friend. He understood it.

"Jarmen," Jazin called again.

He stiffened his shoulders and turned. Jazin slowed when he saw the blaze of red in Jarmen's eyes. Jazin stopped a short distance from him.

"Is there something else that you need?" Jarmen asked.

Jazin sighed and shook his head. "No. Thank you for the work you've done. Your research on the Red Crystal ship has been a tremendous help to Ristéard and his people, and I'm sure that Ristéard appreciates it," he acknowledged.

"Good. If that is all," he said with a bow of his head.

He paused again when Jazin touched his arm. Indecision crossed Jazin's face before he spoke. Jarmen braced himself for whatever condolences his friend might say.

"Believe it or not, Star and I know what you are going through. When she thought I had died, she gave up. It-It was difficult for me to continue as well. I thought for sure I would die in that prison. The thought of losing Star nearly drove me out of my mind," he said.

"But you were not dead—Jane is," he replied in a voice devoid of emotion.

Grief crossed Jazin's face. "There are many people who care about you, Jarmen. I want you to know that we are here for you."

A muscle ticked in Jarmen's jaw. Jazin's concern for him was almost palpable. He bowed his head in acknowledgement before silently turning and walking away. There was nothing he could say because there was only one person in the world he needed to care about him, and she was gone.

He exited the building and crossed to his air bike. In seconds, he was speeding away from the palace. Before he realized it, he had turned away from his starship and was heading for the mountain observatory that overlooked the city. Half an hour later, he parked his air bike and crossed to the doors. The doors slid open as he approached.

Jarmen stood just inside the doors and surveyed the bottom floor. Bittersweet memories flooded him, and he walked forward. Pain radiated through his body, and he embraced it. Emotions, even the painful ones, were a gift Jane had given him.

He crossed to the staircase and slowly climbed them. In his mind, he heard Jane's soft laughter. His steps slowed when he reached the top. The balcony area was clear. There were no reminders of their wonderful evening except the ones he had saved.

Sinking to his knees, he closed his eyes and breathed. The pressure of his grief was too much to hold inside. Throwing his head back, he roared. The muscles along his neck stood out and his fists clenched as he cursed the heavens.

"How could someone so pure be taken?" he moaned, falling forward, and resting his upper body on his forearms.

He drew in ragged breaths of air, wishing with all his being that it had been him instead of Jane. The evidence was clear—she had been assassinated. The weapon had pierced her liver and was tainted with a fast-acting poison. The video feed showed the assassin turning and staring up at the camera. The dark helmet and thick leather jacket concealed the perpetrator's appearance.

The question that remained was why. Why would someone target Jane? She had no enemies.

He straightened and stared up at the stars through the glass ceiling. The communicator at his side pinged. He ignored it. It continued to ping over and over and over until he snatched it from his waist. He was about to crush it, but then he saw the message.

There may be a way to save Jane.

Half an hour later he strode onto his starship with Jon Paul, Luc, and the two bots following anxiously behind him. He passed through the storage bay and continued to the galley. Pouring a glass of water, he ignored the small group as they filed in behind him, but soon placed the glass on the counter and turned to face them.

"She's dead," he savagely bit out in a low voice.

Jon Paul and Luc nodded and replied, "Yes, but...."

They trailed off as his expression became thunderous. Luc scooted back behind the narrow table, pulling Jon Paul with him. Jarmen ground his teeth together.

"Get out," he ordered, walking toward the door.

He stopped when Num stood in the entrance, blocking his way. IQ peered up at Jarmen from between Num's legs. Jarmen placed his hand on the huge bot's chest.

"Before you dismantle us, listen," IQ said.

Jarmen's expression darkened when IQ presented a holographic image of the golden cylinder he had been researching for Ristéard. The knowledge that the robot had been accessing his files without his knowledge infuriated him until a quick scan showed that the source was Ricki's account.

"You should not hack into accounts. That is not part of your programming," he snapped, reaching for the crystal disk displaying the image.

IQ released a sliding, outraged beep and evaded Jarmen's reach with top speeds and sharp maneuvers, spinning his arms to keep Jarmen away. "I'm a robot! I do what I'm programmed to do, even if my actions stem from learning instead of my original coded behavior. If you want to blame someone, blame Jazin and Stan. Jazin requested that Stan find weaknesses in a Kassisan computer system. I think Jazin wanted to keep Stan busy, but I'm just a bot, so what do I know? Anyway, Stan wrote a malware program and decided to hack into Walter's account since he has a Kassisan *and* Elpidiosian account. Why not kill two species with one stone, right? Except the malware worked better than Stan anticipated because it—"

Jarmen sent a command to quiet the small bot's rambling. It wasn't hard to follow what happened next. Stan uploaded the malware to IQ, who uploaded it to Walter. When Walter connected with Ricki, the malware spread to her system and she inadvertently infected Ristéard's.

He was impressed by the human's ingenuity and skills. The fact that those same qualities would get the man killed if Ristéard found out about the intrusion also registered. Stan had found a small backdoor through an old program. The AI software the human was using was able to find a similar weakness in the Elpidiosian software and exploited it. Jazin had been smart to have the human test the Kassisan system.

"You said there was a way to save Jane," he said without emotion.

He stared at the hologram. He saw nothing new, nothing to connect it to Jane. Tiny particles were constantly moving beneath the flexible golden shell, clumping together before shifting and pulling apart. The metal's default state was a vaguely cylindrical formation, but Jarmen knew it had the capacity to form other shapes.

The metal contained a concentrated energy that he found fascinating, but the shell had shielded the internal structure from detailed study. Elpidiosian equipment had not been able to penetrate it beyond a general energy reading and the discovery that it was hollow. Until Jarmen could physically study the item, he could only speculate what the material might be used for. He had certainly never speculated that it could raise the dead.

"IQ has come up with a brilliant hypothesis, haven't you, my smart little friend?" Jon Paul said.

A ripple of lights flashed along IQ's chest at the compliment. "It was hidden in the myth of the Red Crystal ship."

"Hypothesis? Myths? What next? Dreams?" Jarmen scoffed, looking over his shoulder at Jon Paul and Luc.

"What about hope?" Luc replied in a quiet voice.

Bitterness sliced a deep path through Jarmen, and he turned to face the two men. "Hope died with Jane," he said in a voice devoid of emotion.

"What if we stop Jane from dying?" Num asked.

Jarmen twisted toward Num and stepped back. "Stop Jane from dying?" he repeated with a frown.

Num nodded. IQ rolled closer and held out his other hand. Jarmen started, staring at the cylinder lying in the small bot's palm. It was the same piece that he had been remotely studying.

"We told Ricki about our hypothesis. She gave this to us and said you should try," Luc explained behind him.

Jarmen reached out and picked up the gold cylinder. It was surprisingly light... and warm. He took a deep breath, stunned when he felt a connection to the nanobots within the metal. There was something about the technology that was such a familiar mix of organic and non-organic parts. The metal was... alive!

The small clump of crystals twisted and transformed. Deep grooves formed into odd patterns along the sides, and the cylinder glowed.

IQ nodded. "I was playing with it, and Luc said it looked like a key."

"We think it might control the Red Crystal ship," Jon Paul said.

Jarmen rolled the gold cylinder in his palm. Three cylinders had been discovered in the Red Crystal ship, tucked away in a box in the Ancient God's living quarters. The scientists on Elpidios thought they were jewelry. Jarmen had theorized that they were recording devices. Now, as he turned the anomalous cylinder, he could visualize it as a key.

"Num, share the Elpidiosian legend of the Red Crystal ship," Jon Paul said.

Jarmen shook his head. "I know the legend," he stated.

"With a key, you could operate the ship and stop Jane from being killed, couldn't you?" IQ asked, tentatively touching Jarmen's hand.

If a bot could have facial expressions, Jarmen would swear IQ's shimmering eyes were pleading with him. His throat tightened at the obvious love they all had for her.

He closed his eyes, running the probabilities of successfully completing such a mission if the Red Crystal ship could travel through time and space. While the odds were minimal, the outcome of not trying was fixed. Opening his eyes, he stared down at the golden key.

There had been *three* cylinders in the box. He would need the other two.

Curling his fingers around the cylinder, he inhaled deeply as hope began to glow inside him. He held a chance to save Jane in his grasp. How far back should he go? Would preventing her death have a disastrous ripple effect?

"I leave for Elpidios tonight," he announced, looking up.

Jon Paul laughed and placed a hand on his shoulder. "*Non, nous partirons ce soir.* No, *we* leave tonight, my friend. Jane is part of our family. We will go with you."

"Oui! You don't think we'd let you screw up the timelines of the universe without a little help from us, do you, eh?" Luc weakly joked, coming to stand next to them.

"Num is going," Num stated, folding his arms across his metallic chest.

Jarmen looked down at IQ who was turning in an excited circle.

"Someone needs to keep an eye on this gang!" IQ exclaimed.

Jarmen started to shake his head before he stopped and sighed. "Arrive here before dark or I leave without you," he ordered.

He pushed past Num and stepped out of the galley. This was a mission where nothing could go wrong, and if that meant asking for help... a foreign concept to Jarmen... he would ask.

Exiting his starship, he strode over to his air bike, and seconds later he was heading to the one place he had been avoiding—The Cirque de Magik complex. If anyone could help him make the Red Crystal ship disappear, it was the people behind the greatest show in the universe —who also happened to be Ristéard's in-laws.

"Jarmen! Oh, love, come in, come in," Nema said, wiping her hands on her apron. "Walter! Walter, Jarmen is here."

Jarmen stood awkwardly in the narrow foyer of Walter and Nema's travel trailer. They still used their former home during the day before going to the larger home that Torak had built for them. Jarmen scanned the interior. This was the first time he had ever been inside. Everything was adapted for Walter and Nema's shorter stature.

He followed Nema up the three steps to the living room. Walter emerged from the back. Nema waved Jarmen to the long, U-shaped couch, and he perched on the edge of the furthest seat cushion.

"Would you like a drink?" she asked.

"No, thank you," he replied with a slight shake of his head.

Walter climbed the steps and sat down on the couch across from him with Nema by his side. His gaze immediately went to their clasped hands, and his throat tightened. The foreign emotion of guilt rose in his throat.

"Jarmen, I'm glad you came. Nema and I—" Walter paused and looked at his wife. She returned her husband's gaze with a sad, supportive smile. Walter cleared his throat and continued. "We both want to express our… our heartfelt sympathy."

Nema nodded. Tears glistened in her eyes. She gave him a watery smile.

"Jane was like a daughter to us," she said.

Jarmen nodded. "Yes… I know. Jane loved you both very much," he replied.

Stating known facts was a normal part of making conversation, Jarmen knew. Sometimes it was better than silence, even for him.

"If there is anything Nema and I can do to help you, I want you to know that we are here," Walter said.

He returned their earnest gazes with one of his own and realized that he couldn't ask them to put themselves in danger—or alienate their daughter's mate on a mission that had less than a .001 percent chance of success. He shook his head and rose to his feet.

"This was a mistake. I shouldn't have come. I apologize for interrupting you," he said.

"Sit down," Nema ordered in a surprisingly stern tone.

Jarmen sat down in an even more surprising compliance. He stared at the woman across from him. The determined look in her eyes vaguely reminded him of another woman... one from his past.

"Now, let's try this again," Walter said. "What do you need?"

Jarmen tore his eyes away from Nema and looked at Walter with a frown. "I need your help to steal the Red Crystal ship from Ristéard so that I can go back in time and stop Jane from being killed," he stated in a firm, matter-of-fact voice.

Walter's low laugh caught him by surprise. Jarmen tilted his head to the side with a questioning expression.

"We'll have to do it without telling Ricki," Nema warned. "You know she is a horrible liar. She'll never be able to lie to Ristéard convincingly if he asks her if we are up to something."

"She'll be fine. We don't have to tell her everything," Walter said, rubbing his hands together with growing glee. "I can't wait to see Ristéard's face when he realizes his top-secret ship is missing!"

"Ricki is already aware of the Red Crystal ship's capabilities. She has instructed me to... try. Unfortunately, I do not believe Ristéard would be as agreeable. I believe the less she knows of my plans, the better it will be," he replied.

"You don't think it will hurt the planet, do you?" Nema murmured with concern. "Ricki said the ship produced all those red crystals that protect the planet from dying."

"The mountain has enough red crystals to protect the planet for more than a thousand years," Jarmen stated. "They originated from the ship, but have spread through fissures over thousands of years until the entire mountain range has veins of it. The mining and distribution of the crystals are in full scale production. They will be fine."

"What can we do for you, then?" Walter asked.

"I need you to distract Ristéard, his security, and his scientists long enough for me to activate the ship. I would do it, but I will need all my concentration on operating the ship," he explained.

He knew from his connection with the gold nanobots within the key that operating the Red Crystal ship would require a sentient mind able to directly connect with nanobots. Luckily, he was one of the few beings in the universe for whom that would not be a problem.

Walter frowned. "We'll need a map of the interior of the research facility," he said, looking at Nema.

She nodded. "And a list of everyone and their positions and work schedules, as well as any cameras," she continued.

"Stan can handle the tech stuff. We'll need a distraction. No... Ristéard would never let us all into the research facility, and it would be too difficult to set everything up in such a well-monitored space. Ricki said there are people working in there round the clock. If we can't go in, then we need to figure out a way to get the Red Crystal ship to come out," Walter said, rubbing his chin before a grin spread across his face.

"You have an idea?" Jarmen asked.

Walter chuckled. "I think it is about time Cirque de Magik paid a visit to Elpidios," he announced.

"I'll contact Ricki this evening," Nema said.

"The Cirque de Magik— Are you ready for that? Will *everyone* be there?" Jarmen asked, studying the excited expressions on the couple's faces with worry.

Nema rose from the couch and walked over to him. She gave him an overjoyed smile and patted his knee. If anything, the gesture added to his unease.

"Don't you worry about it, dear. We'll make sure you have the time you need to steal our son-in-law's fancy red ship. You just focus on saving Jane. Now, how about a nice piece of apple pie? I baked it fresh this morning," she said.

He found himself nodding as Nema descended the short steps to the kitchen. When he returned his attention to Walter, the man was watching him with a thrilled expression on his face.

"Is there something else I should know?" he inquired.

Walter chuckled and shook his head. "No-no, I'm just imagining Ristéard's face when he realizes what has happened," he said.

"You seem unusually pleased with the idea of stealing the ship from him," he observed.

"You bet your ass I am. It is poetic justice after he kidnapped Ricki. Making a huge ship vanish will be the *pièce de résistance!*" Walter said with another gleeful rub of his hands. "Doing it in front of his royal blue nose is going to be even better!"

"What exactly do you have in mind?" he asked, preparing to adjust his assessment of the risks.

Walter gave him an offended glare. "Magic, of course, my boy. We are, after all, the Cirque de Magik—the greatest show in the universe! There is nothing we cannot make disappear. What happens when Ristéard realizes it won't reappear is a matter we'll deal with later. Now, let's get some of Nema's pie before she remembers I'm supposed to be on a diet," he said.

CHAPTER 11

E lpidios
    One Week Later

"Couldn't we have just gone to Kassis?" Ristéard asked with a wave of his hand.

"You were supposed to come a month ago—and the month before that," Walter pointed out.

Ristéard frowned. "I have a planet to save. I can't just drop everything and come visit," he growled.

"Ristéard," Ricki admonished with a raised eyebrow.

Ristéard's cheeks flushed a slightly darker color. "We were coming next week," he defended.

Ricki's lips twitched in a suppressed smile, and she shook her head. Jarmen watched the interaction, but his mind was elsewhere. He was astonished at how quickly Walter and Nema were able to pack up the big top, animals, and entire cast and crew of the Cirque de Magik, transport them to Elpidios, and set everything up again. It was worthy of any military operation.

"We wanted to see you and Ricki. We miss her so much, especially after what happened to Jane, and with Ricki pregnant...," Nema began, her eyes filling with tears.

Ristéard's stern demeanor softened. "We heard of the accident. I'm deeply sorry for your loss. I know how upset Ricki was when she found out," he said.

Jarmen wanted to correct Ristéard's characterization of Jane's death, but he didn't. He caught Walter's eye and nodded. Walter lifted the corner of his mouth in a secret smile and looked to Stan.

Jarmen bowed his head to Walter before he quietly excused himself. He crossed the expansive lawn of the palace with Stan at his side. Marvin and Martin Rue, the two Kor d'Lur scientists who had taken refuge with the circus when they were stranded on Earth, soon appeared next to them, and the foursome continued in silence. They wove their way through the maze of amusement rides, arcades, and tents until they reached a surprisingly mundane tent at the far end. Stan didn't speak until they entered the dim interior filled with computers.

"Gentlemen, have a seat and watch a true master of the computer at work," Stan said, cracking his knuckles and plopping onto a chair on wheels in front of the long table.

Jarmen looked at the row of holographic displays that appeared. Each screen displayed a different real-time image of the circus. He sat down in the chair next to Stan and watched the human's fingers move across the virtual keyboard.

"With the schematics you gave us and the connections Marvin and Martin installed in the complex, I tied into the security system around the Red Crystal ship," Stan explained.

Jarmen already knew this. He had been monitoring the feeds since they went live and processing the relevant data. What he did not have, yet, was a plan. Working with others introduced so many variables that Jarmen did not know how to account for, but he could not do this alone.

Each of the hologram screens changed to the large tent where the Red Crystal ship was being stored. He still couldn't believe that Walter, with Ricki's help, had been able to talk Ristéard into letting the circus use the ship as a backdrop for their premier performance on Elpidios. Ristéard had reluctantly agreed, but only after setting up heavy security around the big tent.

The real-time vidcom feed showed the restricting perimeter around the ship and the movements of security and scientists. Only a select few others were allowed, and no one, including the scientists and security members, were allowed to approach the ship without either Ristéard or one of his handpicked personal guards accompanying them.

The precautions were understandable. Not only was betrayal a common risk for people in power, but that duplicity had recently happened to Ristéard. His best friend and personal guard, Andras, had tried to kill Ristéard and Ricki. The man's actions had been motivated by greed. Something as powerful and valuable as the Red Crystal ship was definitely worth protecting.

"I need the other two keys to the ship. Pull up the video feed of Ristéard," Jarmen requested.

The bottom right screen changed and an image of Ricki talking to Ristéard appeared. Stan narrowed his eyes and tilted his head as the light caught something metallic peeking out from Ristéard's neckline.

"Aw, man. This sucks," Stan groaned. He adjusted the angle and enlarged it to show twin glimmers of gold hanging from the chain around Ristéard's neck. "Damn, these are going to be tricky to get."

"Is it possible to replicate the key?" Martin inquired.

Marvin shook his head. "No, each ship and each key is designed with slight variations," Marvin replied.

"That's right, I forgot that Glacian mythology was one of your areas of expertise," Martin said.

Marvin nodded and looked at Stan and Jarmen. "While not as interesting or as detailed as the Kassisan and Elpidiosian myths, there was a mention of the same invaders attacking Isotope, the home world of the Glacians, and the appearance of Red Crystal ships to battle them. I've always had a fondness for myths. There is often a hint of truth in the stories of the past."

Jarmen watched as Stan leaned forward and adjusted the angle of the camera. The image enlarged to show the chain around Ristéard's neck. The glimmer of gold shone like twin beacons from the end. Stan sat back in his seat, pulled a small bag out, and began popping pieces of white fluff into his mouth while Jarmen and the two brothers sat forward in theirs.

Stan waved a hand at the screen and mumbled around the popcorn in his mouth, "I saw the gold thingies around Ristéard's neck earlier today. When you started talking gold keys, a light-bulb clicked on. I was hoping I was wrong."

Jarmen's eyes narrowed on the two gold cylinders. He needed them—and he would have them. The question was how to steal them without Ristéard knowing.

"I can see the look in your eyes, man. As Boom would say, 'no worries, mate.' We've got this," Stan added with a laugh.

Jarmen frowned. "You have this? How?"

"Marcus," Stan and the two Kor d'Lurs said in unison with huge grins on their faces.

"So, this living ship was on Isotope. That's an ice planet, isn't it?" IQ asked, looking up at the report flashing in front of him.

"Num no like ice. It makes my joints freeze," Num said.

"We are not going to Isotope," Jarmen replied.

"I might add a heater to your oil reserve. That would be good, eh?" Luc suggested.

Jarmen looked over his shoulder with a frown. "I repeat, we are not going to Isotope," he said.

"What else do we know about the ship we are going to steal?" Jon Paul asked.

IQ tilted his round head and continued scanning the report summarizing the Red Crystal ship's log. "The Ancient Gods arrived in our galaxy and our timeline after they got into some big fight and got their butts kicked."

IQ shook his head. "You'd think with a ship that amazing, they'd be better fighters," he added.

"What if the invaders had even bigger and badder time-travel ships, eh? Then they would be the baddest of all the bad," Luc replied.

"Is badder even a word?" Num asked.

Jarmen gritted his teeth.

"*Non*, but I believe *batter* is a cannabis concentrate. It is named that because it resembles a thick cake batter," Jon Paul said.

"I am not talking about batter. I am talking about badder! Eh!" Luc retorted, grumbling under his breath in French.

Jarmen closed his eyes and breathed deeply. It was a technique Jane had taught him. The thought of Jane sent a shaft of pain through him. He pressed his hands down on the desk and rose to his feet.

"Stay here," he ordered.

He shot a dark look at all four pairs of eyes staring at him. The protest slowly faded from Jon Paul and Luc's eyes.

"I will call you when I am ready for you," he said.

Exiting the galley, he strode down the corridor to the cargo bay. A targeted thought had the platform lowering. He mounted the air bike and exited his ship, escaping into the darkness of the night.

Cool air surrounded him as he gained altitude. Below him, the circus was blazing with bright lights, and he heard the muted sounds of laughter. Citizens of the nearby capital strolled through the arcade games and displays. A spotlight illuminated the sky, guiding visitors to discover the magic of the circus.

He turned away, heading for the mountains and the vault where the Red Crystal ship had been discovered. There were still many questions he needed answers to before he tried to achieve what was nearly impossible.

His heart ached for Jane. If he closed his eyes, he could almost hear her laughter on the wind, her arms wrapped tightly around his waist, and the warmth of her breath against his neck.

"I will find you," he promised, his words whipped away by the wind as he sped toward the distant mountains.

Unit 626 stood in the shadows and watched as the Unit who called himself Jarmen sped away. The mission was proceeding according to plan. The audio device installed in the circus master's mobile living quarters had revealed Jarmen's plans to steal the Red Crystal ship. Unfortunately, the device had needed to be removed before their departure from Kassis. An intense security sweep was performed on every unit before it arrived on Elpidios.

Irritation flashed through 626, but the Unit dutifully activated the communication device attached to the black helmet.

"Status report," Seanna demanded.

"Mission B is in progress. I will inform you when Unit 482 has taken control of the Red Crystal ship."

There was a long silence. The Draka must have detected the slight edge in 626's response.

A movement caught the Unit's attention. Someone was approaching Jarmen's ship. 626 moved deeper into the shadows.

"Draka Specimen 626, do you need a software upgrade?" Seanna finally inquired.

A full-body wave of intense agony ripped through sensitive neurons. As the pain faded, 626 flexed each finger and counted.

"Negative. Program parameter is working correctly. I will inform you the moment Unit 482 has taken command of the Red Crystal ship," 626 replied in a tone devoid of emotion.

"See that you do," Seanna replied before ending the communication.

626 pulled a micro-injector from the leather pouch attached to the utility belt. Placing the injector against the narrow strip of exposed skin between the concealing helmet and thick leather jacket, 626 depressed the button. The chemical compound poured through 626's bloodstream, halting the degeneration of vital organs—temporarily.

626 studied the man who stood outside of the Unit's ship. It was one of the Kor d'Lurs. Stepping back and squatting behind a large boulder, 626 remained still when the man rotated in a semi-circle and scanned the area. The Kor d'Lurs were a mild-mannered species—until they weren't. 626 had no desire to tangle with one of them, much less two.

Settling back in the shadows, 626 waited for Jarmen's return. The Unit would not go without his companions—or rather, his companions would not allow the Unit to go without them. The delay was good. It would allow the drugs regenerating 626's organs to finish working.

CHAPTER 12

In the cave where the Red Crystal ship had been discovered, Jarmen sat at one of the computers set up for the scientists, and scrolled through Ristéard's files.

Ricki's eye for obscure details had been instrumental in finding the Red Crystal ship's location and saving the planet. Jarmen paused, surprised to learn that Ricki's biological father was from Isotope. Jarmen had only been told that Ricki was able to decipher the map and messages embedded on a pair of ancient doors. She had discovered the secret to opening the vault in those carvings.

There might be something there to explain how the ship could travel through time and space. He should see these doors for himself.

Jarmen rose from the console and looked at the vacant area where the ship had been found. Mounds of red crystals, a by-product of the ship, filled the interior of the vault.

Scientists moved through the vault, taking samples, and monitoring the decreasing radiation levels on the planet. His gaze paused on the massive doors.

Three scientists were scanning the doors, documenting the unfamiliar writing and symbols etched into them. He created his own record and sent it back to his ship.

He was scanning the third row when a pattern emerged, hidden within the message. As his mind connected the symbols, they merged until a three-dimensional map formed before him.

In the center of the map was one of the golden keys. He stiffened, realizing that the writing on the doors was… the code for the time-space travel. It was mixed in with nonsense information and symbols.

A sense of wonder swept through him at the Ancients' ingenuity. They had given instructions… in plain sight, but only to those who had the ability to detect and process the data. Because of the nonsense coding mixed into the symbols, a non-living entity, such as IQ or Num, would read the coding as single layers, not multi-dimensional.

He needed the doors closed so he could download the full circular pattern.

It took another hour before the scientists called it a night. He ignored them as they exited the empty cavern. Two security guards stood at attention outside of the massive doors.

"The Empress has instructed you to ask us if you need anything," one of the security guards said.

"I do not require anything. If I do, I will summon you," he replied.

"Yes, sir."

The security guard's glance flashed to the badge Jarmen wore. Thanks to Ricki, he had the highest security clearance and wouldn't be asked to leave. The guard bowed his head and nodded to his companion. Jarmen waited until both men disappeared in the direction the scientists had departed.

Once he was alone, he stood back and activated the doors. The noise of the gears echoed in the chamber as the massive doors slowly slid together and locked into place.

Standing before them, he focused on the embedded code. He was in awe as images began to rise out of the etchings. Billions of globes, each with the golden keys in the middle of them appeared before him. He gasped, his body going rigid as the information poured into his mind. His eyes glowed a deep, blood-red, as trillions of gigabytes of information were downloaded, processed, and linked.

The process took mere minutes, but it left him dazed and disoriented. As the last piece of the puzzle fell into place, he realized that embedded in the code was a vidcom. A shudder ran through him as the surrounding landscape changed.

～

Elpidios

01.2 AAI (After Alien Invasion)

"Commander Starla, General Zephren wished me to inform you that the other captains will be in range of Kassis within the hour."

"Thank you, Carrie, I will be there shortly," Commander Starla replied.

When Carrie left, Commander Starla looked directly at the screen and said, *"Personal entry: Stardate Earth 8514. I'm recording this for historical preservation. In the Earth year 8509, an alien species we call the Death Souls was defeated when we harnessed their own technology. During an early battle, my father, General Zephren Strauss, discovered that the Death Souls' blood contained a rare, red bio-crystal. This element in their blood allowed them to travel through space-time when combined with an element found in the ruin of their ships—a golden living metal.*

"Through his experiments, General Zephren learned that the crystals in the Death Souls' blood could be harvested, grown, and used to create living ships. We call them Zephren ships. In the right environment, we can interact with these ships through the gold element.

"This is when our mission began. General Zephren's breakthrough allowed us to go on the offensive. The space-time activation is controlled through a neural connection between the commander and the ship through a trio of gold keys. I-I-I-I will not go into the specifics as to how the connection works between the ship, the commander, and the living metal.

Jarmen blinked and frowned when a line of corrupted code interrupted the transmission. The disruption lasted barely a nano-second, but it was enough to disorient him. His head began to throb as the data reconnected.

"After the remaining Death Souls retreated from Earth, the Council decided we would pursue them to save other worlds. It is too dangerous to allow the Death Souls to increase in number and rebuild their fleet. Earth's population was almost completely decimated. The Death Souls must never return.

"We first followed them to an ice world. Isotope's environment and the natives' ability to control ice saved them from the Death Souls, but other worlds were not so fortunate.

"A battle on Elpidios has damaged my ship, and it is necessary to leave it concealed in the mountains of this planet. The environment on Elpidios is conducive to the needs of my ship and will allow the crystals the necessary time to regenerate.

"In the meantime, the Death Souls have begun an attack on a nearby planet called Kassis. My crew has been dispersed among the remaining ships. We will continue to fight. We are vastly outnumbered, but will not give up. Today may be our last chance at defeating the Death Souls. May victory guide our hand and prevent other worlds from experiencing this tragedy. Commander Starla Strauss of the Zephren II for Earth's Defense Fleet."

Jarmen frowned when the petite commander ended the transmission. The name immediately struck him as familiar, as did the woman who was human and had similar features and coloring as Star Strauss— Jazin's mate.

According to Kassisan history, an alien species attacked the Kassisan world, nearly obliterating the population of the planet. The Kassisans were saved when fantastic ships appeared out of the heavens. Jazin Ja Kel Coradon's namesake had been the leader of the Kassisan forces and had fallen in love with an alien commander—a woman named Starla.

Jarmen recognized that what he was witnessing was of significant historical relevance. The vidcom proved the legend of Kassis was based on fact.

Most important to his own mission, however, was the knowledge that the Red Crystal ships had originated in the future!

Which means the ships work.

He studied the door again. The threads of the multiverse seemed to reach out to him. In each, he could see that the keys were essential. They energized the red crystal. He *had* to get the other two keys if he was to save Jane.

Four days later, Jarmen stood stiffly in the shadows of the magnificent big top watching the performance. Marvin and Martin stood across from him next to Marcus the Magnificent. Marcus would be up next to perform.

Jarmen carefully studied the Red Crystal ship in meticulous detail. Once again, he was impressed with Walter's powers of persuasion. Walter hadn't stopped at showcasing Elpidios' newest national treasure to its people. No, Ristéard's father-in-law had gone one step further; he had actually convinced Ristéard to allow Marcus to use the Red Crystal ship as a prop in his magic show.

That hadn't stopped Ristéard from being paranoid. The Grand Ruler was extremely cautious about who went near the stage and the ship. Still, Nema and Jarmen had successfully sent IQ and Num to hide in The Red Crystal Ship. Jarmen would likely need all three keys for speed and the ability to time-travel, but with just one, he had found that he was able to open and close the ship's door from a distance.

"Step between the mirrors," Martin instructed.

When Jarmen moved into position, he realized the mirrors were two-way, so he could see the surrounding area, but anyone looking at the mirrors would only see reflective glass. The illusion was in the cut of the mirror and the way it captured the surrounding landscape.

Martin closed him inside. Jarmen breathed deeply, focusing on the Red Crystal ship to keep from feeling claustrophobic. Marcus was doing one magic trick after another, enthralling the crowd who had never seen such a performance before. Martin and Marvin wheeled out the mirror containing Jarmen and stopped next to Marcus.

"And now, ladies and gentlemen, for my greatest feat ever…." Marcus paused for dramatic effect, lifting his arms outward and walking forward. "I will need two brave volunteers from the audience to perform my death defying next act. Two volunteers who are not afraid of death. Two brave souls who will trust me with their very lives! Who in this vast audience is brave enough to look death in the eye and say 'I fear nothing!'?"

"Us! We volunteer!"

"We fear nothing! Eh, Jon Paul? We are the bravest of the brave!" Luc shouted, puffing his chest out and slapping his hand against his chest.

"Ah, we have two enthusiastic volunteers. Step forward," Marcus declared.

The spotlight flashed across the ring and focused on the two fervent Frenchmen who were waving their hands above their heads. It was almost a cringeworthy moment as they scrabbled down out of the stands. Jarmen's sensitive hearing picked up Marvin and Martin's low groans.

"Tonight, before your very eyes, I, Marcus the Magnificent, along with the assistance of my two very eager volunteers, will make an entire spaceship disappear!" Marcus announced with dramatic flair.

"I think not!" Ristéard roared, standing up in the special box seat reserved for him.

"Ah, a disbeliever of my abilities! Ladies and gentlemen, may I present my third and most prestigious volunteer... the Grand Ruler of Elpidios, Ristéard Roald," Marcus announced with a crescendo of volume.

Jarmen breathed deeply. Not being able to control every aspect of this mission was torture, but it must be done. Marcus would be able to do this.

Ristéard scowled and didn't move. Martin walked over to the bottom of the stands where the spotlight was now shining on Ristéard.

"Move now," Marvin told Jarmen.

He stepped out of the mirrored cube and connected with the ship. An opening appeared, and a dark red platform lowered. He stepped onto it, entering the ship while all eyes—and lights—were directed at Ristéard.

IQ met him, swirling in a circle with excitement. The rapid movement was stressful in Jarmen's current state of mind. His objective was to avoid notice until it was time, and though IQ was quiet for the moment, Jarmen was still tempted to crush the little bot under his boot. He reminded himself that Jane would be horrified.

"Where is Num?" he growled instead.

"Watching from the bridge. I love how easily Marcus can distract a crowd. Did you see the holograms of us that Stan created? I could not tell the real us from the fake us!" IQ exclaimed with delight.

The holographic images of him and the two bots were sitting a few seats away from Ricki and Ristéard.

"Yes, I saw," he stated, striding down a glowing corridor toward the bridge.

"You just be ready to open that melty-doorway thingy for Jon Paul and Luc. They'll have the keys," IQ retorted.

Jarmen stepped onto the bridge. His connection with the ship was almost complete. He only needed a few more minutes.

"Jarmen, there is a problem," Num announced, breaking through his concentration.

"What is the issue?" he demanded.

"I-I-I...," Num stuttered before his head jerked back and forth several times.

"What's the matter, you big pile of bolts?" IQ growled, wheeling up to look at the screen.

"My mistake. Ristéard is coming down the steps," Num replied with a slight hint of confusion in his metallic voice.

Jarmen studied the large robot for a moment before nodding. He would have Luc and Jon Paul run a diagnostic on Num after they departed.

He locked his eyes on the two Frenchmen. There was only this one chance to get the keys. They had better not mess this up.

The act below played out as if in slow motion before him. He focused on each movement, recording and analyzing each slight-of-hand gesture while Marcus weaved his special brand of magic on the audience. Most would have missed the split second when Marcus laid one hand on Ristéard's shoulder while the other moved in front of Ristéard, but hidden at the nape of the Grand Ruler's neck, the clasp of his necklace released, and the ends hovered above his shirt. It was accomplished with a magnetic string and the magician's dexterity.

Marcus made Ristéard chuckle. The spotlight flashed to the stands again, this time pinpointing Ricki who was watching the performance with an amused expression, but Jarmen kept his eyes locked on Marcus as he slipped the two golden cylinders off the chain that had been around Ristéard's neck, before adding two fake ones in their place.

Marcus looped the magnetic string to close the necklace clasp, gave Ristéard a friendly slap on the shoulder as he removed the string from the necklace, and welcomed Ricki to the stage as the audience roared their approval. Lowering his hand, the magician slipped the keys to Marvin, who dropped the keys into Jon Paul's pocket.

"Look, Marcus is going to make Jon Paul and Luc disappear now!" IQ exclaimed.

Sure enough, Marcus had Marvin and Martin direct Jon Paul and Luc to the mirrors. The two Frenchmen appeared to be stepping through the mirror. They both turned as if in shock before grinning and waving to the cheering crowd.

Stan's voice came over his headset, "Once Ristéard lowers the red curtain over the ship, that is your cue."

"Affirmative. I will be ready," Jarmen replied.

He breathed deeply and connected with the ship and the multitude of star maps. He was still processing the information and how to think in the fourth dimension.

"Put the platform thingy down," IQ ordered in an excited voice.

Jarmen was already lowering the platform for Jon Paul and Luc by the time IQ made his excited demand. Jarmen retracted the platform the second the two Frenchmen appeared in the loading bay of the ship. The low hum of the ship was muffled by the heavy curtain lying over it and the increased volume of the music.

"Safe journey, my friend. Bring Jane back to us safe and sound—and if you can, bring some Bubble Yum Bubble Gum!" Stan requested.

Jarmen held out his hand for the golden keys as Jon Paul stepped onto the bridge. Relief swept through him when his fingers wrapped around them. He focused, pulling up the multi-dimensional drive.

"You may want to sit down," he warned.

"You don't need to tell me twice, my friend—not with the way your eyes are glowing," Luc muttered as he hurriedly found a seat.

Holographic star maps appeared in front of Jarmen, glowing a brilliant aquamarine color. Three red crystal cylinders grew out of the control panel in front of Jarmen. He aligned each key with its corresponding crystal.

"Are his eyes supposed to be glowing that bright?" Luc loudly whispered.

"Is the ship supposed to be glowing this bright?" IQ questioned.

"Hush, the both of you! Let Jarmen concentrate. Do you want him to blow us up?" Jon Paul growled.

Num tilted his head and hummed for a moment before he shook it in disagreement. "The energy emitting from the keys has a high likelihood of destroying the entire planet because of the disbursement of—"

"I will not blow anyone or anything up," Jarmen gritted out, cutting off the large robot's analysis. "I cannot say that I will not deposit all of you in the middle of a distant planet."

"He doesn't mean that... does he, Jon Paul?" Luc asked.

"Of course not. Now be silent and let him concentrate!" Jon Paul retorted with a nervous look at Jarmen.

Jarmen breathed deeply, blocked out the mutterings of the others, and focused on his connection with the Red Crystal ship. The information flowing between him and the ship was highly complex. A thin coating of sweat beaded his skin as the pressure inside his head grew.

"You may want to put a move on it, Jarmen. Marcus can't drag this out any longer," Stan warned.

"The calculations are almost complete," he growled.

"You've got to hurry, Jarmen. Ristéard will kill us all when he discovers what we've done," Luc nervously added.

"Hey, look at that! It looks almost like you can touch it," IQ exclaimed.

"Don't touch—!" Jarmen hissed.

His warning came too late. The glowing aquamarine orb of the star chart that he was forming distorted when IQ touched a metal finger to it. Jarmen's head jerked back as if he had been shocked when the connection was made.

The explosive energy from the golden keys surged through the red crystal and into the star chart. Information poured through Jarmen. His eyes blazed a ruby red as he processed the command that IQ had unwittingly triggered with his touch.

"Perhaps this was not such a good idea, eh?" Luc groaned.

The world around them tilted out of focus, shimmering as Jarmen locked onto the world that IQ had selected. A small part of Jarmen was aware of what was going on around him. Jon Paul and Luc were frantically securing their restraints. IQ, realizing he had made a drastic error in judgment, had retreated from the bridge. Num stood locked to the floor, his eyes glowing as he stared toward the front viewscreen.

The red velvet curtain fluttered down onto the stage floor. Stan's voice distorted as the ship dematerialized. The last thing Jarmen registered before the ship disappeared was the look of disbelief and fury on Ristéard's face.

CHAPTER 13

U nit 626 slipped through the heavy fabric of the big top. The shouts of guards mixed with the excited whispers of the departing crowd of patrons. 626 pulled the hood of the cloak higher as two more guards rushed by.

A glance at the signal on the communicator filled 626 with a rare sense of satisfaction. The program was working. No matter where Jarmen went, 626 would know.

626 studied the current position. The first stop was personal. 626 broke from the crowd and headed away from the bright lights of the Cirque de Magik. A mental command summoned the transport hidden a short distance away.

626 jumped on the air bike as it slowed before powering the bike away from the city. A half-hour later, 626 secured the air bike in the outer storage specially made for it on the sleek ship.

The space ship was an old Draka gunship that 626 had modified with additional weaponry and a newer, custom-made Kassisan propulsion system downloaded from files hidden within the Draka computer system. This was an advantage that 626's handlers were unaware of—and it would stay that way.

626 discovered the information on Doctor Seanna Labyrinth's personal system. The information was mixed in with other documents that once belonged to the handler's father. Hidden in an encrypted file were the schematics for a prototype engine using the Kassisan crystals and information on a Kassisan traitor named Grif Tai Tek. The now-deceased Alliance-Kassis councilman had been stealing and selling top-secret information to help finance his pet project of trying to over-throw the Ja Kel Coradon royal family.

There was more information about the human women who had captured the hearts and imaginations of the Kassisan people; especially those of Torak, Manota, and Jazin Ja Kel Coradon. 626 had down-loaded the information, then permanently deleted all records of it from Doctor Seanna Labyrinth's computer system.

Also in those files was the mention of a deserted laboratory belonging to Labyrinth's father. No description of the laboratory was given beyond the fact that it belonged to General Cerberus Teivel, the primary handler's father. There were no records of the Draka experi-ments. Not even the location of the lab was in the file.

The knowledge that there were more experiments—another Unit that had survived and was... free—had intrigued 626. Unit 482 had given himself a name, lived among others without fear or a need to be hidden, and had friends—others who actually cared about him—enough to risk their lives for him.

What intrigued 626 the most was that 482—Jarmen—did not need the regenerative medication that 626 required.

Unit 626 programmed the moon of Ala'mont into the ship's navigation system, connected the ship to the Elpidiosians' spaceport command center, and in seconds, 626 had secured the command's approval for departure.

Freedom will finally be within my grasp.

Hidden Lab

On the moon of Ala'mont

The ripple of space was nearly undetectable as the crystal ship materialized a short distance from the moon. This was not where Jarmen had intended to take them. The location was the spot IQ had touched on the star chart. Jarmen had recognized the quadrant, and the moon had formed in his mind.

"Are we there yet?" Luc's unsteady voice inquired.

The unexpected comment reminded Jarmen that he was not alone—not this time. He had returned to the moon base on several occasions since his rescue. The first time had been in an effort to remember who he had been before he was changed. The other times had been to search for information about what had been done to him.

There were rumors that a few others like him had survived, but to date, he had found no evidence to support those claims. He powered down the time-space drive. The glow around the golden keys dimmed.

"Where are we?" Jon Paul asked.

"We are in orbit around the moon of Ala'mont," he replied.

"Why did we come here? I thought we were going back in time to stop Jane's death," Luc said, coming to stand next to Jarmen and Jon Paul.

"We are. This was... not planned," Jarmen replied.

"I'm sorry, Jarmen. I didn't know that would happen if I touched the glowing, globey-thing," IQ said.

Jarmen closed his eyes.

He's still learning, Jarmen. Be patient. I think it is adorable how enthusiastic IQ is about everything.

That was what Jane had said after she brought the robots with her to his lab. It had been the first time any of them had been there. IQ had been buzzing around the lab, exclaiming over the different experiments in development, and the exuberant bot had accidentally activated an incomplete remote space robot, sending it careening around the room.

It had taken Jarmen several minutes to shut down the wayward bot, and the workroom became a mess. Equipment and tools were scattered everywhere. The damaged bot took an additional three weeks to repair. Jarmen hadn't told Jane that—though, she must have figured it out during her daily visits to bring him lunch.

The memory of her wrapping her arms around IQ's round body, her hands tenderly soothing the distraught robot, and her eyes looking up at him with a pleading expression and a hint of wry amusement were not unlike the looks in Jon Paul and Luc's eyes now when he looked back at the two men.

"There was no harm... done," he managed to say. "However, from this point on, none of you should touch anything in the ship without clearing it with me first," he said sternly.

"What about the bathroom?" Luc asked.

"Luc!" Jon Paul hissed.

Luc's expression turned to confusion. "It is not an unreasonable question. I need to go."

"Let me clarify. Touch nothing on the bridge or in any area except the sleeping quarters and the galley," Jarmen replied.

"And the chargers?" Num inquired.

Jarmen lifted his hand and rubbed a spot between his eyes that was beginning to ache. "And the chargers," he added.

IQ asked, "What about—?"

"Only those places that I have listed," Jarmen interrupted, "... until I have had a chance to... human-and-robot-proof the ship."

"Sounds reasonable, eh, Jon Paul?" Luc hastily agreed.

Jarmen breathed and lowered the intensity in his eyes. He frowned as he studied the moon through the viewscreen. Somehow, this location felt right for their first stop. Jarmen analyzed that feeling, but the results were inconclusive.

Was there some subconscious connection he was unaware of? His database and capabilities had expanded so rapidly, he was not certain what information was trying to rise into his working memory.

What Jarmen did know was that he could not leave yet. There was something here... or perhaps something was going to be here... or was once here... or was connected to a parallel version of here....

Jarmen's headache increased in intensity.

"What are we going to do?" Jon Paul quietly asked.

Jarmen realized that he and Jon Paul were alone now. He studied the older man for a moment before responding.

"We stay."

He needed time to learn the space-time function of the ship. This was as good a place as any to do that.

Three Days Later:

The Lab on Ala'mont

Debris from ruined equipment and crumbled rock crunched under Jarmen's boots. Memories of the lab before it was destroyed were still vibrant in his mind. Until he erased them, they would always remain.

He stopped in front of the metal frame where he had been restrained. His fingers brushed the filthy strap hanging from it. He breathed deeply when a rush of memories rose to the surface of his mind. He shut the memories down, refusing to let them distract him, and scanned the rest of the room.

All traces of the experiments had been removed. The rows of cylinders lining the walls were empty save for the wires hanging down like skeletal fingers. Most of the glass enclosures were fractured or shattered completely. The rock floor in front of each cylinder was stained and pitted from the corrosive acid that had eaten away the flesh of the Units imprisoned inside.

He hadn't planned on coming down to the moon's surface. There was no need to visit the lab again. There was nothing left here. The few tidbits of information he had recovered had long ago been retrieved.

No, he had escaped down here because it was impossible to think on the Crystal ship. After three days of listening to the continuous conversations of his companions, he had needed peace and quiet. There was no such thing when he was around the robots and the Frenchmen. Between them and his connection with the Crystal ship, his mind felt as if it would explode.

What I need is Jane's soothing calm.

He realized that only when he was with Jane could he find a place where his mind was at peace. It was as if she had the power to shut down all the noise. Without her, there was no barrier.

He fisted the strap as pain and rage poured through his mind and body when he remembered her lying so still on the table. His body shook with his grief. The Frenchmen were wrong. The pain had not lessened with time.

Metal creaked as he pulled the strap taut. Jarmen wrapped his other hand around the edge of the frame, taking his anger, pain, and grief out on the inanimate object that had once restrained him. His muscles strained as he ripped the frame from where it was bolted to the floor.

Lifting it above his head, he threw the frame across the room. The crash of metal-on-metal echoed loudly through the cavernous interior when the frame struck a bank of charred computer equipment. The frame was embedded halfway through the console.

"Does it help? Throwing things?" an unfamiliar voice asked.

Jarmen twisted in surprise and stiffened when he saw the figure standing near the entrance to the lab. Shock kept him frozen. He remained silent, waiting for the unidentified person to step out of the shadows.

"I had heard that one of the experiments survived. I see it is true," the low voice said.

"Who are you, and what are you doing here?" he demanded.

Jarmen silently cursed his previous distraction and lowered his hand to the laser pistol at his side. He showed no outward expression as the black-clad figure stepped out of the shadows.

"I am… like you. I am Unit 626."

Jarmen took a step back when the woman's eyes connected with his. Caution warred with curiosity. He had never seen a woman during his captivity, but the ring of red glowing in the woman's eyes and her Unit name were undeniable proof.

She started to take another step toward him when she suddenly doubled over. She sank to the filthy ground, landing on one knee. He took a step forward.

"What is wrong?" he asked.

626 shook her head. "My internal organs…."

Jarmen took another step forward, opened his senses, and scanned the cavern. He didn't want any more surprises. When his scan did not pick up any additional threats, he holstered his pistol and carefully advanced on 626. A quick scan of the woman showed that she was not faking her distress. Her organs were degenerating.

He stepped around the charred equipment and knelt beside her, grasping her shoulder when she started to tilt sideways. She gripped his arm.

"What do you need?" he asked.

"There is… a mini-injector… a serum," she croaked.

"Where?"

"In my… bag," she said, turning her head slightly to the left.

Jarmen nodded. He made sure she wouldn't fall over before he rose to his feet and strode to the dark room from where she had emerged. It was Cerberus's old office. He grabbed the black bag that had recently been placed on the dust-laden desk.

When he returned to her, he noted that sweat covered her brow and she was trembling. He opened the bag and placed it in front of her.

626 reached inside with a shaky hand and pulled out a black case. Her fingers fumbled to open it. Jarmen took the case from her, opened it, and combined the micro-injector with a vial, wishing there was time to analyze the chemical compound of the blue agent within the vial. He handed it to her, and she lifted the injector to her neck, depressing the trigger.

A shudder ran through her as the drug coursed through her body. He monitored her, storing the data of her recovery. Almost immediately, her skin changed from a light, ash-tinted purple to a deeper violet.

"What happened to you?"

She breathed deeply before looking at him. "My… body rejects what has been done to it. My organs begin to deteriorate if I do not have medication to stop the degeneration process."

Jarmen frowned. That had been a major issue with Cerberus's experiments. Most of the specimens' bodies rejected the extensive modifications to them. Those prisoners still in the cylinders were either in the early stages of the research or in the last stage of deterioration and would be dissected.

Even the two Units beside him were in the first stages of rejection. He alone had not suffered the same fate as far as he had discerned. The fact that there was a method that could halt the degeneration was a step ahead in the research.

"There were no records of women being used. There were also no women in this lab. Where did you come from? Are there others like us?" he demanded.

"I... don't remember. I was injured. My... memory became corrupted during my escape," she replied.

Concern filled him. He thought the Draka had given up. Over the last ten years, he had continually searched for any signs that they had restarted the program and found none.

Since the defeat of Grif Tai Tek and those connected with him, the Draka had been sanctioned. That did not stop them from causing trouble throughout the star system. In fact, Ajaska Ja Kel Coradon had recently left on a mission to uncover the depth of the Draka's deceit.

"How did you know about this lab?" Jarmen inquired.

626 struggled to rise to her feet. Jarmen slid a hand under her elbow to help her. She nodded her head in thanks.

"I overheard my handlers talking about another lab—this lab. I hoped to discover more information here. In my hurry, I neglected to monitor my vital signs. The medication is effective for a shorter period. If I do not stop the degeneration, I will not survive much longer," 626 replied.

Jarmen remained silent. If 626 was telling him the truth—both about her condition and the new lab, then it would be a death sentence to leave her here. Either her body would shut down or the Draka would find her.

"All data for this lab was destroyed. There is nothing left that will help you," he replied.

626 looked around the lab. "Then I will make my stand here. It is only a matter of time before I am found. I have less than a month's supply of the serum left. I would rather die fighting."

"Were you able to retrieve any data from your lab?" he asked.

626 nodded. "Some... plus I have the serum. If I can reproduce the compounds naturally —"

A shudder shook the complex. Jarmen stiffened and connected with the Red Crystal ship. The sensors detected three cruisers. One of them was firing at the surface of the moon. Another powerful explosion rocked the lab.

"Jarmen, you may want to return to the ship. There are three badasses blasting away at something on the moon," IQ warned.

"Pirates. My transport is concealed," he replied.

"Mine is not. They must be bounty hunters hired by the Draka to bring me back. You must escape. I will distract them," she said.

"No. It is imperative that you not be recaptured. The ship I am on has a medical unit. It is... foreign to me, but I have been able to operate all other components of the ship. It is possible that I can replicate the serum you need with the equipment onboard," he said.

"One ship against three seasoned bounty hunter ships is all but suicide," she argued.

Jarmen's eyes glowed as he prepared the compact shuttle he had taken from the ship. There had been two intact fighters and the transport shuttle. He wished now that he had chosen one of the fighters.

"They won't even know that we were here," he replied.

CHAPTER 14

"Are you sure about this, Jarmen? You know nothing about this cyb—woman. What about—?" Jon Paul began before biting his tongue.

Jarmen understood the Frenchman's hesitancy. He didn't trust 626 either, but if the Draka were reviving their experimental Cyborg Soldier Unit, he needed to know who was in charge and where the lab was located. For that information, he needed the genetically-altered woman.

"I have not lost focus on my quest," he promised.

Jon Paul shook his head. "I never doubted that. What I am concerned about is having another being on a ship that can only be run by someone like you."

"I am aware of that. I have taken precautions."

When he made the decision to bring her back with him, he had immediately set up a series of fail-safes to ensure that 626 could not take over the ship. His focus was on stopping Jane from being murdered, but he also needed to address any new threats that might endanger the Kassisans and the Alliance.

"We will—discreetly, of course—help keep an eye on her as well. Luc has taken her on as his personal mission to ensure that she does nothing bad, but he... we... have our limitations," Jon Paul added.

"Hey, Jarmen, you need to see this. The bad guys are landing on the moon," IQ hollered from down the corridor.

Jarmen sent a silent message to the robot. IQ swiveled on his wheel and rolled back toward the bridge. Jon Paul watched IQ's swift departure with a frown.

"I've added an alert to the robots. I want to know if 626 tries to access them," he said.

Jon Paul's shoulders relaxed. "I should know better than to worry, eh?"

"Yes. I need to monitor the situation on the moon."

Jarmen exited the upper-level crew's lounge and strode down the corridor toward the bridge. He was monitoring the one-sided conversation going on in the infirmary through a comlink. Luc had indeed decided to glue himself to 626.

Jarmen wasn't sure if it was Luc's compassionate side, the fact the Frenchman missed Jane, or his need to protect them all from the female cyborg. Whatever the reason, he figured it would keep at least one of his vagabond crew out from under his feet.

His pace slowed as he neared Num. The giant robot was standing in the center of the corridor. He frowned and ran a brief diagnostic scan over the robot's memory. He pulled back with a hiss when a vivid image of Jane flashed through his mind.

"Jon Paul, run a detailed diagnostic on Num," he ordered, knowing the man had followed him.

"*Oui*, I'll do it now," Jon Paul said. "Come, my big friend. Let me plug you in. I might even give you a shot or two of oil for your joints."

"Num like oil," the robot slowly replied.

He stepped out of the way when Num nearly knocked into him as the robot passed. Jarmen should have requested the diagnostic earlier. Breathing deeply, he entered the bridge. IQ was perched in the captain's chair. Jarmen resisted the urge to rub the aching spot that was forming between his eyes.

"I don't know what they are doing. They hit the freaky lady's spaceship, but they didn't really do any damage to it from what I can tell. Did you know if you twist these crystal things, you can zoom in super close? Like, I could see if the bad guys have boogers hanging out of their noses."

Jarmen shook his head at the little robot. He highly doubted the robot had learned that expression from Jane. He motioned for IQ to get out of his seat.

"I miss the days when I was the captain of the ship. I always had the best seat," IQ grumbled as he rolled off the chair and onto the floor.

"I would hardly call that dilapidated freighter you were found on a ship," Jarmen replied.

IQ released a series of rude bleeps that made Jarmen smile despite the disturbing scene he was monitoring on the moon below.

He opened a link to the vidcoms he had installed in the lab after his first return visit. He wanted to be alerted in case anyone returned to the lab—either the Draka or another survivor. Until now, no one had.

A group of ten well-armed men and women entered the complex series of caves. They moved with military precision. These were no ordinary bounty hunters, and they were not random pirates looking for an easy raid.

"Check everything," the woman in charge ordered.

The group moved systematically through the narrow corridors cut into the moon. While the Draka had destroyed the lab, there had not been time for them to destroy the environmental system. It was still fully functional—thanks to Jazin's timely arrival.

Since no one else had been to the lab since its destruction except Jarmen, he had left the artificial support system active. The bounty hunters still wore their outer protective suits, but he could see their features through their helmets. Each time they passed through a different corridor, a different vidcom activated.

"Clear."

"Clear."

"There's no one here," one of the men called out.

"Everything is destroyed. We aren't going to find anything worth taking."

"I don't care about the equipment. Find the Cyborg," the woman demanded.

Jarmen did a facial recognition search for each member of the team. They were a mixture of species from different planets. The woman who was obviously leading the group was a Waxian—a species known for their mercenary tendencies. His lip curled when he noticed her Drethulan companions. The Drethulans were a cruel, shape-shifting species known for their enjoyment of inflicting pain.

Ajaska Ja Kel Coradon was working with the Alliance, specifically a species called the Trivators, who had personal experience with the Drethulans. Jarmen did not have first-hand knowledge of the Waxians, Drethulans, or Trivators. All information he had about the first two species was limited to the classified reports Ajaska was compiling. The Trivators were often sent in first when a new planet was deemed ready for integration in the Alliance of Star Systems.

Ajaska will not be happy to learn the Waxians and Drethulans are closer than we realized and working with the Draka.

The thought was deeply unsettling. It meant that the threat was spreading closer to home. If the Draka succeeded in their attempts to create more cyborg soldiers, it would have devastating consequences for not only this star system, but for many others. The power of super-soldiers combined with the strength of the Draka, Waxians, and

Drethulans would be lethal to even the strongest, most advanced militaries in the galaxy.

"How is it that the bounty hunter ships have not attacked this one yet?"

Jarmen didn't turn around. He was aware of 626's presence as she approached the bridge—just as she was cognizant of his location. That knowledge did not sit well with him.

"We are shielded," he replied.

"How is it possible to control a ship this size with so few... crew members?" she continued.

Before he could answer, IQ rotated on his wheels. Jarmen bit back the impulse to growl when the robot answered.

"We don't need a large crew. I'm an excellent pilot. Num can handle any communications, and the two idiots are entertainment. Besides, Jarmen could run this thing with no one else. All he's got to do is think and it works," IQ answered.

"Think?" 626 repeated.

"Why would the Draka send a Waxian and Drethulans to bring you back?" he interrupted.

626's attention turned to the screen. He scrutinized her expression. She showed no emotion.

"Perhaps because the Draka know what they have created and don't want to die retrieving me."

～

Thirteen hours later, the bounty hunter ships departed the moon. Unease coursed through Jarmen as he watched them depart. They had left 626's spaceship intact.

"Will we be leaving soon?" Jon Paul asked.

Jarmen nodded. "Yes. I've almost completed my calculations."

Jon Paul sighed and sank down onto the chair to the left of him. Jarmen pursed his lips, knowing the short respite of time he had been given was over. Closing the holographic maps, he sat back in the captain's seat and waited for Jon Paul to speak.

"Luc is with 626 in the galley. I finished running diagnostics on Num like you asked. I am not as good as Stan or you, but I found... something that I believe is unusual. It was not in his programming before," Jon Paul said, holding out a disk.

Jarmen frowned and took the disk. "Did you run a log?"

"Yes. I wasn't sure if you had added anything new to Num's coding so I made a copy of the data. I thought you should review it," Jon Paul said, shooting a worried glance in the direction of the doorway.

Jarmen turned his attention to the console in front of him. With a thought, the crystal changed shape, forming a disk reader. He inserted the disk. Placing his hand on top of the crystal, information flowed through his fingertips.

Computer code flashed through his mind. He had connected enough times with both robots to be very familiar with their programming.

He suddenly paused his search when a line of unfamiliar code popped up. He moved a finger, pulling a copy of the line to the side before restarting his scan. By the time he finished, there were five lines of malware embedded that had not been in Num's programming before. The signature of the programmer was unfamiliar, but the lines and the placement were done by a professional.

Someone as good as myself, he thought.

He ejected the disk and crushed it between his fingers. Jon Paul studied him with a puzzled expression.

"Have you told Luc about your suspicions?" he asked.

Jon Paul shook his head. "*Non*. He has been with the woman. I... do not trust her," he confessed.

"Good. Warn him when you are alone that Num has been compromised. Tell him not to say anything to either the robots or to 626."

"It was not a coincidence that she appeared here, was it, eh?" Jon Paul quietly replied with a concerned expression.

Jarmen stood. "No, Jon Paul... I do not believe it was a coincidence."

He exited the bridge, leaving a troubled Jon Paul behind. A quick search informed him that Luc and 626 were still in the galley and the two robots were connected to their charging stations.

He briefly connected with Num, checking the malware that Jon Paul had downloaded from the bot. His eyes narrowed when he noticed the code had been erased. Jon Paul's download must have triggered it.

Striding down the corridor, he waved his hand. The lift at the end opened. He entered with a mental instruction for it to take him to the third level.

There were four sections to the ship. The bridge and the lounges were on the top level, the second level contained the crews' living quarters and recreation, the third contained the medical bay, the galley, and the transport/service bay areas, and the fourth was for crystal regeneration, weapons, and the propulsion/engineering, level. The first and fourth levels were the mind, heart, and muscle of the ship. He silently reinforced the restrictions to those two levels.

Luc's deep, infectious laugh greeted him as the doors to the lift opened. If there was one thing the Frenchman was good at, it was distraction. He paused at the entrance to the galley.

Luc and 626 were sitting at the table. Each had a steaming beverage in front of them. His senses immediately detected Luc's favorite drink of strong coffee while 626 was drinking a Kassisan herbal tea. They looked up when he entered the room.

"Ah, Jarmen, my friend. Have the bad guys left the moon base yet?" Luc inquired.

Jarmen nodded. "Yes. They have departed."

The grin on Luc's face grew. "We are off to rescue the beautiful Jane now, eh? No more time to waste."

"Once I've made sure 626 is stable," he replied.

Jarmen didn't miss the flicker of interest in 626's eyes or the slight, almost indiscernible, tightening of her lips. She would know her malware had been detected. He locked eyes with her.

"Charon is feeling much better. She had some of my famous quiche. No wonder she has been feeling poorly! What person could survive on space rations their entire life?" Luc declared with a dramatic sigh.

"Charon?" he repeated.

Luc reached over and gently patted 626's hand. 626 tilted her head and studied Luc with a perplexed expression, as if she wasn't quite sure what to do with him. Her reaction pleased Jarmen. It meant that she was not completely in control of her emotions.

Luc cupped 626's hand in his and grinned up at Jarmen. "You did not expect us to continue calling her by a number, did you? Everyone deserves a name," he defended with a gentle smile.

"Is that why you gave the robots names?" 626—Charon—inquired.

"Of course! They are family, eh. We could not run around calling them by numbers all day long," Luc chuckled.

Jarmen grimaced—on the inside. His outer expression remained neutral. The last thing he wanted to do was point out that service bots were an atypical addition to a family.

His thoughts immediately flashed to Jane and her love for the two bots. It reminded him of the reason he was there. Whatever name Luc might call the cyborg sitting next to him, it did not dispel the fact that she was very dangerous—and that they knew very little about her.

"You will be restricted to the second and third levels of the ship. Luc or Jon Paul will always accompany you." He directed a hard, intense stare at 626. "Once we are on our way, I will meet you in the medical unit. I will need a vial of the medication you use to stop the degeneration of your organs. Do not integrate with the ship or the robots or I will eject you into space. Do I make myself clear?"

626's lips flattened and she gave a slight bow of her head in acknowledgement. Luc was looking at him as if he had lost his mind. Jarmen didn't care what the Frenchman was thinking. If Luc interfered, he would find the nearest habitable planet and deposit the lot of them on it—regardless of when or where they were.

"You've made your instructions perfectly clear... Jarmen," 626 replied in a cool, measured voice.

CHAPTER 15

J armen focused on the calculations he was compiling. The star charts were extremely detailed. One slight jerk of his hand and they would be traveling to Goddess-knew-where in the universe.

It wasn't only the location, but the time. He was still processing the billions of gigabytes of information he had downloaded. There was a mathematical formula embedded in the coding, but he was unfamiliar with some of the symbols used.

Until he could process and test his calculations, they would be traveling on a direct path back to Kassis. His plan was to travel back to the morning Jane was murdered, prevent it, and eliminate the person responsible. He determined this plan would be the least likely to cause a disruption in the time/space continuum.

He lifted the gold keys from around his neck and studied them. The metal felt warm to his touch. He wasn't sure if the heat was from his body or if it was a natural characteristic of the living ore that made up the keys.

Positioning the keys over the time/space controls, he studied the alignment of each one. Each key had a different shape... yet, there was a piece of the puzzle missing to make them function properly once inserted. He was sure of it.

Studying the console, he breathed deeply and drew up the video Commander Starla had embedded in the coding on the door back on Elpidios. He replayed the video... then replayed it again, pausing when it distorted.

I-I-I-I will not go into the specifics on how the connection works between the ship, the commander, and the gold elements.

The disruption in the video was like a scratch in one of the old records that Luc liked to play. He rolled the three keys in the palm of his hand. What was he missing? He had the three control columns and the star charts.

The first column handled the integrated engines that powered every aspect of the vessel. The second column handled the environmental, communications, medical, and other controls inside the living crystal ship. The third column activated the navigation and time functions.

He looked up at the glowing aquamarine star map. He could operate the ship normally using the star chart and either of the first two columns. That is how they had traveled to the moon base.

Theoretically, he should be able to activate the time function and simply command the ship to go either forward or backwards in time to the location he wanted using the star chart.

He knew there was something more to it, though. Shaking his head, he connected with the console in front of him and uploaded the video to the ship's computer system.

... I will not go into the specifics on how the connection works between the ship, the commander, and the gold elements.

·   ·   ·

He sat back in the captain's chair and watched the video on the holographic display in front of him. Each time it got to the part with the interruption, the pressure in his head built. He rubbed at the ache. Frustration burned inside him, and he sat forward, leaning his elbows on his knees.

Why would she give so much information about the history of the ship and its capabilities, yet not include instructions on how to activate the time/space function?

"I don't know why she keeps saying that when that is not what she is saying at all," IQ grumbled behind him.

Jarmen looked over his shoulder at IQ. He had barely registered the small robot entering the bridge a few minutes earlier. IQ rolled over to the communication's console and pulled himself up onto the chair.

"What do you mean?" he asked.

IQ pointed to the paused hologram. "She might keep saying she isn't going to tell you how it works but she does keep saying 'Jarmen, '*dic nomen tuum*'. How she knows your name when she has been dead for like… forever, is the question I would be asking. What does '*dic nomen tuum*' mean?"

Jarmen stared at IQ for a moment before he slowly swiveled back to stare at the holographic screen.

"It is Latin," he replied, unsure how he knew that.

IQ rolled his eyes at him. "Yes, but what does it *mean?*"

Jarmen frowned. "It means 'say your name'.

"Why would she want you to say your name when she already knows it?" IQ asked.

Jarmen shook his head. "I don't know."

"Are you going to say it? Do you have to say it in a special way, or can you just say 'Hi, I'm Jarmen' and it opens up something?"

Jarmen stared back at the paused face of Commander Starla Strauss. For the first time, he realized that there was another person in the corner of the room standing off to the left side of her. He zoomed in. While he could get a general impression of the person's size, their features were too blurred to recognize... everything except the eyes. There was a faint, red glow illuming from the person's pupils.

"Jarmen."

Nothing happened.

"Buzz."

Still nothing happened.

"Unit 482."

Nothing changed.

Taking a deep breath, he tried again. "Jarmen... D'ju."

Greetings, Jarmen D'ju. If you are receiving this message, you are still trying to save your Jane Doe. It is good to know that my ship is still functional after all these millennia. My father would be proud. Your visit, while brief, gave us great hope for the future. I have spoken with my father as you requested. He believes there might be a way for you to save your Jane. If you are receiving this message, it is best if you find me to retrieve the information. It would be very dangerous if it fell into the wrong hands.

"What does she mean, your visit? When did you go visit her?" IQ asked.

"Quiet," Jarmen growled.

Almost immediately, he felt a wave of remorse when IQ released a low beep, rolled back several feet, and folded his arms across the front of his round body. Still, he listened intently as Commander Starla continued.

Time and space coexist together. You may travel along the same linear line, but if you do, any change you make that results in you never existing or you never having reason to time travel would mean that you never do time travel.

The timeline would likely reset, and you would disappear from existence. It is what we humans call the Grandfather Paradox... but, there may be a way. If you wish to know the answer, look for me. Good luck, and safe travels. Commander Starla Strauss, Earth Fleet on Kassis, year 01.2AAI.

"Well," IQ said, rolling up beside him. "At least there's hope. We'll travel to Starla Strauss, and she'll tell us the answer."

Jarmen looked down at the small, metallic hand resting lightly on his arm and blinked. He suddenly understood how to operate the time-travel function of the ship, the last piece of the puzzle clicking in place within his mind.

It brought him little comfort now.

He could not shake the feeling that the Jarmen he had seen in the video was not himself. Information was lurking in the depths of his mind. He felt a great and terrible foreboding about what that Jarmen had sacrificed to be there, and what the cost could be if he tried to go to that time as well.

He turned his attention to the three gold keys in his hand.

"I... need time to process what I have learned," he said, looking at the small bot. "IQ, I need you to keep this confidential."

IQ blinked at him. He knew he could just erase the bot's memory of what just occurred. Before Jane, he would have done it without a thought, but now... now it didn't seem right.

"You can trust me, Jarmen. Mum's the word. I won't tell anyone, not even Num," IQ promised, crossing his hand in front of his round body.

Jarmen smiled. "Thank you."

The familiar tightening in his chest occurred once again when IQ beeped a happy note. Thoughts of Jane chatting with IQ, explaining things, giving the metal bot a hug, flashed through his mind. She was so patient with IQ, ignoring the fact that the bot wasn't a living creature, but a mass of circuit boards, wires, and an energy pack.

But... am I so different?

The thought gave him a pause. *Are any of us any different? Jane loved us not for what we are, but for who we are.*

Another scene from *Tales of Two Galaxies* rose to his mind. The scene where Suzanne stood before the angry mob who had marched to the old inn to execute Jarmen.

"You call him the monster, but who are the ones with the spears and swords? Who are the ones chanting to kill with hatred in their hearts? Who are the ones fed by rage, fear, and distrust? He is not the monster. You are. You have given up the very essence that makes you different from a mindless killer: compassion, love, understanding, and empathy. His flesh, his veins, his heart may look different, but they make him no less alive. It is his compassion and his ability to love that give him life. He is not the monster. If you wish to see who the real monster is, look at each other and tell me what you see when you do!

He rubbed his thumb over the thin scar running up the inside of his arm.

"I will return. Stay on the bridge... please," he murmured.

Exiting the bridge, he strode down the corridor. He took the lift to Level 4 and stepped out. The engine room was the only spot on the ship where he felt confident that no one would bother him. He walked among the columns of glowing crystals that fed the ship. Running his hand along one column, he could feel the pulsing life contained within the amber stone.

"Jane, I need your guidance," he breathed, bowing his head as intense grief struck him.

CHAPTER 16

Two hours later, he stepped back onto the bridge. He had spent the time reviewing the message from Commander Starla, running calculations, and conjecturing different scenarios. In the end, he had decided that this was a decision he could not make alone. Perhaps… in another timeline he had. In fact, Jarmen was somehow certain of it.

The others were still in the galley. There were not a lot of other places to go on the ship with the restrictions Jarmen had imposed. IQ followed behind him, chatting about how he was going to have to make sure he recorded all their exciting adventures for Stan and the others.

"Marvin and Martin were very insistent that Num and I document everything. They were really envious that we were getting to go on this adventure," IQ confided.

"IQ."

"Yes, Jarmen?"

"Nothing…," Jarmen replied with a sigh, unable to cause the light in the little robot's eyes to dim by telling him to be quiet. "What exactly did Marvin and Martin say?"

Silence fell over the small group as Jarmen and IQ entered the galley. A quick scan showed Jon Paul, Luc, and 626 at the table while Num was bent over, looking at the alien replicator. Num straightened.

"I am making dinner. Would you care for something, Jarmen?" Num politely inquired.

He shook his head. "No… thank you, Num. I need to speak with all of you."

626 started to stand, but Luc reached for her hand. Jarmen tensed when his eyes connected with hers. Memories of his time in the lab flashed through his mind. It was impossible to ignore the similarities between them when he looked at her.

"This will include you," he stated.

626 sank back into her seat, her features devoid of emotion. He stepped closer to the table.

"Tell us," Jon Paul quietly encouraged.

He dipped his head. "The door that enclosed this ship on Elpidios had a video message encoded within it. This video gave me information about the history of the ship. I saved a copy, and I have discovered a new message within in it."

"It is good, eh? It is what you needed to take us to Jane?" Luc asked, perking up.

"It is… complicated." Jarmen took a breath. "To save our Jane, the Jane from our timeline, we would need to go back three millennium… to learn a theory. Traveling that far back would mean crossing many cosmic events that could alter the course of our path or kill us."

Everyone's eyes widened.

"If we do make it, anything we change could alter our present to such an extent that we never have the opportunity to time travel in the first place. Everything we did would become undone—and we would cease to exist. This is the Grandfather Paradox.

The others were looking very uneasy at this point, but he was not done.

"A parallel Jarmen has already been in our timeline's past with Starla," he said, "which means he likely already tried to save Jane in his own past, and he has avoided being erased, but he cannot return to his own timeline without dire consequences.

"Learning about the Grandfather Paradox has increased the chance that we will not make the same decisions that he has, but his presence has also helped me understand that at any point in our journey, we run a significant risk of traveling to the exact time and space that a parallel version of us does. This would destroy the timeline, erasing the existence of every living being within our time."

Jarmen paused. No one tried to fill the silence. Everyone was struck speechless.

He continued. "I believe that Jarmen left Starla's space and time after she gave him the information he needed. The message Starla sent was for us, not for the parallel Jarmen. Jarmen has left to pursue the theory, so it is unlikely we will run into him in Starla's time. Our next step from there, however, would have a much greater risk of destroying the timeline—if we even make it that far."

He paused.

"You are saying there is no hope?" Jon Paul finally asked, his voice filled with disbelief.

"*Non… non*! There is always hope, eh, Jarmen?" Luc insisted.

Jarmen's face was expressionless.

"I am saying that we have a decision to make. All this time, I have been thinking that I cannot live without her—but, I have also been thinking about what it means to be a monster. It may be time to... think beyond myself, and consider the lives of people other than Jane. The risk to learn this theory, the risk to time travel at all... it may be too great. We do not have to do this."

"I do not understand," Luc said. "If you stop her death in our timeline, then everything will be alright, eh? All will be solved."

"*Non*, Luc. It is like the chicken and the egg question," Jon Paul stated.

"Ah... Now I understand," Luc said glumly.

"What does a chicken and an egg have to do with this?" IQ asked.

Luc turned to IQ. "Which came first... the chicken or the egg? You cannot have one without the other."

IQ's eyes brightened as he processed that information. "Interesting."

"*Oui...*," Luc continued with a ruffled brow, "and in this time travel scenario with the chicken and the egg, both the chicken and the egg disappear? Like 'Poof! None of that nonsense!' kind of disappear? Is Jarmen both the chicken and the egg?"

"Yes, and Jane would not be saved."

It was quiet for a moment as the group absorbed that.

"You must save her," Num said, stepping closer to the table and resting his big hand on Jarmen's shoulder. "Jane must not die."

Jarmen looked at Num with fear and hope and gratitude. "You wish to travel three thousand years into the past to learn how saving Jane is possible? Even though something could go wrong and we could cease to exist?" he asked.

"Definitely!" Luc said passionately before a flicker of doubt crossed his features. "But... we *could* still exist, just not in this timeline, perhaps, maybe, eh?"

Jarmen pursed his lips, gave Luc a brief nod, and looked at 626 who had been silent during the discussion. Her features were pale but composed. She was staring at Num. A brief scan showed that she was not trying to connect with the large robot. No... there was a different expression in her eyes, as if she were trying to process a complex calculation.

"What is your decision?" he asked, curious about her thoughts.

She pulled her focus away from Num and stared back at him with an unblinking gaze. She seemed almost confused by his question. She looked down to her hand which was still entwined with Luc's before she looked at Jarmen again.

"You must... save Jane," she slowly said, as if the words were a foreign concept.

"Then it is decided. We try. I need to do more calculations before I attempt a jump," he replied.

Luc released a deep sigh and gave the group a crooked grin. "Well, at least we have time on our side, eh? That is a good thing."

Jon Paul groaned at the pun while IQ snorted out a beep that made everyone cringe. A dry laugh made everyone look at 626. She looked almost as surprised as everyone else by the sound that had slipped from her.

"You made a joke," she stated.

Luc chuckled and patted the back of her hand. "Yes, *ma chérie*, I made a joke," he laughed.

Jarmen shook his head as he exited the galley. There was something about this strange group that changed a person.

Ten hours later, Jarmen commanded the three columns to activate the time/space drive.

"Prepare for activation," he ordered over the com system.

He removed the keys around his neck and inserted them into the columns one at a time. The star map flickered in front of him as he connected with it.

Initiate command Kassis year 01.2AAI.

The globe in front of him sank down between the three columns. Brilliant bands of gold light shot out from each of the columns, sweeping through the globe and connecting before interconnecting with Kassis. The hum of the ship was soothing. Veins of red light lit the interior walls of the ship.

The shift was almost imperceptible. His connection with the ship was the only indicator that something had occurred. The star map showed a slight change in the alignment of some stars... and the life and death of more than one.

Jarmen could feel the thread of time as they moved along it. The ship accelerated with a force that would have melted the outer hull of any known starship in the galaxy. The crystal ship changed shape, becoming more aerodynamic as it sped backwards through time. The rising heat on the hull of the ship was fed into the engines, becoming unlimited power.

A slow, steady vibration in the ship resonated inside him, matching his own heartbeat. It was as if he and the ship were one. He closed his eyes, feeling the pulse of the engines, the heat against the hull, and the life and death of celestial bodies throughout time as they passed.

Jane, I wish you could see this.

A small smile curved his lips. If ever there was such a thing as an out-of-body experience, he believed he was experiencing the closest that a living being could encounter. Power surged through his mind along with knowledge.

The faster the ship accelerated, the slower time moved until it almost stood still. He was no longer Jarmen, but part of the living ship. Lifting his hand, he could see a faint red glow clinging to his flesh, and he understood that particles of the ship coated his vulnerable flesh to protect it.

As the time he selected drew closer, the hum of the ship slowed until it faded. His disconnection with the time function left him slightly disoriented. He opened his eyes and stared out into space.

"Jarmen, Luc wanted to know if you wanted something to dri-nk. What is that?" IQ asked.

"Trouble," he replied.

He stared tight-lipped down at the planet. Bright flashes of light dotted the surface. They had arrived on Kassis... during the alien invasion that would change the course of Kassisan history.

"Is that Kassis?" Jon Paul asked behind him.

"Yes. Jon Paul, please tell Luc that I must wait for that drink. Also tell him, 626, and Num to prepare for battle."

"*Oui,*" Jon Paul responded.

"You did it! We're alive!" IQ twirled his upper body in excitement. "I knew you could do it! I wasn't worried at all!! What do you need me to do? Do you want me to handle the weapons? I enjoy blowing things up. Bombing Bill and I have had so much fun," IQ chortled, rubbing his hands together.

Jarmen grimaced at the squeak of metal-on-metal and shook his head. "That won't be necessary."

"Aw, Jarmen. I'm really good at blowing things up," IQ grumbled.

"That is what I'm afraid of," he replied. "I think you should keep an eye on 626. I will be distracted. I need someone to make sure that she does not take advantage of my inattentiveness."

IQ rubbed his hands together again and nodded. "Watch the evil b— witch. You've got it. I'll keep both of my eyes on her."

Jarmen breathed a sigh of relief and returned his focus to the planet below.

Dozens of enemy ships were engaged in combat against the sleek Red Crystal ships. The fighting between the two alien forces would have been equal if the human-built crystal ships had the same numbers as their enemy. Jarmen connected with the communications systems.

"Red Squadron One, take out that mothership," a woman's strong voice ordered.

"There are too many, Commander," the fighter squadron leader responded in a terse tone.

"I don't care what you have to do. Find a way."

An analysis of the voice matched Commander Starla Strauss's voice from the vidcom. Jarmen turned his attention to the mothership that was the focus of the battle. It was the link to the fighters. If the mothership was eliminated, the fighters would fall.

The controls under his palms heated and he directed an intense laser blast to the rear engine section. An analysis of the situation warned him that continuing to blast the ship would have little effect on it. The ship was repairing itself as fast as the ships were damaging it.

An idea formed in his mind and he ran the calculations to see if what he was considering would work. When he came up with an eighty-six percent chance of success, he decided to proceed. There was a fourteen percent chance that he could blow his own ship to pieces, but it was a risk that was necessary for his allies to win.

He was certain of that in a way he could not explain, and he was surprisingly not worried about ripple effects on the timeline. He felt his actions slide within a groove that had already been created for him in this time and space.

"Secure yourselves for impact," he instructed over the com system.

Taking a deep breath, he merged with the ship in a way he hadn't so far. Thin, microscopic elements extended from his fingers, embedding into the crystals of the command console. His body stiffened and his eyes widened, glowing a brilliant red as his mind connected with the living ship.

Crystals formed up his fingers, over his hands, and up his arms. His breath caught as he merged with the alien life contained within the ship. Memories contained within the crystals poured through him. He would have jerked free if the crystals weren't holding him in place.

The gold keys dissolved, flowing along intricate channels previously unseen in the crystal. He connected with the pulsing form, awed at the power contained inside the living gold elements.

The Goddesses' blood.

He knew the minute the realization came to him that what he was experiencing was something unique. There were no memories of Commander Starla connecting with the ship on this level. As the crystal flowed over his body, its energy pulsed through him.

What is your command?

The voice was melodic, yet he could not ascertain if it was male or female.

Destroy the mothership.

Life should be protected, not destroyed.

The species destroys planets and all who live there. We must stop them before they do.

The crystals hummed, as if in distress. He could sense the ship's horror. A strange need to comfort the ship swept through him, and he thought of Jane. What would she do?

New life will grow from the ashes; life that will be full and give abundant energy not only to the planet below, but many other worlds.

He shared his memories with the ship. The beauty of Kassis and the crystal cities as well as the healing powers of the crystals on Elpidios. The ship shuddered.

Command confirmed.

Images flashed through his mind, and the ship morphed. The bow of the ship became long and slender before flaring outward into a shape that resembled a spearhead. The hum grew until Jarmen's body shook with the power surging outward.

With a thought, the crystal ship burst forward to collide with the alien mothership. Part of the enemy fleet noticed their approach and turned to intercept. Any that got too close disintegrated from the intense heat. The smaller ships shattered, raining crystal fragments on the planet below. The fragments lit up as they entered the planet's atmosphere.

"Commander, another ship has appeared!" a human fighter pilot warned.

"Fall back!" Commander Starla ordered.

"Commander… it looks… it looks like… the *Zephren II*!" the fighter pilot exclaimed.

"Impossible! Fall back. That is an order," Commander Strauss reiterated.

"The mothership…. The other ship is…."

The fighter pilot's voice ended on a hiss as Jarmen crashed the *Zephren II* into the underbelly of the alien mothership. The outer hull of the alien spaceship cracked and splintered before exploding along the blazing gash the *Zephren II* had run through it. By the time it exploded, the *Zephren II* was already engaging with the alien fighters who were retreating to the planet's surface.

He destroyed as many as he could before they breached the upper atmosphere. Thick, cumulus purple clouds darkened the planet's surface. The crystal ship passed through, appearing on the other side of the clouds.

The night sky below was not black but a rich, dark blue. The color reminded Jarmen vaguely of Lady River Knight's eyes, especially when she was angry. Around him, brilliant flashes resembled falling stars, the center a dark red rain that turned blue as it struck the surface of the planet.

On the surface, scorched soil and devastation greeted him. The few remaining enemy forces were locked in battle with the human resistance in the air and with the Kassisan forces on the ground. Lacking the connection to the mothership, the huge insect-like alien invaders fell swiftly under the combined forces.

Jarmen engaged the shields and the *Zephren II* shimmered before disappearing. In the distance, small Red Crystal fighters appeared, running down the last of the enemy as they charged a lone figure standing on the top of a hill. He knew without zooming in who the warrior was. The knowledge caused his throat to tighten with emotion.

Jazin Ja Kel Coradon, the original ruler of Kassis.

His eyes followed a single fighter that landed a short distance away from Jazin. He was watching history in the making. He would need to be very, very careful with what he did next.

CHAPTER 17

"Aw, Jarmen, why do we have to stay here?" IQ whined.

"Because the fewer interactions between us and anyone from the past, the less likely there will be complications," Jarmen patiently replied.

"It isn't like we'll be doing anything," IQ grumbled.

Jarmen breathed deeply, thought of Jane, and squatted down in front of the small robot. IQ rotated his eyes to opposite sides, trying not to return his gaze. The robot's obduracy struck a chord in Jarmen that made him want to laugh. He reached out and laid his hand on IQ's shoulder.

"I need you to trust me on this, IQ. I only need a few minutes with Commander Strauss. Once I'm finished, we will be leaving. While I'm busy, I need you to keep an eye on 626," he said.

IQ's eyes rolled in opposite directions. "You said that before. She isn't doing anything but sitting there looking pale and purple. I think Num and Luc do a better job watching her than me. They keep her dazed and confused."

"They do a good job, but no one can do it as well as you do, my little friend," Jarmen quietly replied.

Jarmen almost fell over when IQ threw his short metal arms around his neck in a surprise hug. Once again, he marveled at how emotional a pile of wires and metal could be thanks to a little creative programming.

"Jane always said you had a heart. She was right," IQ declared.

Jarmen rested his temple against IQ's as emotion swept through him. "So do you, IQ. So do you."

He released the bot and rose to his feet. "I will return. Remember, stay on the ship. Kassis is not like your memory chip says it is."

"No worries."

He patted IQ's head before he guided the bot off the bridge. He sealed the upper level, still unwilling to trust 626. He clutched the three gold keys around his neck. As long as he had them, she could not operate the time travel aspect of the ship, but he did not know if she could access the same functions that he had been able to access when he held one key and opened the ship's door.

She had promised that she would not, however, and she needed his help to produce the serum naturally. Exiting the ship, he paused and looked around the devastated landscape.

The blood of the deceased alien invaders soaked into the ground, the crystal particles in their plasma changing the upper layer of soil as it interacted with the chemical makeup of the planet. The creatures' bodies disintegrated, leaving nothing but a red dust in the air.

In the distance, fires burned, silhouetting the remains of a ruined village and a group of Red Crystal star fighters. He rolled his shoulders before setting off in the direction of the fighters with a sense of déjà vu.

∾

"Kil mai ta eff mauway!" *Stop and identify yourself!* the Kassisan male guard ordered in a sharp tone.

The ancient Kassisan language flowed through Jarmen's mind and he bowed his head, partially concealing the glow of red in his eyes. Already his teak-colored trousers, white long-sleeve shirt, and coffee-colored leather jacket and boots set him apart from both the time-travelling humans and the Kassisan natives.

"Ki taka makki," he responded. *'I come in peace.'*

From the shadows nearby, Jazin Ja Kel Coradon's deep voice could be heard addressing the guard. Beside him, Commander Starla Strauss of the Earth forces stepped into the light, her weapon aimed at Jarmen's chest. He bowed to her in greeting.

"Commander Strauss," he said in English.

"Have we met?" she dryly inquired, not lowering her weapon.

A slight smile curved his lips. "In another place... and time. Most assuredly in another life," he added.

She frowned, but she lowered her weapon. "Explain yourself," she ordered.

He nodded to himself as he integrated the information she had just provided. The other Jarmen had not yet arrived. That meant he would be the one to convince Starla to send the message that his younger self would find—and the other Jarmen would arrive sometime before she recorded that message.

It would be fine. He had miscalculated, but he would only be here a few minutes, and as long as he did not exit this space and time at the precise moment that the other Jarmen entered, everything would be fine.

He looked up. Her hushed hiss of surprise and Jazin's warning growl told him they noticed the red glow of his eyes. He returned Jazin's hostile gaze with a cool, calm one.

"I mean no harm to you or to Commander Strauss," he explained in old Kassisan.

Jazin stepped forward. Two guards on either side matched his steps. The others circled around them. Jarmen kept his hands slightly out to his side, palms facing forward to show he was unarmed.

"Who are you, and where did you come from?" Jazin demanded.

"My name is Jarmen D'ju. I believe the rest of the explanation would best be conducted in private," he answered with a flickering glance to Starla who was watching him with a guarded expression.

She touched Jazin's arm. "I agree. This is not a conversation for out in the open. I think it would be best if I speak with him alone."

He could see that Jazin was suspicious, but also curious. Jazin nodded and motioned for his guards to fall back.

"If you insist. I must see to my people. Many were wounded in the invasion," Jazin stated.

Starla nodded. "Thank you. I will instruct my crew to help yours. I will assist as soon as we are finished."

Jazin ran the backs of his fingers down her cheek. Jarmen bowed his head in respect, fisted his hand, and pressed it against his chest in the age-old symbol of fidelity to Jazin. Jazin responded with a sharp nod before turning and striding away.

Jarmen returned his attention to Starla. She was staring at him with an inquisitive expression.

"You have my ship, the *Zephren II*?" she asked, more as a statement than a question.

"Yes."

She lifted an eyebrow.

"It's good to know that it survived. Are you a by-product of the ship?" she inquired as they strode across the uneven ground toward the *Zephren I*.

He frowned and shook his head. "No. Why do you ask?"

She gestured toward his face. "Your eyes… they are the same color as the crystal, and you connected with the ship. Only someone with… special abilities can do that."

"True, but my enhancements are not unlike your own."

She paused and looked at him with an intensity that reminded him of Star from his time. She reached out and gripped his arm, turning it so that his wrist was exposed, and gently rubbed her thumb along the scar on his wrist.

"Not quite the same, I think."

Zephren I was almost twice the size of *Zephren II*. Crew members studied him with curiosity as he followed Commander Starla through the corridors. He refrained from connecting with the ship. The last thing he wanted to do was appear hostile. They entered the commander's event room. Starla turned to face him.

"When are you from?" Starla asked.

He hesitated a moment before he decided the truth was the best course of action, or at least as close to the truth as he could go.

"The future. More specifically, three thousand four hundred sixty-four Kassisan sols. I could give you to the exact millisecond, but I don't believe that would be of any use," he replied.

"Three thousand…."

Her voice faded, and she stared at him in silence. He looked past her to the view outside the ship. From the bridge, he could see the vast destruction caused by the invading alien forces, but also the beginnings of new life.

"The crystals from the aliens' blood will provide tremendous power to the planet, as well as building material," he said.

She followed his gaze. "They are reacting differently than they did on Elpidios."

"The soil and the atmosphere are responsible. Elpidios has more radiation, less oxygen, and fewer ionic, covalent, and metallic minerals for the crystals to bond with. Elpidiosians have adapted to the radiation, but over time, it will increase, and the planet will begin to die. You are the one who saved them. You hid your ship in the mountains. The crystals will eventually absorb the radiation and save the planet."

"Three thousand years from now," she repeated with a touch of awe in her voice.

"Yes."

"Why are you here, Jarmen D'ju from the future? I'm sure it was not to thank me for hiding my ship on a planet. And be sure to tell me how you found it… and how you can command it," she added.

"We have met before. You embedded a message near the ship that was meant for me. You explained several things, including how to operate the space/time function of the ship."

She frowned. "Continue."

"I wish to save the life of someone. You told me about the Grandfather Paradox, but you said your father might know of a way to change my past," he said.

She stiffened, shook her head, and turned away. He watched in anxious silence as she walked over to the viewports and looked out. She gripped the sill. He stood next to her.

"What is… was… her name?" Starla asked.

"Jane. Jane Doe."

She stared at him with an astonished expression. "Jane Doe?"

"Yes."

She sighed and shook her head. "It is a theory, you understand. No one has come close to proving its veracity. Keep that in mind, please. My father has posited that we may exist in a multiverse that consists of strings that are woven around each other and the other multiverses. We know these as timelines. Sometimes, a string creates a loop. He says it is why we sometimes feel like we have been somewhere before or lived a past life. At that juncture, the loop creates a spot where the past, present, and future meet.

"If you could calculate where and when that spot is and travel along the loop, you could theoretically save Jane and continue from that point on as if the event never happened. There are many natural phenomena that change the rules of the universe within a local area, and my father has applied this concept to time-travel. He calls it the *Zephren Loop.* The theory has not even been vetted mathematically, never mind practically."

"Did you not use a Zephren Loop to save Earth?"

"No, we didn't. Back then, the only information we had indicated that trying to keep the invaders from arriving would mean we never created time travel. So, we used the ships' ability to teleport and we restarted certain fights several times. The invaders did the same. We could feel that we had battled more times than we actively remembered. It was more than an intuition; it was something like knowledge and emotions that had no context. Eventually the invaders decided to find easier prey, and we followed."

"Do you have your father's research on Zephren Loops?" he asked.

"No... but I can ask him for it," she said.

"Please, ask him," he requested.

"I will send you the information as soon as possible... if he is willing to share. You must understand, this is just a theory and he may be hesitant to share it with you, especially with your ability to command one of his ships," she cautioned.

"I understand. I will be aboard the *Zephren II.* It is best that I not be away from it for very long," he said.

"I will contact you soon."

He bowed his head before turning and exiting the bridge. Once he was outside, he breathed deeply and studied the terrain again. His gaze locked with Jazin's a short distance away. He had known the man wouldn't be far from Starla. Lifting his hand to his chest, he again showed he was no threat to him, his people, or his future mate before he turned in the opposite direction and made his way back to the *Zephren II*. As the darkness engulfed him and he moved farther away from the village, he searched the sky. Above him, crystal fighters patrolled the area for stray alien invaders.

He thought of Luc, and with a smile he thought, *At least I have time on my side.*

"I can't believe this is Kassis," 626 commented.

"It has been over three thousand years. The changes are to be expected," he replied.

"Then it's true, the time function does work."

"I have work to do," he said in a neutral tone. "Please go with Luc to the medical unit. I would like him and Num to run a complete scan on your system."

He rose to his feet, ignoring Luc's disapproving expression. Exiting the galley, he headed for the lift. A scan of the bots showed no new intrusion by 626.

He spent the next two hours working and listening to Luc over the com. Luc was charming 626 with tales of the adventures he and Jon Paul had before Jarmen found them on a dilapidated freighter. The men had lived a rather colorful life among the pirates who had captured them before they eventually won their freedom, the bots, and the freighter in a card game.

He was almost finished with both an analysis of the serum 626 was using and a new calculation for their return to the present when a message pinged the *Zephren II's* communication system.

"This is Jarmen," he responded.

"Jarmen, I have the information from my father. I can transfer it to the *Zephren II's* computer system if you like. He was hesitant at first, but after explaining the situation, he agreed," Starla said.

"Please do. Thank you," he replied.

"You're welcome. My father's only request is to let him know if you do prove his theory correct. Whatever you do, take care of my ship. I may need it again one day."

Jarmen registered the hint of amusement in her voice.

"You won't."

"Sending the information now. I must stress that this is not information that should be shared lightly. My father also wanted me to warn you that the longer you are in the past, the greater the chance for disruptions."

"I understand. The information will go no further than myself. We will be departing immediately," he promised.

"Thank you for your help, Jarmen D'ju. I hope you save your Jane Doe," she replied before ending the transmission.

He entered the lift, connecting with the ship's computer. By the time he reached the bridge, he had downloaded all the information and was processing it. Hope swelled inside him.

"Jarmen... is everything alright?" Jon Paul asked.

He blinked and realized he had been staring out of the front viewport.

"Yes. Prepare for departure," he instructed.

"*Oui*. We are going to save Jane?" Jon Paul asked.

He looked over his shoulder and said, "We are one step closer."

"Each step is a good one, Jarmen. We will get there, my friend."

Jarmen gave a brief nod and stared out of the viewport again. "Yes, we will."

Once he was alone again, he focused on the complex equations that Zephren Strauss had proposed. Finally... finally, he was seeing the hope that Jane whispered to him.

You just have to believe, my love.

He closed his eyes and embraced her presence.

"I do, Jane. I believe."

CHAPTER 18

T wo Weeks Later:

Jarmen silently cursed as he gripped the controls, struggling to compensate for the damage to the power crystals of the ship. The calculations he had inserted into the drives were incorrect.

"Power levels at forty percent," the computer stated.

"Damage assessment," he ordered.

"Cracks have appeared in columns five, sixteen, eighteen, and twenty-four," the computer responded.

One-sixth of the engines were in danger of collapsing if he didn't pull out of their current track. The crystal ship shuddered.

He gritted his teeth and slowly began bringing them out of the super-luminal tachyons drive. The ship was literally on the verge of shattering.

"Jarmen," Jon Paul anxiously called behind him.

"Everything is under control," he bit out.

"It doesn't sound like it is under control."

He turned a heated glare to 626.

"I said I have everything under control. You are not allowed on this level."

She raised an eyebrow. "Since it is quite likely that we'll soon be floating in space, I didn't think it mattered if I ignored your order. Do you need assistance?"

"No. Get back down to the lower level," he ordered.

"If you keep going, we're going to need a lot more duct tape," IQ chirped.

Jarmen smothered another curse and counted to ten... just the way Jane had taught him to do. The ship was responding to his silent commands, and the decreased strain on the engines appeared to have slowed the cracks forming along the columns.

He breathed deeply when the *Zephren II* emerged out of the superluminal drive. The moment they were free of the wormhole they had been pulled into, he cut power to all but four of the crystal engines.

"Wow! Would you look at that! Is that Kassis?" IQ exclaimed.

"No," he replied.

"Where are we?" 626 asked, her voice filled with hesitation as she stepped onto the bridge and walked over to stand near him.

He quickly retrieved the key to the space/time controls, leaving only the other two keys to maintain the ship's normal operations and environmental systems. He had used too much energy during this last jump to control everything remotely. The time/space column lowered back into the control console in front of him. Surprise swept through Jarmen when 626 didn't take her eyes off the huge, blue and white double planets in front of them.

"I... am not sure," he confessed.

She shook her head. "I don't recognize these planets."

He cleared his throat. "That is because they are not located in our universe."

"What do you mean?" she asked with a frown.

He pursed his lips for a moment before he decided that the others deserved to know.

"We crossed a thread connecting our universe to a parallel one. There are thin corridors that link each level of the multiverse," he explained.

Her lips parted. He could sense her awe and fascination as she leaned forward, her eyes locked on the beautiful celestial bodies before them.

"How did you do this? I know the theory has been proposed, but it was always more of a myth than a serious possibility."

A slight smile curved his lips at the eagerness in her voice. "It is no longer a myth," he said, not answering her question.

"Are we going to check it out?" IQ asked, rolling up to his other side.

He connected with the ship's scanner. The planet contained the proper chemical balance to sustain their life forms. He did not detect any orbital technology, which meant that the lifeforms on the planet were probably not advanced enough for space travel.

"Warning, ship hull integrity has been compromised on Level Four. Emergency protocols have been implemented," the computer suddenly announced.

Jarmen grimaced. There was more damage than he initially realized. The computer had sealed off Level Four. He would only be able to access the engines when the ship was in a safe environment.

His attention moved to the planets. Whether he wanted to or not, they would be landing. He just hoped that their presence didn't cause irreparable harm.

Jarmen tiredly rubbed a hand down his face as he walked around the last crystal drive column. He had barely rested over the last three days, instead focusing on the repairs to the ship. The sixteenth column had suffered the most damage and was taking the longest to repair. He studied a deep crack in the column. The living crystal was reforming, but it was taking time.

Fine filaments of microscopic crystals flowed downward into the cracks, adhering to the ragged edges that had opened under the pressure of their journey.

The external integrity of the ship was no longer compromised, but he would need everything in excellent working condition if they were to return to their universe.

He ran his hand down along the column, feeling the pulse of the crystal under his palm. The crystal should finish repairing itself in another couple of hours.

He ran another round of diagnostics as he focused on analyzing where his calculations were off. They should have looped back to their own timeline's past. If his revised calculations were correct, they had exited the loop at the top where it intersected with a parallel universe.

"What'cha doing?"

Jarmen silently groaned when IQ's tinny voice pierced the relative quiet of the engineering room.

"I am plotting a course back to our universe. Why are you here?" he replied.

"I'm charged and have nothing else to do. There isn't any chatter on the coms... well, except for Jon Paul and Luc," IQ replied.

IQ wheeled up next to him. Jarmen looked down at the little bot, noticing that there was something off about it. IQ's eyes weren't glowing quite as brightly as they had before.

A strange feeling of concern coursed through Jarmen, and he turned to the bot. He had been so absorbed in the repairs that he had spent little time in the upper levels. Squatting down, he placed his hands on either side of IQ's round head and connected with him. A swift diagnostic showed all IQ's systems were functioning properly. He did not detect any malware.

"Where is Num?"

IQ rolled back several inches and raised his arms. "He's... with the others. Luc gave him an extra hot oil treatment, and they wanted to make sure the oil was worked into all of Num's joints."

Jarmen frowned when the little bot swiveled and slowly rolled around the engine room, lightly running his metal fingers along the crystal columns. Rising, he studied IQ and ran through the diagnostics he had scanned again. IQ looked at him several times before turning away.

"What is wrong?"

IQ paused, rolling back and forth on his single wheel. Jarmen folded his arms across his chest and waited. He knew if he was patient IQ would eventually respond. The bot was incapable of remaining quiet for long.

"I miss Jane," IQ replied in a low voice.

Jarmen's eyes widened. Stanley's emotional response programming for the bots was continuing to learn and adapt. He had noticed the change over the past year, but he didn't realize the bots could experience grief —and depression.

"I... miss Jane as well. I promise I will not stop until she is back with us. I have been working on new calculations while I've been down here," he said.

He jerked back in surprise when IQ sped over to him as fast as his small wheel could go, threw his arms around his waist, and buried his round metal face against Jarmen's stomach. Unsure of what to do, he reached down and awkwardly patted IQ. The little bot hummed in an uneven pitch.

He closed his eyes as he suddenly remembered another hug. He fought to capture the fuzzy image. A woman with blonde hair, dancing brown eyes, and a round face emerged.

Buzz, you're a genius! I never would have made it through that test if not for you."

Pain seared behind his eyes, and he breathed deeply as he tried to hold on to the fleeting memory. The image blurred and faded. He opened his eyes, blinking several times to clear the spots dancing in his vision.

"I will... transfer the telecommunications and some other basic operating duties over to you so that you may help me with the ship," he said in a strained voice.

"Wow! You mean you'll let me pilot the ship?" IQ exclaimed, dropping his arms, and rolling back to gaze up at him with glowing eyes.

Jarmen frowned. "No, that is not what I mean."

"Aw, come on, Jarmen. I'm a great pilot. I bet I could fly this thing. I'm a robot like you, after all," IQ whined.

"No... you are not. Not a good pilot, and not like me. You are a mediocre pilot. This is an advanced ship. I will give you some control over communications and a few other areas. If you argue, the only thing you'll be able to work is the food replicator," he warned.

"Jon Paul and Luc would have let me," IQ grumbled.

"I will not get into a discussion of Jon Paul and Luc's ability to pilot a ship. They are best left to function in the kitchen," Jarmen retorted in a stern tone.

"Okay, so who do you want me to contact first?" IQ inquired, rubbing his hands together.

Jarmen winced at the sharp sound of metal-against-metal and rubbed the aching spot between his eyes. Sympathy did not come without a price, he decided.

"I do not want you to contact anyone. I want you to *listen* and notify me if you intercept any outside communication. We do not want anyone to know where we are. The inhabitants of this planet, if there are any, may not deal well with having visitors from another world."

"Oh, okay. No chatting up the freighter chaps... if there are any. That sounds boring—but I can do it," IQ replied.

"Good."

Jarmen noted the light in IQ's eyes was shining a bright, cheerful red again. Satisfied that he had handled another crisis, he started to turn away when something occurred to him. He turned back to IQ as the bot rolled toward the exit.

"IQ."

IQ swiveled on his wheel to face him. "Yes?"

"What did you mean when you said 'There isn't any chatter on the coms... well, except for Jon Paul and Luc?'" he inquired.

IQ perked up. "Oh.... They went for a walk."

There was now a heavy rhythm beating between Jarmen's eyes. He rubbed the spot. Surely the bumbling Frenchmen wouldn't have left the ship. He connected with the ship's sensors as dread built and knotted his stomach.

"Computer, location of crew members," he requested.

"Android system called IQ is located in the engineering room with Commander Jarmen D'ju," the computer responded.

IQ released a low beep and slowly rolled backwards toward the door. The bot froze when Jarmen sent a silent command. The bright red glow in IQ's eyes flickered, and the small bot crossed his arms over his round stomach, nervously tapping his fingers against his smooth, metal body.

"Ah, Jarmen..."

"Computer, location of Jon Paul and Luc," he growled, taking a step closer to IQ.

"Ah, Jarmen, maybe now might be a good time to tell you...."

"Crew members Jon Paul, Luc, Num, and passenger 626 departed the ship three hours, forty-two minutes, and thirty-three seconds ago," the computer responded.

Jarmen clenched his fists and glared down at the bot who was doing his best to look in any and every direction except at Jarmen.

"Where are they?" he demanded.

IQ beeped in distress.

Impatient with the robot's procrastination, Jarmen scanned IQ's memory. A low, foreign curse slipped from him, spoken in a forgotten language. He pushed his way past IQ, strode out of the engine room, and headed for the lift.

"Computer, scan area for missing crew members," he ordered.

"Scans have detected multiple lifeforms approaching. Crew members of the *Zephren II* have been found. They are approaching at a rapid pace bearing the following coordinates," the steady voice of the computer responded.

"Jon Paul and Luc had comlinks. I was listening to them. Well, I was listening until I needed to charge. Everything was fine. They were enjoying some fresh air," IQ hurriedly explained as he rolled after Jarmen.

Jarmen winced when he connected to the comlinks Jon Paul and Luc had taken with them. The shouts and heavy breathing indicated that everything was not 'fine'. The information pouring in from the scanner that they had turned off also indicated that everything was not 'fine'.

"The lot of you better hope the cloaking shield still works," he snapped.

IQ looked up at him in the lift as they swiftly rose to the upper level.

"What happens if it doesn't?"

Jarmen gritted his teeth and didn't answer.

"Run, Num, run!" Luc yelped as he ran past his larger, more cumbersome friend.

Num shook one of his big feet. Pieces of wood fell from between his joints. He swiveled and raised his middle fingers at the shouting hoard slowly gaining on them. Luc glanced back in time to notice the gesture and winced. Perhaps he shouldn't have been playing with Num's programming earlier.

"I've decided this was a very, very bad idea," Luc huffed, ducking as a spear flew past him.

"You are just now figuring that out? You should have at least brought a weapon," 626 growled, keeping slightly ahead of Num.

"Jarmen said we were not to interfere with the local population. He is going to leave us here," Jon Paul groaned.

"Only if he finds out. It isn't like we knew there was a local population. He said the planet *could* sustain life, not that it did!" Luc defended. "Num, you need to move it faster, my friend. We do not want you to end up as a sacrifice again, do we, eh?"

"Num no like this planet," Num responded, pushing a dead tree branch as thick as Luc's body out of his path.

"Jarmen's specific instructions were to stay on the ship so that you did not interfere with any lifeforms," 626 snapped, bending to pick up a rock and firing it over her shoulder.

Luc whistled with appreciation when the rock struck the closest creature, causing him to topple to the ground. He cursed and dodged behind a tree when several creatures threw their spears at them. One of the spears wobbled in the bark of the trunk, inches from where he stood pressed against the other side. Luc hiccupped when Num passed him, and then took off running again.

Behind them, dozens more small creatures swung from the trees or scampered through the thick, fern-covered forests, chasing them, and throwing small, poisoned spears. They wore masks and furs—very brief, gaudy furs. Their arms, legs, and torso were bare except for colorful tattoos.

"We're almost there," Jon Paul called over his shoulder.

"Num, what are you doing?" Luc demanded when he saw the large robot hopping on one leg.

"He's got a spear stuck in his knee joint. It has pierced the oil line running down to his foot," 626 replied.

"Oh. You need to hop faster, my big friend. We can't carry you," Luc encouraged.

"Argh!" 626 growled.

Luc almost fell when he turned to see what the cyborg woman was doing. She had pivoted and run past him to Num. Grabbing the spear embedded in the back of Num's right leg at the joint, she ripped it free. She grasped a portion of her shirt, tore a long strip off, and stuffed the piece in the hole of the oil tube so it wouldn't seize.

"Now, run," she snapped.

Num took off running again. Unfortunately, the few seconds it had taken for her to come to Num's aid had given the creatures chasing them time to gain some ground. Luc glanced over his shoulder again. The creatures were about the same size as Walter and Nema, but that was where the similarities ended.

Luc's eyes widened with dismay when he noticed that the clearing where the Red Crystal ship had been was now empty.

"Jon Paul, he's done it. Jarmen has left us," Luc wailed, unable to keep the panic from his voice.

"No, he hasn't. He wouldn't. He knows you are too stupid to survive on your own!" 626 snapped.

Luc wasn't as confident as their new female friend. Surely IQ would have informed Jarmen that they weren't onboard? Or worse, IQ had informed Jarmen, and Jarmen had decided to leave them behind. All kinds of terrible thoughts were beginning to form in his mind before relief swept through him.

"Jarmen! You didn't leave us," Luc cried.

"Don't give him any ideas!" 626 growled.

The dark expression on Jarmen's normally composed features sent a shiver of unease through Luc. If he wasn't having such a hard time drawing breath, he might have tried to ease the tense situation. Instead, he focused on trying to run a little faster.

"Luc!" Num called.

Luc looked over his shoulder, and dismay filled him when he noticed that Num was now dragging his right leg. The native creatures were overwhelming the large bot.

"Aaugh!" IQ roared as he charged, whizzing past Luc like a small, oversized but vengeful bowling ball.

Jon Paul grabbed Luc's arm and steadied him as 626 turned to stand slightly behind Jarmen who was holding a laser rifle firmly against his shoulder. Luc's immediate reaction was panic that *now* Jarmen was going to shoot them for leaving the ship. He swallowed his protest when he saw the creatures chasing them suddenly stop and fall to their knees.

"Will you look at that! They think IQ is a deity or something," Jon Paul breathlessly commented with a thread of amusement.

"You mess with my friend; you mess with the wrong robots!" IQ barked, sending tiny bolts of electricity out through his palms.

Luc frowned and glanced at Jon Paul. "I didn't know he could do that. That is something new, eh?"

"Neither did I. It appears to be working, though," Jon Paul chuckled with relief.

Those close to the irate bot shrieked as the bolts of energy shocked them. Luc and Jon Paul hurried back to Num who was clumsily rising off the ground.

"Aw, my friend, you are a mess! You are going to need a good cleaning and another oil bath, eh?" Luc murmured.

"That's right! You better beeping run!" IQ shouted, lifting his fist, and shaking it at the retreating creatures.

Luc warily studied Jarmen's stony expression. Jon Paul grimaced and raised an eyebrow at his husband as they walked by Jarmen in silence. Luc shook his head at 626 when she paused next to their furious friend.

"It could have been worse," she stated.

"Yes, it could have. I could have left you all here," Jarmen retorted before turning on his heel and striding back toward the crystal ship.

Luc swallowed and threaded his arm through 626's. "He doesn't mean that. He wouldn't have left us."

She looked at Jarmen's retreating back. "Oh… I think he would."

CHAPTER 19

J armen worked with a furious, silent fervor to finish his second
set of calculations. Exhaustion plagued him, and he knew that he
was going to need to rest and recharge before he tried to return
them to their own dimension.

Pulling the keys out of the columns, he almost knocked over the half-
full cup of tea that Luc had silently placed next to him. Beside the cup
was a partially eaten sandwich that he had taken only a few bites out
of while working on his calculations and checking on the final repairs
to the engines.

He tiredly sat down in the captain's chair and drew the plate of food
onto his lap. He had just taken a bite when Jon Paul stepped onto the
bridge. His scowl of warning made the Frenchman pause in the
doorway.

"Luc and Charon have finished cleaning and repairing Num. He's
recharging," Jon Paul said as a greeting.

"You are all lucky to be alive," he replied, his expression still severe.

Jon Paul blanched, nodded, and gave him a crooked grin. "As Charon has said, it is amazing that we have survived this long," he admitted, walking over to sit in the communication's officer's chair.

"Why do you do that? Insist on giving 626 a name?" he asked before finishing his sandwich.

Jon Paul shrugged. "We all need an identity. A name helps us have a purpose... a... place in this world."

Jarmen nodded, understanding all too well. Wasn't that the reason he gave himself a name when the scientists tried to deny him a face? He tiredly closed his eyes and bowed his head. She was still a potential enemy, but his persistence in using the number her tormenters had given her... it suddenly seemed much more cruel than she deserved.

A sense of peace descended over him when he imagined he could feel Jane's presence. Curling his fingers around the plate in his lap, he opened his eyes and looked back at Jon Paul. The man silently rose and took the empty plate from his hands.

"You need rest. I promise we will behave," Jon Paul said.

"I need to...."

Jarmen's voice faded when Jon Paul shook his head and gave him a stern look.

"You need rest, my friend. We have all the time in the world. What are a few hours, eh?" Jon Paul interjected.

"626?" Jarmen inquired before he huffed. "I mean Charon?"

"Luc is with her. We will make sure the ship is safe. I believe you instructed IQ to keep an eye on her as well. That little bot takes his duties very seriously. Besides, he is feeling very proud of himself at the moment. We've got this, Jarmen. We will behave," Jon Paul promised with a chuckle.

He grunted and rose to his feet. Weariness made him sway. He gave a brief nod of acknowledgement.

"Either you or IQ need to remain on the bridge at all times. I will return in a few hours," he instructed.

"I will take personal responsibility," Jon Paul assured him.

Jarmen gave Jon Paul a brief nod before he exited the bridge. He took the lift down to the quarters he had chosen. Entering the dark room, he rolled his shoulders to ease the tension in them.

Twenty minutes later, he exited the bathroom. The hot shower had relaxed him. He crawled under the covers and rolled onto his side. A deep sigh slipped from him as he stared at the empty space next to him. Sliding his hand over the cool sheet, a deep sense of melancholy hit him, and he closed his eyes against the shaft of pain.

"Oh, my Jane," he murmured.

Exhaustion pulled him down, and as he drifted to sleep, a small smile curved his lips as he embraced the memories of his time with Jane. The universe was more vivid and colorful with her in his life. He imagined her hand curling around his, and the feeling was so real that he gasped.

"I miss you so much."

He knew he was dreaming, but he didn't care. Jane was in his arms, and he never wanted to wake. Her face was flushed with happiness, and her laughter was like music to his ears. She had been teasing him, saying she would beat him to the bridge.

They had raced to the crystal bridge that crossed the winding river in the park. He had given her a head start, watching with breathless wonder as the fading light danced over her glowing skin. Her long red skirt swirled around her legs, giving him a glimpse of her bare limbs. Her feet were encased in a pair of matching ballerina shoes. A three-quarter sleeve white peasant blouse with a thin belt finished off her outfit. Her shoulder-length brown hair danced around her, brushing her rosy cheeks as she held her arms out and twirled to see how far behind her he was.

"Jarmen, it isn't a race if you don't run," she teased, laughing.

"What do I get if I win?" he called.

She bit her bottom lip, her eyes twinkling with love.

"A kiss."

"What do you get if you win?"

She slowed and took slow steps backwards. She was so beautiful that his heart ached and he took a step forward. Her gaze softened and she lifted a hand in his direction.

"You."

"Then I will let you always win."

She wiggled her fingers, motioning for him to come to her. He surged forward, capturing her hand and pulling her into his arms. She wound her arms around his neck and stared up at him with so much love in her eyes that he felt as if he was drowning in the beautiful brown depths. She stepped back, pulling him with her as she stepped onto the bridge.

"I win."

A low groan slipped from him as she kissed him. He wrapped his arms around the spare pillow on the bed and slipped deeper into sleep, a slight smile on his lips as he relived that night.

Time seemed to slow for a fraction of a second before everything returned to normal. The change was so subtle that IQ didn't even appear to register that anything was different. Jarmen immediately checked their position.

The journey this time was smoother than the first, but the readings were coming back wrong. They were in the correct universe, but he had been forced to exit before he was ready due to warnings of an impending solar disruption from a nearby star. He wouldn't have any trouble determining their exact location. It was the exact time that had him concerned.

I'm sorry, my love. It would appear the universe is determined to make our reunion a challenge, he thought with wry amusement.

The few hours of rest had helped clear his mind and reinvigorated his determination. The dreams of Jane had also helped. They had given him a sense of peace and calm. He was so calm that he only felt aggravation instead of rage when he heard Charon behind him.

"What happened?" she asked.

He gritted his teeth and turned. Charon stood at the entrance to the bridge with Luc and Jon Paul hovering nervously behind her.

"You are not supposed to be on this level," he reminded her.

Her lips tightened, and annoyance flashed across her face before she schooled her expression into a blank mask. Her glance slipped to the holographic globe shimmering behind him, however. He silently sent her a warning.

"My apologies. I was... concerned when I... felt the change," she murmured with a bow of her head.

"Everything is fine," he tersely replied.

"Come, *ma chérie*. I told you it was nothing, eh. Jarmen has everything under control. I was about to introduce you to this wonderful creation called hot chocolate. It will melt in your mouth and make everything feel much better," Luc gently coaxed, sending Jarmen an accusing glare.

Jarmen remained silent. Charon's gaze slid over the glowing holographic globe again, her attention pausing on the three control columns holding the golden keys. He stepped in front of them, blocking her view.

"This hot chocolate sounds... fascinating. If it is as good as the other supplements you have given me, I'm sure it tastes delicious," Charon replied.

Jarmen remained where he was until Charon and Luc left. Jon Paul sent him an apologetic smile before he hurriedly followed the other two. Jarmen felt a tug on his pant leg. He looked down at IQ.

"Is 626 bad?" IQ asked.

Jarmen debated how to answer and sighed. Stanley's emotion program was making life more difficult than he could have ever expected. He didn't know how Jane dealt with living with both the bots and the two Frenchmen. It was like having... children!

"I hope not," he finally replied. "I need to review what has happened."

"I'll check for any communication traffic. Who knows, maybe there will be something interesting going on!" IQ responded in a suddenly cheerful tone.

"That sounds like it will keep you busy."

IQ's disgruntled *humph* told Jarmen his response was not received happily. He rubbed the spot between his eyes. A pang of longing for Jane's gentle guidance swept through him.

Soon, my Jane. Soon, we will be together again, he vowed.

Two hours later, he had determined that he must have misread a symbol in his calculations because they were nowhere near Kassis. They were near a small planet in the Kepler-10 star system. Kepler-10 was in the opposite direction of Kassis.

Of course, IQ's off-key singing might have played a small factor in my miscalculations, he thought with a wince when IQ hit another wrong note.

"Hey, Jarmen, I'm picking up a strange signal. It's weird because the signal is being transmitted through the ship's system to the navigation and communication consoles. I didn't do it. You aren't doing it, are you?" IQ called from where he was plugged in to the ship's console.

Jarmen connected with the communication system. A dark, thunderous expression swept across his face when he heard the nearly imperceptible signal hidden within the ship's network. He swiveled on his heel, his mind scanning the ship for 626. She was in the medical lab with Luc, Jon Paul, and Num.

Breaking into a jog, he exited the bridge and headed down the corridor. Less than two minutes later, he was striding into the medical unit on the third level. Luc stood up from his chair near the bed. Jon Paul turned from where he was studying the medical panel. Num was standing over 626. She was lying on the medical bed, her skin a dull, pale purple and her eyes glazed with pain.

She sat up and stared at him with a wary expression. Num moved aside, sensing his rage. Jarmen strode over to the bed, and in a flash, had one hand wrapped around 626's neck.

His eyes blazed red as he scanned her. In her weakened state, she offered little resistance. She wrapped her hand around his wrist, but she didn't fight him. He dragged her off the bed and backed her up against the wall. Behind him, Luc sputtered with outrage.

"Jarmen! What are you doing? This is no way to treat a lady, eh, my friend?" Luc choked out in protest.

"She is no lady. She is a—"

His fingers tightened. 626 stared back at him with eyes devoid of emotion. She didn't struggle.

"What happened?" Jon Paul asked, his voice calming.

"She connected with the ship and sent us here. I want to know why," he growled.

"I... did... not... c-connect with it," she stated.

"My calculations were changed. The instruction was sent to the computer system through the internal controls. There is also a signal being sent into space with instructions to intercept us," he retorted.

"I did not—" she insisted.

Jarmen pressed his hand against 626's temple. Microscopic sensors in his hand pierced her skin, pushing through flesh, bone, and brain matter. 626 didn't flinch. Instead, she kept her eyes locked on his face.

Vivid images flooded his brain. He saw a lab, masked faces, and muted voices. Everywhere there was pain—and a sense of defiance.

A woman's voice instructed 626 over and over to do things her body was not originally designed to do. Agony—physical and emotional— almost always accompanied the woman's instructions. Above all, there was a desire for revenge.

His body stiffened with shock when he saw Jane's face. Over and over, images of Jane in different places. There was Jane—smiling and chatting with the robots at her humble home. Another of her joking with Jon Paul and Luc. A different time when she was talking with Walter. Scenes of him and Jane together—talking, kissing, and holding each other. Those particular memories almost drove him away. He gritted his teeth, determined to know everything. A new scene emerged. It was the morning of Jane's death. Jane was laughing with River, Star, and Jo at the café.

The image darkened with tunnel vision. She sped toward Jane, clutching a short spear tipped with a fast-acting poison. Jarmen recoiled. The moment she stabbed Jane burst to the front of her mind. His stomach roiled, and the familiar feeling of nausea rose up his throat and over his tongue.

She is responsible. She killed my Jane.

"Jarmen, no!" Jon Paul shouted in horror.

Without realizing it, he had pulled his laser pistol and was pointing it at 626's head. She had slid down the wall and was now sitting on the floor. Her eyes were dull, her face emotionless.

"Let him. It… is no more than I deserve," she said, not looking at anyone else but Jarmen.

"Why? *Why* did you kill her? She-she never harmed anyone. She-she was no threat to you or anyone else," he choked out.

626 lifted her chin. "I did it to get to you… to get to this ship. There was no other way. I was doing what I was ordered to do. It is what we were made for—to follow orders."

Jarmen shook his head. "No, we are more than killing machines. We were someone… once," he growled.

626 scoffed and leaned her head back against the wall. "In the few memories I have of before, I was nothing different. My people were bred to kill each other and anyone else who gets in our way," she replied, her voice threaded with pain and resignation.

"That is not true, Charon," Luc protested.

"Luc… don't!" Jon Paul warned.

Luc glared at his friend and lover. "We all deserve a second chance, Jon Paul," he argued.

Luc walked over and knelt next to Charon. He cupped her hand in his and pressed it against his cheek. Jarmen sneered at the compassionate gesture. Luc didn't know what he knew—that 626 was right, she was nothing but a killing machine.

"Luc, move away," he ordered.

Luc looked up at him and shook his head. "*Non*, Jarmen. I will not let you harm Charon. She is under our protection. She is very sick."

"She is going to be dead soon," he snapped as the memory of 626 killing Jane threatened to choke him.

"If you wish to put us on the nearest planet, then so be it, but I will not let you kill her," Luc declared.

"She is the one who *murdered Jane!*"

Luc nodded. "*Oui,* I know."

"Luc!" Jon Paul hissed with dismay.

"You... know... knew... that 626 killed Jane, and you said nothing?" Jarmen demanded.

"I suspected. It was a little too convenient for her to suddenly appear, and she was wearing the same utility belt that the killer was in the video," Luc replied with a shrug.

"Why didn't you tell me?" Jon Paul asked, his voice filled with hurt.

Luc raised an eyebrow at his lover. "Because you would have told Jarmen. Why do you think I have been staying so close to her? Num and I would never let her hurt any of you, would we, Num?" Luc said, looking over at the large robot.

"Why?"

The soft, bewildered question seemed out of place in the medical unit. 626—Charon—was staring at Luc with a confused, almost vulnerable expression on her face. He sensed her emotion was real.

Luc lifted her hand to his lips and kissed her knuckles. "Because as you say—you were ordered to do what you did... and because Jane would forgive you and want us to help you."

"She... Jane... is lucky that you care for her," 626 murmured. She looked up at Jarmen with a determined expression. "I... am sorry for what I did. I have never felt that way before, but I do this time. I hope you save her. I hope you save your Jane."

Jarmen lowered his weapon when 626 closed her eyes and suddenly tilted to the side. Luc caught her with a curse. Her skin color turned ashen. Another scan showed she was going into multiple organ failure.

He holstered his weapon, stepped forward, and scooped her into his arms. He placed her on the medical bed. His mind was connecting to the medical scanner. She needed advanced care.

"Num, engage the regeneration unit and keep her heavily sedated. She is not to leave the medical unit under any circumstance. I have a new derivative of the compound she has been using for you to try," he ordered.

"*D'accord*. Num, you heard him. We need to take care of Charon," Luc responded.

"You are not going to let her die?" Jon Paul asked, gripping Jarmen's forearm to stop him from leaving the room.

Jarmen looked back at 626 lying still and pale against the white sheets. "Not until I get all the answers I need," he said before he pulled away and exited the room.

Once outside the room, he leaned back against the wall. His breaths came in heavy gasps. It took a few seconds for him to realize that his body was trembling and his vision was blurred.

"My beautiful Jane," he groaned in a shuddering breath as he realized that Jane was dead because of him.

He sucked in deep breaths and forced his eyes open. Pushing away from the wall, he walked with leaden feet back toward the lift. He had work to do, and he would not let anything stop him.

CHAPTER 20

Fatigue slowed his movements as he ran a myriad of tests on both the space/time functions of the crystal ship and on Charon's bio-regenerative experiments. Concern about what damage the other cyborg might have done had slowed his progress over the last four days. Because of the delay, he had skipped resting and only nibbled on the simple meals IQ had delivered via Jon Paul and Luc.

He was going through each system line-by-line, trying to determine what she may have accessed and who she had been trying to contact. While his mind ran the tedious tasks, a separate part clung to Jane's soothing influence.

The rage he felt at knowing he had Jane's killer on board and his own role in her fate still roiled with a bitter taste inside of him. He didn't trust himself anywhere near 626... or Luc. He was still angry with the Frenchman, even though he understood that the man was acting in good faith.

He brought up a hologram he had taken of Jane weeks before her death. Her laughter wrapped around him, filling him with the warmth of her love. The image of her face, glowing with excitement, as she shared Stanley's new upgrade for the bots made him smile. He lifted his hand to cup her face when she turned to him.

"I love your smile," he murmured.

His fingers brushed through the holographic image, momentarily distorting it. A shudder ran through him, and he dropped his hand back to the controls as the scene faded to be replaced by a map of the new star system they were in.

He needed rest, but the idea of closing his eyes for even a few minutes filled him with dread. He straightened and stiffened his shoulders when he heard footsteps behind him.

"How is 626?" he inquired, already knowing the answer.

Jon Paul snorted. "*Charon* is stable—barely—as you well know. Even the adjusted compound is lasting a shorter amount of time with each dosage. How are your calculations going?"

"I am almost finished with my latest test," he replied.

"Uh, Jarmen?" IQ called.

Jarmen rubbed the ache at the bridge of his nose. IQ had been blissfully quiet since his return to the bridge. Well, as blissfully quiet as the small robot could be.

The bot had discovered how to download music from nearby worlds using the communication system and was playing someone called John Prine. Anything was better than IQ's renditions of spaceport melodies.

The folksy music had a surprisingly pleasant combination of music and storytelling, but the biggest draw was that it kept IQ entertained. It took Jarmen a split second to realize that the music had stopped.

"What is it IQ?" he asked.

"I know I'm supposed to only be monitoring the communication's system, but since there was nothing exciting going on out there except a bunch of people screeching about their search for a stolen *Lexamus IV*

Class Starship, I decided to connect into the long-range scanner and check out the local exoplanets in case you wanted to drop off that cyborg b— witch somewhere," IQ explained.

"And?" Jarmen asked, trying to hold on to his patience.

IQ's eyes opened and closed at opposing times. "This crystal ship's detection system is way better than any I've seen before. The Kassisans could learn a thing or two about—" IQ paused and bleeped when Jarmen released a low, frustrated growl. "Ok! I think I found the missing *Lexamus IV* that some guy named Kelman and the Drethulans are looking for! It's heading for Kepler-10. It is damaged, but still moving for now. From what I've been able to download so far, that planet is filled with Gartaians. Those are—"

"I know what a Gartaian is!" Jarmen snapped.

"Well, bite me. How was I supposed to know that? Oh, yeah… you're half computer. Duh! I just thought you might be interested because the communications traffic you *requested* that I monitor kept referring to a Trivator named Dagger, and I thought that was strange because wasn't Ajaska working with a species called the Trivators?" IQ replied.

Draka, Drethulans, Gartaians, and Trivators were not a good mix— especially when the Trivator was stranded on a damaged ship with a bunch of creatures that could eat virtually anything—and did.

Gartaians were gray mammoths that lived in the swampy areas of the planet Kepler-10. The creatures stood almost four meters high—13 feet high—and weighed in at over ten thousand kilograms or ten metric tons.

A series of three tusks in varying sizes protruded from each side of its mouth, allowing it to uproot trees and other debris in its constant search for food, as well as provide protection for itself. It could eat and digest anything.

The Gartaians' tongues could extend almost two meters—or six and a half feet—and drag its prey into its wide mouth where thick, flat teeth ground whatever it found before it swallowed the remains of its prey.

Jarmen connected with the long-range scanner and communications system and verified for himself that IQ's assessment was correct. He silently cursed and glanced down at the control panel in front of him. The test program he was running had taken the engines off-line. He had been unwilling to make another jump until he had tested his calculations.

It would be several hours before the engines would be back online. He looked back at the scanner again. The *Lexamus IV* was traveling at a fraction of the speed that it was capable of, which meant the engines or the hull were damaged, perhaps both.

"What are you going to do? If it is a friend of Ajaska, then we must help them, eh? It is the right thing to do," Jon Paul asserted.

Jarmen released a long, frustration-filled sigh. "Yes, it is the right thing to do," he replied, already entering the coordinates into the navigation system.

He stiffened when he felt Jon Paul's hand on his shoulder. "Jane would be proud of you, my friend."

Jarmen briefly closed his eyes and gritted his teeth. This mission was turning into a kaleidoscope of bizarre rescue undertakings. First, 626—Charon—and now a Trivator in a stolen *Lexamus IV* spaceship with a group of mercenaries on his tail.

I promise, my love. I will find you—after we rescue half the galaxy.

Deep down, Jarmen could almost hear Jane's amused laughter and see her dancing eyes.

I know you will. I'll be waiting, her soft voice whispered in his ear.

It sounded so real that he half turned and scanned the room.

Jarmen rolled his shoulders to ease his tense muscles. He lay back on his bed in the dark cabin and closed his eyes. He had decided to take advantage of the downtime before the engines came back online to get some much-needed rest. The last thing he wanted to do was confront hostiles when he was not at full capacity.

At least I don't have to worry about the others taking an unexpected stroll outside the ship this time, he mused.

He had made Jon Paul and IQ swear that they would not touch anything. A brief check showed Num in his charger and Luc sitting with 626—Charon. His expression twisted when he used the name the others had given her, but acknowledging her right to an identity was about who he was, not who she was.

Images from his brief connection with Charon filtered through his mind, bringing back painful memories of his own. He recognized many of the machines in her memories. He shut down that line of thought, knowing that if he didn't, he would not get the rest he so desperately needed.

As his mind and body relaxed, the dreams came as he knew—hoped— they would. He needed to feel Jane's presence, her touch, her... love. He felt as if he were breaking into fragments.

"Everything will be alright," Jane whispered.

"How do you know? How can you be so sure?" he asked.

"Because our love is too great for death to hold us apart. Sleep now, my darling Jarmen," she comforted.

A low groan slipped from his lips and he rolled onto his side. Her soft fingers caressed his brow, chasing away the dull ache. The last of the tension melted from his body. His last conscious thought was that her words of love were the same as those Suzanne spoke to Jarmen in *Tales of Two Galaxies.* Her gentle caress brushed along his cheek and his jaw.

I felt her touch— he thought, lifting his hand to his tingling flesh.

"I have made coffee. It is nice that most of the items we are familiar with were already in the replicator's memory bank, eh? It is still hard for me to believe that humans could have flown something like this," Jon Paul stated four hours later.

Jarmen grunted out an unintelligible response as he entered the galley. His plan was to grab a quick drink and a nourishment bar. He hadn't expected to be greeted with coffee and the delicious aroma filling the room. His stomach growled with appreciation.

Jon Paul handed him a cup of steaming coffee but didn't immediately release the cup. Compassion gleamed from the man's eyes. It was as if Jon Paul knew he was losing his grip on reality.

"Thank you," he said, remembering how Jane used to tease him about being polite.

Jon Paul released the cup with a slight smile. "I have prepared you a delicious breakfast. It is important to start your day good; and nothing says good better than a homecooked meal."

Jarmen slid onto the bench seat and warily watched as Jon Paul uncovered several dishes and began piling food onto a plate. He had slept deeply and woke refreshed, but was still disturbed by his memory of the last few seconds before he lost consciousness.

Jane's voice and her touch seemed so real—but how could she know about that scene from *Tales of Two Galaxies*? The only thing she had known about the story was what he had shared with her. He felt ridiculous for expecting his imagination to give Jane only the information she had known in life—but deep down, he could not shake the feeling that she was real. This concrete proof that she was either not real, she was not Jane, or she was gaining more knowledge than she had in life was troubling.

He glanced around the galley before connecting with the ship to monitor the location of the others. Luc was in his cabin—asleep, most likely. Num was with 626 in the Medical Unit. IQ was on the bridge—playing an old human game where a yellow creature with a large mouth was eating dots and trying desperately to avoid the ghostly shapes that were chasing it.

Jon Paul placed the plate in front of him and sat down across from him. Picking up the fork, he began to eat. The food was delicious, and his stomach rumbled with pleasure. He couldn't remember the last time he had eaten.

"Jarmen, there are a few… matters that Luc and I have been wanting to discuss with you," Jon Paul said.

"What type of matters?" he asked around a mouthful of food.

Jon Paul folded his hands in front of him. "Once we rescue Jane…"

Jarmen's hand paused in mid-air before he placed the fork next to his half-empty plate.

"Go on," he said.

Jon Paul swallowed before stiffening his shoulders. "Once we rescue Jane, Luc and I think it would be good for you and her to… for you to consider… Jane is like a daughter to us, and we—"

"What are you trying to say?" he ground out, growing impatient.

"What Jon Paul is saying is that we think you should ask Jane to marry you," Luc said in a voice raspy from sleep. "Ah, coffee…. The elixir of the Gods."

Jarmen blinked. The two men had been discussing him and Jane getting married? He picked up his fork and began eating again.

Marriage? He frowned. The Kassisans had a ritual where they claimed each other as life mates. Was marriage the same?

"Jon Paul, is there more food?" Luc asked before releasing a sigh of contentment when he discovered the covered dishes. "This is why I love you. You make wonderful breakfasts… and coffee."

Luc filled a plate and carried it and his coffee to the table. Luc paused to kiss Jon Paul's temple before he sat down on the bench.

A flash of emotion that Jarmen didn't understand hit him. He slowly chewed his food as he contemplated what he was experiencing.

Envy.

He was envious, and not just of their relationship with each other.

"How did you do this?" he asked, looking back and forth between the two men with a frown.

"How did we do what?" Jon Paul asked.

Luc smiled. "Can you not see it, Jon Paul? It is a beautiful thing, is it not, eh?"

"See what?" Jon Paul demanded.

"You two, the robots, Jane... even 626—Charon. There is a connection between you. How did you create it?" Jarmen asked.

Jon Paul's puzzled expression cleared. He looked at Luc and smiled. There—there was that look again—that connection.

"The same way you have created it, Jarmen. It is love... respect... compassion... empathy. We are your family, and you are part of ours," Luc explained.

Jon Paul wrapped his arm around Luc's shoulder. "You are smart sometimes, eh, Luc?" he teased.

Luc gave an ostentatious glare. "I am always smart! I just don't show it that often."

A snort of disbelief caused both men to look at Jarmen. It took a split second for him to realize that the sound came from him. Jon Paul and Luc's infectious laughter caught him by surprise, and a deep, unfamiliar chuckle slipped from him.

I love the sound of your laugh.

His amusement died when he swore he felt tender fingers caressing his cheek and Jane's lilting voice in his ear. He curled his fingers around the metal fork. The metal bent under his firm grip.

"The engines will be back online in an hour. I need to program our path to Kepler-10," he said, rising to his feet.

Jon Paul and Luc watched him exit the galley with matching deep sighs. He knew he was being rude, but he needed time alone—to think. Was the voice in his head and the touch on his skin a sign? If so, what did it mean? Rationally, he knew it was impossible, but deep down, he needed to know that Jane was still alive somewhere—in some time—and that they would once again be together again.

CHAPTER 21

An hour later, the main engines were back online and Jarmen had programmed the Crystal ship's trajectory to the *Lexamus IV*. The cloaking shield had kept them hidden while he ran extensive simulations of their next space/time jump. He felt confident he had finally worked out the errors in his calculations and hoped there would not be any more unexpected stops.

"Num, how is your patient?" he inquired.

"I have kept her sedated as you requested. The changes to the medication you suggested are showing promise," Num replied.

He curbed his mixed reaction to the news.

"Keep me posted," he ordered.

While he could monitor the medical unit's information, he wasn't there in real-time to observe 626's reaction to the changes he made to the medication keeping her alive. His goal was to reverse, and possibly put into remission, the cyborg's organ degeneration.

Luc's words from earlier, about how helping 626 was what Jane would have wanted, echoed through his mind. If the Zephren Loop worked, if he was able to stop 626 before she attacked Jane... if he found out who had been controlling 626... then he would feel better about his decision to help the cyborg. Either way, he *would* discover who sent 626... and make them pay.

Breathing deeply, he engaged the drives. The familiar shimmer of the ship as it changed shape for the hyperdrive was reassuring. Only the two main columns were raised. The third one that controlled the space / time engine remained inactive.

The ship shot forward. He monitored the engines as their speed increased and determined they would reach their destination before the engines maxed out. The amount of energy the red crystal engines could produce was astonishing. The damage sustained earlier had been completely repaired.

Less than an hour later, IQ's tinny voice exclaimed, "There's Kepler-10! Do you want me to hail the *Lexamus IV* and let them know we are here?"

"No."

"Aw, Jarmen. What's the use of me being your communication officer if you don't want me talking to anyone?" IQ complained.

Jarmen glanced at IQ and scowled. "You are not my communication officer. You are... just supposed to listen."

IQ tapped a command into the console. Jarmen scowled a warning at the small bot who blinked innocently back at him.

"You've given our position away," he growled.

IQ snorted and turned his back to him. "I've been researching the Trivator and have determined that surprising him is not advisable. He has left behind many dead people. You may be determined to make sure we have the same end, but I am here to take care of us. You're welcome."

Jarmen gritted his teeth and resisted the urge once again to reprogram the little bot. Instead, he returned his attention to their arrival. He would send Jon Paul and Luc to greet the Trivator. If he was lucky, maybe the Trivator would adopt the bonnie pair.

I'll even throw in 626 as a bonus. Maybe the Trivator will kill her for me! he spitefully thought.

He adjusted the ship's configuration so the vessel wouldn't sink into the soft soil. The last thing he wanted was to be stuck and defenseless with his crew, a deadly Trivator, and a herd of Gartaian. The outer hull expanded. Below, unseen except on the control monitor, a large sheet of crystal formed into a wide flat base seconds before the ship touched down, distributing the ship's mass over the unstable surface.

"Jon Paul, Luc, I want you to greet the Trivator. I will monitor the situation from the ship," he announced over the communication system.

The hurried footsteps pounding down the corridor towards the bridge warned him that the men not only heard him, but were not thrilled about his orders.

"What do you mean you want us to greet the Trivator? Wouldn't it be better for you to go? You are...." Jon Paul waved his hand in Jarmen's direction before he stopped and looked at Luc, trying to find the right words.

"A natural born killer?" Luc suggested.

Jon Paul winced and scowled at his lover before he looked back at Jarmen. Jarmen was surprised by the flash of amusement that ran through him at the almost panicked expressions on the two men's faces. They had faced down pirates, a furious Kassisan royal, and who knew what those creatures were on the world they had landed on before he found them, and *now* they were panicking?

"It is not necessary to kill us if you are still mad about Charon," Jon Paul warily exclaimed with a nervous expression.

Jarmen sighed and shook his head. "It is better if the Trivator sees someone who is less of a threat than I am. I can assure you, one look at the two of you and he will know he isn't in danger."

"I will go, Jon Paul. Out of all of us, IQ and I are the two least threatening ones," Luc offered.

"*Non!* I will not let you go into the face of death alone. I will be by your side as I have through everything else we have faced," Jon Paul declared.

Jarmen gritted his teeth to keep from throttling the dramatic duo as they stared at each other with solemn expressions.

"Neither one of you will be in danger. I will monitor the situation. The danger will be outside of the Trivator's ship. I can operate the ship's defense system faster and more accurately than any of you, and I will not give 626 the opportunity to take over the ship in my absence. There are two life forms on the Trivator's ship, and one is human. This is another reason why a human should go."

"Don't worry, Jarmen. I'll stay by their side and defend them," IQ stated.

"This is acceptable—if it will make you feel better," he replied with exasperation.

"Then we will go face the danger with our heads held high, eh, Jon Paul," Luc said, threading his arm through Jon Paul's.

"Num go, too," Num said, pausing in the doorway to the bridge.

"Fine, all of you go!" Jarmen growled.

"Someone is in a bad mood," IQ quipped as he rolled by.

"There is another human. I wonder who it is," Luc said, rubbing his hands together.

"Jarmen," Jon Paul began, his expression worried.

He held Jon Paul's gaze. "I will not harm Charon while you are gone," he promised in a low voice.

"Thank you."

Jon Paul's equally quiet response made him wince internally. He turned away and scanned the area for the Gartaians before he activated the platform. In all honesty, he could use the peace and quiet… even if it was only for a short time.

He listened as the group departed, their chatter noisy and unconcerned about what they might face as they crossed from ship to ship. He turned his attention to the communication IQ had intercepted. He identified potential threats while he assessed the damage to the Lexamus IV spaceship and monitored 626.

All of this was taking time away from his real mission, and guilt weighed heavily on him. It was tempting to repair the Trivator's ship and leave the two Frenchmen, the bots, and 626 with the Trivator and human. Even as the idea formed, he dismissed it. If he was honest with himself, he needed all of them… including Charon.

Jane would be proud of you, my friend.

Jon Paul's haunting words kept echoing in his head. Was this a test? To see if he was worthy of Jane? Pain struck him as Charon's confession of why she attacked Jane resurfaced. He clenched his fists and cursed as the world blurred around him.

"Jane would have been safer if she had never known me," he murmured.

A crushing weight settled in his chest.

"Ah, Jarmen… you *are* seeing the huge, scary Trivator with the very big blaster in his hand, aren't you?" IQ asked through the communication link.

"Yes, IQ. I am aware the Trivator has weapons," he calmly replied. "Will you please inform Jon Paul and Luc that I can hear their argument."

"Hey, guys, Jarmen says he can hear you," IQ announced.

"Yes? Did you hear that Luc is having second thoughts about our visit here? He believes we should have taken a right at the second star and traveled to Neverland instead," Jon Paul teased.

"What's Neverland? Have we been there before?" IQ inquired.

"*Non*, IQ. It is an inside joke. I have no wish to be Captain Hook's cannon fodder on this trip, eh," Luc defended.

"The Trivator is not carrying a cannon.," Num responded. "He is carrying...."

Jarmen tuned out the large robot's rambling description of the weapons the Trivator was holding. Instead, he focused on learning about the man and his human companion. A frown creased his brow as he read about Dagger and the human woman called Jordan Sampson.

Pain suddenly pierced him between the eyes. He stumbled backwards and fell to one knee as the world tilted around him. Bracing his hand against the floor, he tried to push past the debilitating agony. His stomach roiled, and he fought to keep from vomiting as blurred visions danced in the haze and the black spots interfering with his vision.

He keeled over, landing heavily on his left side. A whimper slipped from his clenched teeth as the pain in his head increased. He rolled onto his back and stared up at the ceiling, breathing through his nose as a vision of a blonde woman emerged. A smile curved her lips, and her dark brown eyes danced with mischief.

"*Hey, Taylor, do you want to hang out tonight?*"

"*I can't. Hunter is taking Jordan and me for flying lessons.*"

"*That saves me from growing gray hair.*"

Taylor's snort of laughter coursed through him as if she were on the ship's bridge. The sound was so real, he lifted his hands and braced them against his ears. He closed his eyes, trying to hold onto the vision when it changed.

"Buzz, have you seen what I did with my tablet? I could have sworn I left it on the table."

He stiffened when he glimpsed a reflection in the mirrored surface of the small café. He saw a young man with an easy smile. His dancing brown eyes were ringed with gold. The images blurred in his mind and the ring of gold changed to red.

"Shewta!" The Trivator curse flowed from him as he jerked into a sitting position.

The room spun around him. Bracing one hand against the floor and the other to his head, Jarmen breathed deeply as the dam in his mind burst and a torrent of memories left him dazed and confused.

I had a name before! I... knew Jordan... and Taylor.... I was a...

The knowledge of who and what he was before left him shaken. He ran his hand over his face. None of his features looked the same. The experiments and the physicians' scalpels....

They tried to erase any memory of my life before... including how I looked.

The thought left him nauseated. He drew his legs up and leaned forward to rest his arms against his knees as memories of his past filled in the blank spaces. He'd had a family, friends, a career.

I had fallen in love.

That memory shocked him like none of the others. He had been in love, or thought he had, with Taylor Sampson... a human woman from Earth. They had been best friends.

He staggered to his feet, swayed, and reached out to grip the edge of the long bank of crystal. Jon Paul's voice came over the communication console again. Connecting mentally to the communication system was too much for him in his current condition. He bowed his head. Reaching out, he touched the console controls.

"Bonjour, monsieur. I am Jon Paul and this is Luc," Jon Paul stuttered. "Would you happen to know what year it is back on Earth?"

"Dagger, they *are* human!" a soft voice exclaimed behind the man.

"Ah, Jarmen, I think we are good here. The woman reminds me of Jane. I don't think she'll let the Trivator toast us. Do you want to come out and meet them?" IQ asked.

"Not yet. I... have things I must attend to here first. Assess the situation and have Num send it to me," he forced out between gritted teeth.

"Okay. More important things... like what? You aren't planning on killing Charon, are you? She kept Num from being dismembered, so I like her now, you know?" IQ retorted.

"I'm not killing anyone. Just... make contact and have Num report back," he ordered.

"Fine! I think they will be more fun than you anyway," IQ replied.

Jarmen ended the link and pushed away from the console. He sank down into the captain's chair and braced his head between his hands. Memories flooded his mind, and he drowned, disoriented and disconnected. Some memories didn't make sense.

It is like I am seeing my life from multiple angles all at once....

He jerked his head up, ignoring the excruciating pain that flared at the movement. His eyes widened and glowed as information embedded within his memories filtered through. His lips parted on a hiss of astonishment as everything suddenly became clear.

He looked around the interior of the ship as if seeing it for the first time... and yet—not. He rose on surprisingly steady legs and stared out the front viewport. It hadn't been the Draka or scientists who had blocked his memories.

It was me... an alternate version of myself... from a parallel universe...

CHAPTER 22

J armen splayed his left hand over the glass and stared at 626's peaceful face. She was in the regen cylinder and wouldn't wake until he changed the sedative. He was shocked by the emotion coursing through him now. Gone were his feelings of hostility and rage.

"I… understand now," he murmured, closing his eyes and bowing his head.

You are a good man, my love. Help her find her way, and you will find me.

Peace flowed through him as Jane's whispered words floated through his mind. Each of his alternate selves had gone through this journey before him. Their knowledge flowed through his mind.

The Jarmen who had once been Buzz, and who had loved and lost Taylor Sampson only to discover Jane, was not him… at least, not the Jarmen he was now. He was not the Jarmen who had traveled to Jane's childhood to kidnap Jane and her mother. He was not the Jarmen who had brought them to present-day Kassis. The move had meant Jane and Jarmen could never be together, but she was safe and she had a chance to be happy, so Jarmen knew he would have been willing to do what his alternate-self had done.

He was also not the Jarmen who had failed repeatedly to stop Jane's death and used the Red Crystal ship to attack the Drethulans. He was not the Jarmen who had never understood what it felt like to be part of a family.

The question was: how did Jarmen have the memories of parallel Jarmens *before* he was kidnapped and experimented on? Because Jarmen did know one thing for certain: his other selves had shielded his mind to protect Jane. Cerberus would have used her to control him… and he would have done whatever the man requested.

Just as 626 has done.

∾

Jarmen glared at his crew. They were being their usual boisterous, irritating selves. Jon Paul and Luc poured on the charm with Jordan Sampson while IQ flirted outrageously with her. A brief scan of IQ's programming showed that one of the men must have been playing with his coding again.

"So, are you attached, in a relationship, seeing anyone?" IQ asked, walking his fingers up Jordan's arm.

"IQ, she belongs to the Trivator," he snapped.

Jordan giggled and tilted slightly to one side. Only IQ's arm and body kept her from sliding to the ground. Her mate, Dagger, lifted an eyebrow.

"I told Jon Paul that I liked his programming better than Jarmen's," Luc replied with a wink as he set a glass down in front of Jordan with a bow. "Only the best wine for my beautiful lady."

Jordan turned when the little robot pulled himself up onto the table. She grinned and leaned forward to brush a kiss across IQ's brow.

Jarmen shook his head at the display. He was going to have to have a talk with Jon Paul.

"IQ, off the table," Jarmen ordered with a low growl. "Jon Paul, you should not change his programming."

"But I think he is adorable!" Jordan said.

"You shouldn't encourage him," Jarmen warned, his eyes softly glowing as he found a way to vent his frustrations. "He—"

"Jane liked him the way Jon Paul programmed him, eh," Luc interrupted. "He made her laugh."

Jon Paul walked over to the table and placed a tray in front of Jordan. "Here, a feast fit for a beautiful princess. The food on this ship is much better than what we have."

"So is the wine, eh?" Luc added with a low moan of appreciation.

Jarmen turned away to focus on the repairs he and Dagger were making to the *Lexamus IV*. He had joined the group several hours earlier. After a brief, tense introduction, the Trivator called Dagger had cautiously welcomed him. He suspected Luc, Jon Paul, and the two robots had a lot to do with that.

Dagger ate one of the small appetizers Jon Paul had prepared. His eyes widened with surprise, and he reached for another helping.

Dagger and Jarmen spoke briefly about how the aggravating Frenchmen's cooking saved the men's lives every day before Dagger abruptly changed the subject.

"Where did you get your ship?"

Jarmen debated how much to say before he shrugged. He was an equal match to the Trivator despite their size difference. He was also not concerned about the man trying to steal the ship from under him. The Trivator wouldn't be able to operate the ship without the keys or the knowledge.

"I stole it. I needed it, so I took it."

"Why did you need it? Where did you steal it from, and are the ones you stole it from going to come looking for it here? I won't allow anyone to put Jordan in any more danger than she already is."

Jarmen's hand moved in a blur of speed when he saw a knife in Dagger's hand. He deftly disarmed him. Jarmen suspected that he was only able to do so because of the modifications to his body and his surprise attack.

Dagger returned his stare with a cold, calculating one. Jarmen twirled the knife between his fingers before he offered the blade to Dagger, handle-side out. His message had been sent and understood. If he had wanted to harm anyone, he would have done so already. Dagger carefully took the knife and set it down next to his plate.

"I am no threat to you or the female," he promised.

"That was a good visit, eh? We should do it more often," Luc mumbled later that evening.

"Oh, Luc. You warm my heart," Jon Paul replied, helping Luc onto the crystal ship when he staggered.

Jarmen shook his head. The two men were both more than a little drunk. They had enjoyed chatting with Jordan while he worked with Dagger on the *Lexamus IV*. He didn't ask Dagger about his captivity. There was no need. Jarmen knew all-too-well what men like the Drethulan, who had held Dagger, did to those they held prisoner. He had been to the *Hole* and had witnessed the savagery of the fight rings.

No, he hadn't asked questions, but he had observed. He didn't miss the way Dagger's gaze constantly sought Jordan. Nor did he miss the way Jordan responded to Dagger. It reminded him so much of himself and Jane that he felt a physical pain.

It was also impossible to miss the man's internal struggle to control his emotions. There was a primitive aura to Dagger's demeanor that warned others to proceed with caution. Watching the other couple had been like looking in a mirror.

"We will leave first thing in the morning," he announced, striding onto the ship.

"I have forgotten about Charon. I have left her unattended, Jon Paul. What if she needed one of us?" Luc fretted, casting a blurry glance around the interior of the ship as if he was trying to remember which way he was supposed to go.

"626—Charon—is stable. She is in the regen. Num will watch over her while we rest," he replied.

"Ah, good. See, Jon Paul! I told you he would not kill her... or us, eh. He is a good man," Luc slurred with a lopsided grin.

"You are always right, Luc. Now, it is time to sleep. I think it has been too long since we've had such good wine! It is embarrassing to think we cannot hold our liquor! We are the masters of holding our wine!"

Jarmen refrained from telling either of the men that the 'wine' they were enjoying was probably more potent than any they would have enjoyed back on their world. Instead, he sent a silent command to IQ, instructing the small bot to make sure the two men made it safely to their cabin. It would be just his luck if they managed to somehow fall out of the ship.

"We save Jane now?" Num inquired.

"Very soon, my friend. First, we will make sure the Trivator and his mate are safe. It is... what Jane would want," he replied.

Num nodded. "Yes, Jane would be happy."

Jarmen remained where he was, watching as Num lumbered after the others. He stood in the bay as his menagerie of misfits slowly disappeared into the interior of the ship. IQ was talking up a storm; Jon Paul was reassuring Luc that Jordan had enjoyed their company; and Num was on his way to sit with Charon.

Jane, you would be very proud of our small family, he silently thought.

I am, but I'm even more proud of you. You have finally recognized what it means to have a family.

He smiled as the soft reply echoed through his mind. There was still some minor tweaking to do on his calculations, but he wanted to join Num in medical. With the knowledge of his other selves came additional data that might help Charon. It was time to test their theories.

Early the next morning, there were four Drethulan starships in orbit. It didn't take long for Jarmen to determine each of the ships' capabilities and the number of fighters they hosted. Dagger's skill as a pilot combined with the modifications Jarmen had added to the *Lexamus IV* would make sure the couple could quickly escape.

He was sure the Trivator was already aware of the fighters approaching at a high rate of speed, but he still warned him, just to make sure. The *Lexamus IV* should be fully operational, but there had been no time to test the ship.

"Kill them," Dagger tersely responded.

"Of course," he replied.

Blasts exploded across the ground, ripping up the soft soil and leaving deep holes that quickly filled with water and muck. Fortunately, Dagger had already implemented evasive maneuvers. The blasts missed the *Lexamus IV*. From his cloaked crystal ship, Jarmen locked on the attackers and opened fire. He quickly phased the ship using the time/space function to move a millisecond into the future to a position well away from where he had just been and killed a few more. He phased again, reappearing higher above the ships.

"Red One...." Dagger's calm voice flowed through the ship's communication system.

"I'm on him," he replied.

He fired on the fighter behind the *Lexamus IV*. It exploded in a rain of fire that sent the Gartaians stampeding. The *Lexamus IV* was larger and not quite as agile as the fighters, but it was three times more powerful. Jarmen watched with appreciation as Dagger guided his ship in a maneuver that scattered the fleet of fighters, making it easier to pick them off one at a time.

"*Red One*, I'm reading six fighters."

"Three," Jarmen replied with grim satisfaction as three of the small enemy ships disintegrated under the force of the crystal ship's defense system.

"I'm taking us up and out. There will be four starships waiting for us to break through. Expect more fighters."

"Affirmative," Jarmen responded.

The *Lexamus IV* swept past the crystal ship, followed by two fighters. The enemy was not expecting another ship to be waiting for them. They were defenseless when he opened fire. Both fighters exploded; their fiery remains scattering along the length of the canyon.

The crystal pulsed under Jarmen's steady hands as he rose through the atmosphere and past the planet's orbit. He could feel the energy flowing through his body. He locked his focus on the scanner and the four Drethulan starships, moving before Dagger emerged from the planet's orbit.

The living crystal responded to his commands, changing form until it was long and sleek. Additional crystal formed around the front and he increased the shields before accelerating.

The ship shot forward. Under his skillful control, the crystal ship shimmered, locked in a suspended state between solid and fluid crystal, and aimed for the largest Drethulan starship. Fighters poured out of the ship, but they didn't get far as the crystal ship shot through the starship like a spear.

The shields, reinforced by the thickened layer of crystal, held. The crystal ship appeared on the other side, undamaged. Jarmen watched dispassionately as the Drethulan starship imploded, taking most of the fighters and starships with it during the initial explosion and the resulting debris field.

"What are you doing?! *Êtes-vous fou? Vous venez traverser ce navire ! Essayez-vous tous nous tuer ?* Are you crazy? You just went through that ship! Are you trying to kill us all?"

"The Trivator and his mate are under attack," he replied, angling the ship toward his next target.

"We are going to die, eh? Before we have even saved Jane," Luc moaned, holding a hand to his head.

"Luc, for the very last time, we are not going to die!" he gritted out.

"*Red One*, this is *Lexamus IV*. Status report."

"The largest attack ship has been destroyed along with its fighters. Two of the other ships were severely damaged in the explosion. I will destroy the last ship before I depart," he responded.

"I don't know how you did that and survived, but I sure as hell wish I had a ship like that. Thank you again for your help, Jarmen," Dagger said.

Luc released a loud groan behind him. "I need a drink. I am definitely a lover, not a fighter."

Jordan's giggles made Jarmen's lips twitch with amusement. He wanted to hear Jane laugh. If he had to keep the two Frenchmen alive to do that, he would.

CHAPTER 23

S ome Time, Space, and Many Universes Later:

"Jarmen is going to kill us! I don't care what he said. Well, I do... but, he was also very specific."

"He only told us to stay off the bridge so we did not distract him," Jon Paul replied.

"I am supposed to be the reckless one, Jon Paul, not you! You know exactly what he meant," Luc muttered.

"What are we supposed to do? Let Earth be annihilated?" Jon Paul retorted.

"That sounds better than us floating in space," IQ chimed in.

Luc scowled at IQ. "You would survive. You don't need air. Jon Paul and I... we would not last thirty seconds."

"Then maybe you should get Charon to do it. She might last longer. She isn't completely organic," IQ suggested.

"*Non*, IQ. Jarmen no longer wants to kill her. It has taken a lot to get him to accept her, eh? We do not want to go through that again. Besides, she is still unconscious, and Jarmen would know the second she was awake," Luc argued.

"Num, you need to set the camera up over there. We do not want whoever watches this to see too much of the ship. IQ, you are sure you know how to operate this camera?" Jon Paul asked.

IQ glared back at Jon Paul. "I'm a robot. Of course I know how to operate a vidcom."

"Jon Paul, are you *sure* about this? Perhaps what we saw is another Earth. We have been to many universes and times, perhaps we are mistaken, eh?" Luc said.

"You saw what was happening, Luc. We can't take the chance. We will be careful. I'll make the video and IQ will put it in the archive of that fancy Alliance ship that is battling it out with the Drethulans. The Trivators or whoever is running the show will get it the day the Drethulans plan to attack Earth," Jon Paul responded with a determined expression.

"The vidcom is ready. Num go check on Charon now," Num said.

"Yes, Num. You should not be here just in case Jarmen kicks the rest of us out. We may need you to come get us, my big friend," Luc called.

"Are we going to do this thing or not because I'm not so sure my circuits can handle floating in space. I can just see my big, round body floating around while everyone and their brother tries to pop me one with their laser cannons. Jarmen being the first to take a shot," IQ muttered.

Luc shot IQ a reproving expression.

"You were the one who suggested this! Did you forget that, eh?"

IQ rolled his eyes in different directions and moved behind the vidcom with low curses that he must have learned from Bombing Bill. Jon Paul straightened, cleared his throat, smiled at the camera, and began to speak. Luc anxiously glanced at the door to the galley. Jarmen was supposed to be running through his calculations again.

For a cyborg with a computer-like mind, Jarmen had been having a hell of a time figuring out how to work the whole time/space/loop-de-loop thing. Jarmen's latest attempt had sent them across time, space, and the galaxy! They had ended up in the Earth's orbit and near the end of a hundred-year war with the Drethulans. There hadn't been a lot of the Earth left by the time the aliens had finished battling for it from what they could see.

While he and Jon Paul stared in horror at their former world, Jarmen had been busy hacking the closest Drethulan Battle cruiser's computer system to find out what was going on. Fortunately for them, IQ had been plugged into the communication system at the same time and was getting a memory load of information.

Luc was grateful the Red Crystal ship had a concealing shield. The hordes of alien spaceships battling it out both above and below the Earth's orbit was enough to make him start muttering some long-forgotten bible verses that he'd learn as a child.

The Alliance forces were out-numbered a thousand to one. Even the powers of the Red Crystal ship with Jarmen's great mind at the controls wouldn't have been able to save them if they joined in.

Luc forced himself back to the present. Well, the present that they were currently in. A shudder ran through him when the ship shook. The humans and the Trivators were not going down without a fight.

Jon Paul growled under his breath and waved his hand at the video equipment that had been hastily assembled.

"How do you expect me to warn them if you do not have the sound working? IQ, you are supposed to know how to operate this machine, *oui*?" Jon Paul demanded.

"Jon Paul, you better hurry. Jarmen will not be happy if he discovers we are sending this. He swore he would eject us into space if we mess up again," Luc repeated as his anxiety grew.

"How is this messing up? We are simply sending a small message," Jon Paul argued.

"Technically, any interference with history could potentially change the course of it," IQ said.

"Bah! Jarmen has been messing with your programming again," Jon Paul replied with a wave of his hand. "I will be careful."

"The video is currently running," IQ stated.

"What? *Oi!* People of Earth...," Jon Paul began.

Luc snorted, interrupting Jon Paul. He stepped in front of the camera. Luc shook his head with disgust and waved his hands in the air when Jon Paul scowled at him.

"*Non! Non!* If you say it like that, they will think they are doomed. You must give them hope, Jon Paul. Not make them believe they are about to encounter the War of the Worlds! *Oi!* You must say it like this... My friends, there are very bad aliens coming on.... What is the date again, IQ? *Oui*, yes, they are coming. We cannot tell you more for fear our uptight friend will eject us into space, but we felt a need to share with you the dangers. And now, we must go."

"Luc, you believe that is supposed to be a better transmission than telling them that a species called the Drethulans are coming?" Jon Paul scoffed, looking at the other man in disbelief as the vidcom faded.

"Of course I think it is better! Now, IQ, you must upload this to the Trivator ship, but you must make sure that it does not go out until... whatever the date these horrible Drethulans decided to attack," Luc ordered.

"IQ, do this. IQ, do that. You two just want *me* to be the one who gets in trouble if this all goes south," IQ grumbled.

Jarmen shook his head ruefully. He was in his own universe now, and as of this morning, that was no longer where he wanted to be.

I'm also a hundred and sixteen years off.

His plan now was to find Jane when she was a child. All this time, everything had been about being with Jane, but finally, after countless failures, Jarmen had started to yearn for a new path—and last night, an alternate version of himself had come to him in a dream. He gave Jarmen two names, a time, an address—and a universe. Jarmen could not see his own Jane again, not even a younger Jane.

There had been flames in the dream. He didn't know if that was related to the story Jane had told him about when she was a child or not. All he knew was there was a sense of urgency to find and protect her when he woke.

He stared down at the planet. This was Jane's home world. This was the home of the members of the Cirque de Magik. Yes, they would have been long gone by now, but it was still important that he do what he could to save Earth before he left.

I need to warn them.

Opening the com to request either Jon Paul or Luc's assistance, he paused when he heard them talking. It appeared his family was once again creating havoc in the multiverse.

"Jon Paul, you better hurry. Jarmen will not be happy if he discovers we are sending this. He swore he would eject us into space if we mess up again."

"How is this messing up? We are simply sending a small message."

"Technically, any interference with history could potentially change the course of it."

He listened with growing amusement as they made a horrible recording that would probably not have any effect. Anyone with half a brain watching the video would probably dismiss it as a hoax.

Still, it is better than me recording it and scaring everyone.

Their hearts are in the right place.

"Yes, sweet Jane, their hearts are in the right place."

He listened to IQ's whingeing with a shake of his head. The file would need to be placed in the Trivator's archives, scheduled to be uploaded to the *Star Raider,* and received by the right people… along with some actual footage of the ongoing battle, if it was to be believed.

He intercepted IQ's transmission, added the footage, and connected with the *Star Raider's* computer system. Ten minutes later, he was guiding the Red Crystal ship along the timeline.

There is just one last stop before I see you. I promise, my love. You will like this gift.

Jane's lilting laughter echoed through his mind. He could almost hear her saying *'Promises, promises.'*

His eyes glittered with determination and sadness. "Oh, I promise. Because our love is too great for death to take you so young."

To hold us apart, she chided.

Jarmen didn't reply.

～

Earth

"I told you to get inside, Vivian," Samuel Davidson snarled.

"Mommy, it will be okay," the little girl murmured.

The child's soft words would have been missed by anyone else, even if they were standing a few feet from her. Vivian, a petite woman in her late twenties with brown hair caught up in a messy bun, scooped the little girl up in her arms.

"Samuel, I can't help it if Mr. Roberts kept part of my check this week. I missed a day," the woman pleaded.

"Shut the—"

The human male's words were drowned out by a speeding car that was blaring music. Jarmen's sensitive ears were ringing from the volume, even from several feet away! He couldn't imagine how the human inside the car could stand it.

He stood in the empty lot across the street from the dilapidated single-story home. The house had weeds growing in the front yard almost as tall as little Jane and paint peeling from the siding.

Samuel slammed the door of the old Ford pickup truck. The woman flinched, obviously terrified of the man. Samuel was carrying two cartons, one in each hand, as he followed the woman and little girl into the house. A quick scan showed the cartons contained alcohol.

"You want Num to go in the house?"

Jarmen shook his head. "No, Num. I think it might be best if I handle this."

"Did you see her? Did you see Jane? She is my size!" IQ exclaimed.

Jarmen sent a silent warning to both robots. He hadn't planned on them coming, but they had refused to stay behind on the ship. He suspected that his protection programming for Jane had taken on a new life.

"What are we going to do, Jarmen? We can't leave her there," IQ said.

"No, we cannot leave her there," he agreed.

He stiffened when the screen door opened, and the little girl slipped out onto the unpainted front porch. She didn't go far. She sat down on the top step. Behind her, the man's raised voice was easy to hear through the screen door.

Jarmen focused once again on the little girl. Susanne Davidson, age four and a half. She was small for her age and far too thin for his liking.

He motioned for the two robots to step back into the shadow of the overgrown brush when a group of teenagers walked past them. One of the boys yelled a crude comment to Susanne, causing the other boys to laugh. Anger pulsed through him.

"Just say the word, Jarmen. I'll toast them and see how funny they think that is!" IQ growled.

"Num step on them," Num offered.

When Jane wrapped her arms around her waist as she had done when he first met her, Jarmen almost agreed. Darkness was falling, and Jane reluctantly rose when her father opened the screen door.

"Get in the house! Didn't I tell you not to go outside?"

"Sam, leave her alone. She's been couped up all day long. Suzy sat real quiet all day in the storage room. Mr. Roberts said I can't bring her to work no more. That a restaurant isn't a daycare. I'm thinking maybe I could clean houses… or office buildings. If I do it in the evenings after everyone goes home, I can take her with me."

"You just want to go out looking for another man," Sam snapped.

"It ain't that, Sam. I promise. It'll be for just a couple of months. Suzy will be five and can start school in the fall."

"I told you, you ain't leaving me, Viv! I warned you about what would happen if you tried!"

Jarmen breathed deeply as Jane slipped between the arguing couple. His fists clenched when the man reached down and shoved Jane between her shoulder blades. The woman's voice rose in anger, and she stepped between the man and Jane.

"Don't you touch her!" Vivian snapped.

"Try to stop me! She should have listened when I told her not to go outside," Sam snarled.

Sam tossed the nearly empty beer can into the tall grass of the front yard. When Sam pulled his belt off with a snap, Jarmen had seen enough.

Vivian's urgent voice telling Jane to go to her bedroom was barely audible before the screen door slammed shut. A second later, the wooden front door closed, and a woman's muffled cry rang out.

"Stay here," Jarmen ordered.

He strode across the empty lot, across the street, and through the broken metal gate. His steps were so light, they didn't make a sound on the cracked, weed-invaded walkway that led to the front porch. He leaped up onto the porch and was through the door less than thirty-seconds later.

The interior of the house was dark, lit only by a single lamp coming from a room off to the side. He walked to the light, following the sound of a belt striking flesh and the muffled cry of a woman. She lay on the dirty kitchen floor with her arms and hands cupped protectively around her head. The man stood over her, his belt-fisted hand raised.

Before the man could strike again, Jarmen moved. His hand wrapped around Sam's wrist, crushing the fragile bones under his grip. Sam's cry of alarm and pain was cut short by the hand he wrapped around the man's throat. He lifted Sam off his feet and held him in the air.

"Go to Jane," he told the woman.

Vivian sniffled and tried to catch her breath. "J-J-Jane?"

"Susanne. Go to your daughter Susanne," he said.

"Who-who are you?" Vivian asked.

He didn't want to frighten her, but he needed her to leave the room for what he was about to do next. This... human... did not deserve compassion. He had killed Vivian in another life and had nearly killed Jane. He would not be given another chance to succeed.

Turning to look over his shoulder, he stared into Vivian's shocked, tear-stained eyes, allowing her to see the full wrath of his anger blazing in his glowing eyes. She gasped and stumbled backwards, releasing a startled scream when gentle hands caught her before she fell.

She looked up into Num's face. Vivian's eyes widened and her lips formed a perfect circle before she fainted. Jarmen nodded to Num.

"Take her to Jane. Where is IQ?"

"He is talking with Jane," Num said. "We wanted to protect her."

The glow in Jarmen's eyes softened with understanding. "You did good, my friend. You both did good."

Num picked Vivian up, cradling her in his arms, and tilted his head to the side. "Good. Because Jon Paul, Luc... and Charon are here, too."

626 appeared in the doorway behind Num. Jarmen raised an eyebrow as she stepped aside to let Num out of the cramped kitchen. Sam's gurgling pulled his attention back to the human who was turning a faint shade of blue under his grip. He opened his fingers and let the man drop to the floor.

"You should be on the ship," he said, not looking at 626.

"Jon Paul and Luc wanted to come, but did not want to leave me alone. I'm not sure if it is because they were afraid something would happen to me or something would happen to them. It would appear that I am now their designated protector on foreign worlds."

He frowned and looked at her. "This is their world."

"Not anymore," she said, stepping up to stand over the man whimpering on the ground. "This male was supposed to be Jane's protector?"

"Who the fu—? Who is Jane?" Sam moaned.

Jarmen squatted in front of Sam. Sam's eyes widened with terror as he got his first real look at Jarmen. The terror turned to horror and confusion when he looked at 626. Jarmen was expressionless when the man wet his pants and frantically scooted backward until he was pressed against the dirty cabinet door.

"Susanne. You hurt her. I will now hurt you," he vowed.

He rose to his feet. The touch of a hand on his arm caused him to pause.

626 shook her head. "Your Jane would not want you to kill him." She turned and looked down at Sam. "Go to her. There is no telling what those bumbling fools are filling her head with. I will take care of this."

Jarmen studied 626... Charon's charged expression. He had never seen her so full of emotion.

He turned to the cowering man. "You will never... ever... harm another woman in your life," he said before he bowed his head to Charon and exited the kitchen.

Behind him, Sam's cry of terror was cut short. He paused in the hallway and closed his eyes. A deep peace settled over him. He... they... had changed the timeline. It just wasn't his own timeline.

Time after time, he had tried to find the magical loop that Zephren had theorized, but each of his calculations had failed. With his last failure, there had been only one thing he could do—set Jane free.

CHAPTER 24

"Who are you? Are you a superhero... like Ms. Marvel on TV?"

Jarmen slowed to a stop outside of Jane... Susanne's room. He looked up at the ceiling, unsure if he had the strength to enter. A movement out of the corner of his eye caught his attention. His reflection stared back at him from the mirror attached to the wall at the end of the hallway. He saw the monster named Jarmen D'ju from *Tales of Two Galaxies,* not the Jarmen that Jane had known.

"Non, fillette, we are not superheroes; but we are your friends. I am Jon Paul and this is Luc," Jon Paul introduced.

"I'm IQ. I'm the smartest robot in the whole universe. That's Numnu—"

"That is Num. He is a very strong robot," Jon Paul hastily added.

"He is. He can carry my mommy. Is she sick?" Susanne asked.

Jarmen leaned back against the wall and listened to Jon Paul quietly reassure Susanne that her mother was fine. She was just tired and taking a brief nap.

"Sam was being mean to her," Susanne murmured.

"Your father will never be mean to you or your mother again, *fillette*," Jon Paul promised.

"He's not my real daddy. Mommy said my real daddy died before I was born because he never acted like this then. Are you going to help my mommy and me?"

"Yes, *fillette*. We will make sure that you and your mommy are safe, eh, won't we, Jon Paul?" Luc said.

"Why don't we just take them back to Kassis with us? We can take care of them there," IQ suggested.

Jarmen closed his eyes and bowed his head. His heart was breaking; and yet, his sense of peace had not abated. She would be saved—in more ways than one. Inhaling deeply, he held his breath for a moment before he sent a silent command to Num.

"Jarmen says you are to make sure Susanne and her mother are taken away from here and to somewhere safe before you return to the ship. He left a bag for them near the front door," Num instructed.

Susanne giggled. "Jarmen. That's a funny name. I like it. Will I meet him too?"

"*Non*. Jarmen... is busy at the moment. He is a very special man, though," Jon Paul replied.

Special... a monster who was destined to love a woman he would never have.

The glow of his eyes in the mirror seemed to mock him believing he could have ever found lasting happiness. After all, hadn't Suzanne in *Tales of Two Galaxies* been ripped from the arms of the monster who loved her?

He shook his head, pushed away from the wall, and strode back the way he came. Pausing by the front door, he pulled a small black bag from his pocket and dropped it. There were enough precious gems in it to take care of Jane and her mother for the rest of their lives.

He pushed open the screen door. Charon had left the front door open and was standing on the front porch. She studied his face before she turned to look at the street.

"The body?" he inquired.

She shook her head. "I've taken care of it. It is amazing what happens to organic material when a laser pistol is on maximum."

He was about to say something when she held out the weapon. He paused, then took the pistol. She started down the steps in front of him. He reached out and touched her shoulder. She partially turned and looked up at him with a raised eyebrow.

"Thank you."

Her lips curved at the corner. It wasn't much, but it was a smile. She bowed her head, turned away, and strode down the path.

IQ, you and Num need to get back to the ship before you are seen, he ordered.

He paused once more at the end of the walkway to look back at the sad, dreary home. He had done what he could to protect his Jane. Hopefully, she would never have to fear for her life again. Turning away, he disappeared into the darkness, knowing he was leaving a piece of his heart on Earth.

The chatter of Luc and Jon Paul alerted him that they had returned. He looked up from the star chart he was studying. He had left Charon and the bots in the galley while he headed for the bridge to begin plotting their course back to Elpidios. He needed to return the Red Crystal ship to Ristéard.

"Everything is taken care of?" Jarmen inquired when the two men stepped onto the bridge.

"*Oui.* Luc and I made up a story that we were lawyers for a distant relative that Vivian did not know she had. We said that her second cousin on her mother's side had died, and there were no other heirs. She did not believe us until we gave her the gems... and a little cash that we had in an old account from before we were kidnapped. It is amazing how much interest it had accrued while we were gone, eh, Luc," Jon Paul said.

"*Oui!* We did good," Luc replied with a grin.

"We helped Vivian pack and called for a ride-share to pick them up. We didn't even know they had such things until she told us. We have been gone a long time," Jon Paul chuckled.

He tried to smile at their amazement but couldn't. "Thank you for your assistance. Please let Charon, IQ, and Num know that we will be leaving within the hour."

"Where will we go now?" Jon Paul asked.

Jarmen looked up from the star chart. "I will return Charon to Ala'-mont to collect her spaceship, then we will return to Elpidios."

"You will not try to reach Jane again?" Luc inquired.

Jarmen stared down at the globe for several seconds before he shook his head. "No. She is safe now, so there is no need. Please prepare for departure."

The journey back to the future was much smoother. He was now more confident about his calculations and how the crystal ship's space/time function worked. Despite the barriers he tried to erect to ensure his solitude, he didn't get it. If Jon Paul or Luc weren't with him, IQ, Num, and even Charon kept him company.

He glanced over at where Charon was sitting. When she first started appearing on the bridge, he had tersely reminded her of his earlier orders. She had ignored him and plopped down in the communication officer's seat that IQ liked to claim. Three days into their journey, he had finally given up on trying to drive her away.

"You know, I could take a look at that formula and see if I can figure it out," Charon commented, draping one leg over the side of the chair and tapping her fingers on the console.

He pursed his lips and shook his head. "No."

"Do you think this Ristéard would lend me this ship?"

He shot her a surprised look before he scowled. "Not in a million years."

She sighed and tilted her head to the side. "Yes. I could see that might not be wise."

He was silent before curiosity got the best of him and he blurted, "Why would you want to borrow the ship?"

Charon studied her fingernails for several seconds before she answered. "I don't know. I... would like to know where I came from before—" She paused and shook her head. "Who am I kidding? I was probably just as broken before the Draka purchased me."

He turned in his seat, his eyes focused on her face. "You remember who you were?"

She lifted one shoulder in a shrug. "Not everything, but enough to piece together that my life before the Draka wasn't any better than after. What about you?"

He lowered his eyelids to conceal his eyes. Jane had said that a person's eyes were a window to their soul. His soul felt raw and exposed. His memories were filled with joy and despair. He had been loved... at least in some of his timelines.

"There is nothing left for me in the past," he said.

"What about your future?"

He stiffened. He suspected that she was asking it more for herself than for him. That was the way he responded, because he couldn't— wouldn't think of his own future. It was too bleak a picture.

"It isn't mine you should be asking about, but your own. What are your plans?" he countered.

She smiled... a genuine smile. "I'm going to hunt down and kill the Draka who did this to me."

"I will help you," he said.

She shook her head. "No. This is something I need to do alone. It's... personal."

"I understand, but you aren't the only one they have hurt."

She grimaced, contemplating what he was saying. When her lips curved and a surprisingly mischievous gleam appeared in her eyes, it was obvious that her time with Jon Paul, Luc, and the robots had an influence on her. He vaguely wondered if perhaps one or both of the men had been playing with *her* programming.

"How much of a hurry are you in to return this ship?" she suddenly asked.

This time he was the one who raised an eyebrow. "As Luc would say... we have all the time in the world."

Her laughter reminded him of Jane. The gnawing ache flashed into pain, and he turned away lest she see the raw emotion in his eyes. He breathed, focusing on the idea of revenge. If he couldn't be with Jane, then he could devote his life to stopping the ones behind her death.

"We'll need to drop the others off first on Kassis," he said.

"Non!"

He turned in surprise. Standing in the doorway to the bridge was Jon Paul, Luc, and the two bots. IQ pushed through the group and rolled over to him. He raised his eyebrows when the little bot placed his hands on his rounded hips.

"If you are going after the bad guys, you need us! We are your crew," IQ growled.

"We are more than your crew! We are your family! And Charon's! If there is going to be justice, then we want to be a part of it," Jon Paul declared.

"Num go, too," Num stated.

"It looks like Marcus's disappearing act will have to last a little longer, eh? Where do we start?" Luc piped in, rubbing his hands together.

Jarmen wanted to protest that the mission would be too dangerous for the group. As Luc once said, he was a lover, not a fighter. The protest died on his lips when he studied the determined expressions on the two men's faces.

"This is what you can expect from the Draka...." he began.

~

Geylur Prime I

"Dr. Labyrinth, I have the reports you requested," Lieutenant Hast said.

Seanna reached for the report and turned away. Her blunt dismissal of Palatine's trusted assistant was on purpose. She knew the General had left Hast behind to spy on her. Ever since she lost communication with Unit 626, his attitude had become more threatening.

She walked into her lab, passing cylinder after cylinder of lifeless rejects. Unit 626 was the only one to survive. She paused in front of one glass tube, laid a hand on the glass, and studied the deteriorating corpse inside. The flesh of the Marastin Dow was peeling off his internal adamantium skeletal frame.

"What made her different? The same process was used for each of you. What made Units 482 and 626 different?" she murmured.

"I don't know about Jarmen, but for me it was revenge."

Seanna stiffened and dropped her hand. In the reflection of the glass, she studied the object of her puzzlement. She slowly turned, sliding her hand into the pocket of her lab jacket where she kept several small but deadly explosives. She stared at Unit 626 through the eyes of a scientist, noting the subtle changes in her experiment.

"You've returned," she said.

"Wasn't I suppose to?" Charon sarcastically inquired.

"Do you require a software upgrade?"

Seanna stepped back when a savage expression crossed Unit 626's face. She silently cursed that the controller for this unit was in her other pocket. Dropping the file in her hand, she shoved her hand into her pocket and pulled it out at the same time as Unit 626 wrapped her hand around her neck.

"Stand down," Seanna choked out, lifting the controller.

Unit 626 smiled. Seanna was shocked! The units were not programmed to smile. They were not programmed for any emotion.

"Shut down authorization—"

Seanna's words were choked off as Unit 626 squeezed her fingers. She depressed the button on the controller. When nothing happened, she pressed it again and again. Darkness edged her vision, and she dropped the controller and clawed at the hand holding her against the cylinder.

"Don't kill her yet. We still need information."

Seanna blinked. Over Unit 626's shoulder, a man with glowing red eyes appeared. She opened and closed her mouth, trying to speak. Her gaze frantically moved to the doorway.

"There is no one alive to come to your rescue. Now, there are a few questions that you will answer."

Seanna tried to shake her head, but a pair of hands—one from Unit 626 and the other from Unit 482—pressed against her temple. A whimper of pain slipped from her as the nanofilaments embedded in their fingers pushed through her flesh.

"No!"

A shudder ran through her when Unit 626 leaned forward and whispered in her ear. Dropping her right hand to her side, she tried to reach into her pocket for the explosives, only to discover they were gone. Her eyes shifted to Unit 482. The gleam in his eyes darkened when he rolled one of the small explosive balls between his fingers.

She knew in that instant that her death would not come swiftly... or mercifully. Closing her eyes, she tried to resist the pair of cyborgs' search for information, but it was a fruitless endeavor. She was no match for the creatures she and her father had created. Monsters who now had names.

"As you die, remember my name. It is Charon."

"There are no other labs. None of the subjects here survived," Charon said.

"Not here, but there were two that survived Ala'mont. They were earlier experiments," he replied, studying the report that had been scattered across the floor.

"I thought you had gone through all the data from there," she said.

Jarmen looked up from the report and nodded. "The data on the computers. This report was not entered into the mainframe. It is from a scientist who left before Teivel destroyed the lab."

"How was he not killed?" Charon asked, looking over his shoulder at the report.

"It seems he faked his own death."

"Where did he go?" she murmured.

"I don't know. A Tearnat named Joren Tralang helped him escape," he replied.

"Uh, Jarmen, Charon, we have incoming hostiles. I think it is time to go," IQ announced over their com systems.

"How many?" he asked.

"I count four cruisers. I have to agree with IQ. I think it would be best to go. Once they start landing, they are bound to sit one of those big ships on the crystal ship, and we may not want to flash our ship's capabilities," Jon Paul answered.

"I think the Draka will receive our message that they are messing with the wrong monsters. Let them stew on it for a while. We should regroup on Kassis in a month's time and plan how we are going to find this scientist. After such an adventure, I could use some down time before we begin the next," Charon stated with a smile of satisfaction.

Jarmen nodded in agreement, glancing at the column of glass cylinders. Yes, they had left a clear message—one that not even the Draka could miss. War was coming... and it wasn't against the adversaries they had been expecting.

General Palatine Namla stared dispassionately at the row of cylinders. He walked by each one, noting from the bits of remaining uniforms the men were wearing who they were. That was the only way to identify the men who had been trapped in the acid.

He paused at the last. Inside was a surprisingly intact specimen. The acid had eaten away the flesh, but the adamantium frame remained. Strips of a white lab coat floated around Seanna Labyrinth's body. He stiffened when her hand suddenly reached out and splayed against the glass enclosure. Her eyes blazed with a bright yellow ring as she jerked back and forth in an effort to free herself from the wires that had caught on the coat she was wearing.

As she struggled, several small metal balls fell from her pocket. He studied them as they fell with a graceful sway toward the bottom of the cylinder. It wasn't until the red light activated that he realized what they were. By then, it was too late.

EPILOGUE

K assis:

Six Months Later

Jarmen swallowed as he navigated his air bike along the winding path to the observatory. It sat like a silent sentinel atop the mountain. He had avoided everything and everyone since his return.

Six months ago, he had returned Charon to her ship on Ala'mont. After that he had taken Jon Paul, Luc, the robots, and the Red Crystal ship to Elpidios. Then, he had disappeared before anyone could stop him.

One month had turned to two and then to six. There had been no need to hurry. So far, the search for the missing scientist had turned up nothing, and he wasn't sure if he wanted to know if the others had a plan to find him. They could message him if it was really important. Jarmen just needed time.

He had spent the past few months exploring a new planet he had unexpectedly found. The new world was more conducive to life than the moon he had originally settled on, and he was contemplating moving to it.

The planet appeared to have been abandoned after an exploding sun had decimated nearby planets. The cosmic debris had created an asteroid belt that would have challenged the most skilled pilot. The reverse polar field had nearly destroyed his ship until he reversed the polarity, pushing the asteroids away from the ship instead of trying to block them.

The asteroid belt was locked by a second, smaller sun that provided the perfect atmosphere for the lush planet that had survived the exploding star. It was a very appealing isolated world with great, empty cities. During his time there, he had only documented one ship coming and going. It belonged to a freighter pilot who never stayed long.

He wished that he could have taken Jane there. She would have loved the beauty of the planet. Pain lanced through him, but he was getting better at dealing with his grief. Whenever it grew too much for him to handle, he would remember the good times they had together. The nights, instead of being the time he thought he would dread the most, were filled with dreams of Jane.

You have given up hope, my love. I told you not to.

Her soft words echoed through his mind. He shook his head. The last month, her voice and the feeling of her presence had grown stronger and stronger until he thought he would rip his own flesh from his body in an attempt to stop the torture.

She's gone! No, she isn't. She is living a happy life on Earth.

He depressed the foot pedal on the air bike and sped up. Jane was alive. She was real. She just didn't know him. She had a happy life without him.

Tears burned his eyes at the thought. He didn't know why he was torturing himself this way or why he was heading to the observatory on Kassis as the stars glittered above. All he knew was that he needed that connection with her—one more time.

Tomorrow, he was to meet Charon. She had information on the scientist and wanted to share it. He had tried to get her to send it to him, but she insisted that it was too dangerous to share it over the com systems in case it was intercepted.

He slowed the air bike as he reached the top of the mountain and coasted to a stop in front of the observatory. Dismounting the bike, he paused and took several deep breaths. He looked up at the sky. Tonight was a brilliant night. The stars shone above in the clear, crisp autumn air.

"I wish you could see this, Jane," he murmured.

Pulling his eyes away from the heavens, he looked at the double doors to the observatory. Memories of helping Jane off his air bike, her cheeks flushed and her hair disheveled from the ride drew him towards the doors. His boots barely made a sound as he crossed the thin layer of gravel.

The doors silently slid open, and he entered the dim interior. As he walked to the center of the rotunda, he studied the stars lighting up the floor. He turned in a slow circle.

"Helma, Darmona… Gamma T'mer," he quietly named as he walked along the lines that connected the three bright points.

Looking up, he followed the patterns of the stars through the glass ceiling. A faint light glowing on the second floor drew his attention. He scanned the building. There was no one there.

He walked over to the staircase and slowly climbed up to the upper balcony. A startled hiss slipped from him when he saw a small table draped in white set up with two chairs. His body trembled with emotion, and he wondered if his mind had finally snapped. He had dreamed of this night so many times.

He walked over to the table. There were three candles flickering in the center. Place settings for two, with crisp white napkins neatly folded on the plates, invited a couple to a romantic dinner.

Pain and rage rose inside him, threatening to choke him. Was this someone's idea of a joke? Shaking at the thought that anyone could be so cruel, he lifted his hand to smash the table only to stop when IQ wheeled out from the shadows.

His eyes widened with anguish as he stared at the small bot. "How could you? Who... who put you up to this?" he choked out.

IQ wheeled forward and held out a single red rose. He instinctively reached for it. Through tear-blurred eyes, he stared down at the exquisite blossom. The petals felt like Jane's skin, and he wanted to crush it against his flesh.

"Don't keep her waiting. She has waited long enough, eh?"

Jarmen blinked and turned confused eyes to Luc. He was dressed in a pair of baggy pants, a white tunic, and wore a strange, tall white hat that sat just a little off-kilter. Next to him, Num stood straight, a towel draped over one arm. He wore a bow tie around his neck.

"Who is— Who—?"

His gaze followed Luc's hand when he waved it toward the staircase. Jarmen walked toward the stairs as if in a daze. He slowly descended, pausing halfway down when a vision wearing a royal blue blouse and white peasant skirt stepped out from behind Jon Paul and looked up at him.

"Jane—" he breathed.

"Jarmen!" she cried, lifting her arms toward him.

~

The Day Before:

Downtown Crystal City

· · ·

"I need to go. I'm making dinner," Jane said, giving an apologetic smile to the group of women sitting in the cafe. "I promised Jarmen I would give him some cooking lessons tonight."

"Now that is true love," River teased.

"You should try showing him how to wash dishes," Jo joked.

She shot Jo a confused expression. "Why?"

"So you can *turn on* the dishwasher!" the three women responded at the same time.

Jane chuckled and shook her head. She rose from her seat and grinned. She would have to remember that line... when she showed Jarmen how to wash dishes.

"I'll walk you out," Star offered, starting to rise from her chair.

"That's okay. I'm just parked over there," Jane replied with a wave of her hand.

"We'll see you later," Star replied.

She smiled and waved a hand before exiting the café. Pausing on the curb, she looked back and forth to make sure the road was clear. The light to cross changed, and she started across. She was almost to the other side when the sound of an air bike revving caught her attention. She glanced up in time to see the bike cross the intersection, heading straight for her. She cried out and froze in terror.

"Jane!" Star screamed.

A figure dressed in black grabbed her and twisted her out of the path of the air bike. They hit the ground with a breath-stealing jolt. She lay stunned, even as the purple-skinned woman who had tackled her rose to her feet. A second later, twin sets of hands reached down and helped her up off the ground as a small crowd of pedestrians gathered around her to make sure she was alright.

Jane twisted and looked down at the ground where she had fallen. She swore she saw a vision of herself lying on the ground. It was as if time had split open for a second and she was seeing what could have happened if she hadn't been saved. She lifted her hand to her head and shook her head to clear it. When she looked down again, there was nothing there.

"Get her to the ship," the woman ordered.

"*Oui*, we will keep her safe."

Jane looked up in confusion. "Jon Paul, Luc… what's going on?"

"We have to get you to the ship, *ma chérie*," Jon Paul said.

"Oh, Jane! You look so alive! Doesn't she, Jon Paul?" Luc exclaimed, wrapping her in a huge bear hug.

She stood sandwiched between them, dazed, but managing to squeak, "What is going on?"

Jon Paul stood back and began ushering her down the sidewalk. She looked over her shoulder, trying to see the strange, purple-skinned woman who had saved her, but she wasn't there. Jane hadn't even thanked the woman!

"It is a tale of love, time travel—" Jon Paul was saying.

"Ferocious little creatures who almost dismantled Num, an assassin who has become part of our family, and Jarmen," Luc finished.

Her heart skipped, and she quit resisting them. "What about Jarmen? Has something happened to him? Is he hurt? Where is he?"

"He is waiting for you," Jon Paul said.

"*Oui*. In the future," Luc added.

"In the future?"

They entered a city park and emerged in a clearing that appeared empty… except for a shimmering red platform. IQ waited at the top, rolling back and forth with a nervous energy. The little bot stopped when he saw them.

"Num! They're here! They've got Jane! Charon did it!"

Jane stumbled to a stop and looked back and forth at the beaming Frenchmen. She took a step back and rested her hands on her hips. The bag containing her purchases bumped against her leg.

"What is going on? What did Charon do? Who *is* Charon?"

"She is the one who saved you," Jon Paul said.

"*Oui.* But she killed you first," Luc added.

"It is a long story, but a very interesting one," Jon Paul promised her with a wave toward the platform.

"We have come a long way to find you, Jane. Jarmen needs you."

Luc's softly spoken words registered through her confusion. She nodded and started walking toward the platform. Her confusion and awe grew as she stepped into the Red Crystal ship.

I wonder if this is where the Wizard of Oz author got the idea for Dorothy's red ruby slippers, she vaguely thought.

~

Near the café:

From the shadow between two buildings, Unit 626 watched with narrow eyes as the two men hurriedly guided her target away. Confusion coursed through 626. She knew she had struck the woman. She had felt the impact, saw her go down, but… Jane was walking away.

626 replayed the scene trying to understand how the woman had survived. The data pouring in did not make sense. Two conflicting scenes were playing out, one overriding the other. It was as if… time had been rewound. There was the moment when she had assassinated Jane… and saved her at the same time!

626 scanned the disbursing crowd, searching for the woman who had looked uncannily familiar.

"Notify Labyrinth that your mission is complete."

Unit 626 swiveled and stared at the woman standing behind her—the woman who was a mirror image of 626.

"Identify yourself," the Unit demanded.

"I will after you notify Labyrinth that your mission was successful," the woman repeated.

"Is Labyrinth working on cloning?"

Unit 626 gripped the long, tubular spear with the sharp, poisoned blade on the end and warily watched the woman step closer. Every feature was identical to hers.

Except her eyes. There is something different about her eyes.

They were the same color and glowed with the familiar red ring around the pupil. Her pallor was a deeper purple. She looked healthier, but it was her eyes that kept pulling 626 back. There was emotion in them. Sorrow and regret could be seen.

And knowledge. She knows something I don't.

"I will ask you one more time. Who are you?" 626 demanded.

"You."

626 snarled and lashed out at the woman. At the last second, the woman twisted away, gripped the spear, ripped it out of her hands, and struck. Looking down, 626 paled at the sight of the embedded spear.

"Shit, that hurts!" the woman hissed.

626 stared in disbelief when a matching wound appeared on the woman's side. 626 groaned and fell to one knee when the woman jerked the blade out.

"I... don't— There is—"

"Poison. I know. I know. I brought an antidote," the woman growled.

626 fell as the poison spread. The woman pulled an injector out of a slender utility belt around her waist and injected herself before she pressed a second dose into 626's neck. The relief from the numbness spreading through her was almost immediate.

626 started to sit up, and the woman pushed her shoulder, forcing 626 to lie down.

"I've got to clean and seal the wound," the woman muttered.

626 lay on the ground, watching the woman work. The woman injected several doses before sealing the wound to facilitate faster healing. Her mannerisms were identical to her own. Cloning was possible, 626 knew, though it had been banned centuries ago due to the short life span of the cloned units.

"How can you be me?" 626 asked.

The woman gave her a knowing glance. "Labyrinth sent me on a mission to kill the woman Jarmen—Unit 482—cared about. I was successful." She paused before she shook her head. "He has a cure for us—you. He cured me. Here take this. It will start the process. I already gave you one dose. He also removed the control device Labyrinth inserted. I'm not sure how much more to tell you, just that if you want your freedom, contact Labyrinth, and tell her the mission was a success; then find the abandoned lab on Ala'mont."

"What happens when I do that?" the Unit asked.

The woman laughed. 626 started. It was the first time she had ever heard herself laugh. Not only that, there was genuine amusement dancing in her eyes.

"Let's just say the rest is history. Listen to the crazy humans, don't mess with the bots, and whatever you do, don't piss off Jarmen!" the woman warned.

"What would happen if I did?" she asked warily.

The woman rose to her feet and held her hand out. 626 cautiously took it. The woman pulled her to her feet and then took several steps back.

"If he doesn't threaten to kill you—which he will want to, but he won't —he might leave you somewhere in time... or worse, some parallel universe with savage tree people. If you don't follow through—you-I may never find our freedom which we do in this timeline unless you-I've screwed things up. I'm hoping that since I'm here, you're going to listen to me," Charon added with a sardonic smile.

When she started to turn away, 626 reached out and gripped the woman's wrist. The woman looked at her with a calm, compassionate expression.

"Who are you—really?"

"I'm Unit 626, but my friends call me Charon."

626's eyes widened at that, and in stunned silence the Unit watched the woman disappear around the corner of the building. She touched her side. Already it was healing, but she also felt different. She scanned her body. The nanobots that were working on her wound were not disintegrating as they usually did. She cradled the precious vials the woman —Charon—had given her.

Lifting a gloved hand, she connected the secure line.

"Mission A complete," she relayed.

"Prepare for Mission B," Seanna ordered.

"Affirmative," she replied with a hint of a smile.

Present Day:

"Are you sure he will be there?" Jane asked, looking at the observatory.

"Yes, he is here. Charon saw him enter a short while ago," Jon Paul assured her.

She ran her hand over the white peasant skirt she was wearing. She was still trying to wrap her head around the fact that she was now six months in the future. Only a few hours had passed for her, and those hours had been strange.

She felt as if she had been locked in a dreamworld. Now that she was awake, she never wanted to sleep again. On the Red Crystal ship, Charon had tried to explain that time travel was an exact science.

"We just haven't quite figured out the 'exact' part yet," Jon Paul had chuckled. "There was a theory that would allow Jarmen to do this, but he never got it to work. Without that, he was unable to change the event that had caused him to time travel in the first place—your death."

Her heart ached for Jarmen. The fact that he thought she was dead, or at least in a place where they would never be together again, broke her heart. Tears burned her eyes when she thought about what it would have been like if their positions had been reversed.

"Come. Let me guide you inside."

Jane followed Jon Paul into the observatory. Her heart was pounding when she saw the empty foyer. What if they were wrong? What if he had disappeared and never returned to Kassis? What if—?

"How could you? Who... who put you up to this?"

Jane looked up when she heard Jarmen's voice.

"Don't keep her waiting. She has waited long enough, eh?" Luc's voice echoed from the upper balcony.

"Who is— Who—?"

From behind Jon Paul, Jane watched as Jarmen slowly descended the staircase. When he was halfway down, she stepped forward, unable to contain her relief.

"Jane—"

"Jarmen!"

Charon peered over the edge of the balcony at the couple below. They were dancing… well, they were swaying together. They were too busy kissing to call the slight movement of their bodies dancing.

She looked over at Jon Paul when he reached the top of the stairs. He was beaming. She straightened and raised an eyebrow at him.

"I'm glad you were right. I was beginning to have my doubts," she confessed.

Jon Paul waved a dismissive hand. "I knew he would come here first. It was a magical night. One does not forget that, does one, Luc?"

"*Non,* one does not forget," Luc agreed with a sigh. "I am glad I made something that will only taste better the longer it sits. I do not believe they are going to want to eat any time soon."

"Well, they might not want to eat, but I do," Charon retorted, turning away.

Jon Paul and Luc chuckled.

"It takes a lot going through time, eh?"

"It takes a lot not getting myself killed by an irate Grand Ruler. For some reason, he doesn't like it when someone borrows his Red Crystal ship," she replied.

"I think you are tired from seeing yourself. You gave your twin quite a shock, eh? How is your side, by the way?"

Charon rubbed her healed side where her present-self had stabbed her past-self. "I've had worse."

"Man, I can't wait to see Jarmen's face when he learns that Stan was able to figure out the Zephren Looptey-loop theory. I guess it took a human to understand all that human gibberish he was drooling over. Whoever heard of Clojure code?" IQ said.

"Well, you will have to wait until tomorrow to see it. He and Jane will be a little busy tonight," Jon Paul chuckled, casting one more pleased glance in the direction of the staircase where soft, romantic music drifted upward.

"How are you here?" Jarmen moaned between kisses.

Jane laughed and caressed his damp cheeks. She didn't know if the moisture was from her tears or his. Her heart swelled as she tenderly kissed him again before sighing and laying her head on his chest. She closed her eyes and listened to his heartbeat for a few seconds before she answered.

"Let's just say we have a very determined family that has grown by one since yesterday," she said with a happy sigh.

He stopped and tilted her head back. She let her love for him shine through.

"I can't believe you would travel through time and space for me! The adventures you went on sounded scary," she said.

"The scary part was being away from you."

"Oh, Jarmen."

She kissed him again.

"When Charon saved me from her past self, and Jon Paul and Luc suddenly appeared and carried me off to the Red Crystal ship—" She paused and shook her head before continuing. "They were babbling about time and space and me dying and having to save me…. It was too much to understand at first. Then, Charon appeared again. She showed me everything. Oh, Jarmen. I was terrified at the thought of losing you, I can't imagine what you must have gone through. I love you so much."

"Our love is too great for death to hold us apart," he quoted, pulling her tightly into his arms and threading his hands through her hair.

A soft sob shook her body. She held onto Jarmen. The vidcom that Charon had shown her had left nothing out, but Jane didn't really understand how the time/space/multiverse worked. She just knew that another version of her was still back on Earth with her mother. She was glad. She hoped that her mother had found happiness, and that Susanne had as well.

Whatever misdeeds Charon had perpetrated, she had more than made up for it by not giving up on finding a way to reunite the two lovers that she had torn apart. Jane ran her hands up Jarmen's back. While it had only been yesterday for her, it had been much longer for him. Tilting her head back, she threaded her hands through his hair.

"Jarmen," she murmured.

"Yes, my Jane."

"I'd like to go home now so I can hold you in my arms."

"I would like that, my sweet Jane. I would like that very, very much."

∾

Planet Raia:

"What have you found out?"

"My sister said there's a huge wedding planned for the end of the month at the Cirque de Magik compound on Kassis," Joren Tralang replied.

"Did she say who was getting married?"

Joren chuckled. "You know who is getting married—Jarmen D'ju to Jane Doe. I guess the timelines are fixed now?"

"Almost. There are a few more that need a little tweaking."

"Aren't you afraid that you might get it wrong?" Joren curiously questioned.

"No. Not anymore."

"What are you going to do next?" Joren asked.

There was a long pause. The silence was broken only by a deep sigh as Joren impatiently waited for a response. The man on the other end of the communication smiled to himself.

"Zephren, are you there? Please tell me that you aren't going to a wedding. You know that you are still being hunted."

Zephren chuckled. "Yes, I think I'll be going to a wedding. Don't worry about me. I have time on my side," he replied with a smile.

Zephren Strauss sat on the platform of the Red Crystal ship he had created so long ago in another time and place, and studied the birds gliding above him. A deep sense of satisfaction coursed through him. His theory had worked. He had finally corrected one timeline, and would help correct the others; but first, he had a wedding to attend.

AUTHOR'S NOTE

Thank you for traveling on this amazing adventure with me. This story about love, loss, family, hope, and never giving up is very dear to my heart, and I hope you'll feel the same!

This is not the end! One thing that made Jarmen's story complex was the multiple series that he was in and the dynamics of the characters. There are always characters that I fall in love with. Charon (Unit 626) is one of them. I can't wait to see what new adventures there will be for the Lords of Kassis, Jarmen, and the rest of my worlds. The next story in this series will be Ajaska's! The King of the Lords of Kassis is about to meet his match! In the meantime, I have many other series to love. Turn the page to discover The Alliance.

When Earth received its first visitors from space, the planet was thrown into panicked chaos. The Trivators came to bring Earth into the Alliance of Star Systems, but now they must take control to prevent the humans from destroying themselves.

USA Today Bestseller!

Alone in a world gone mad with just her younger sisters, Jesse Sampson has learned to use the darkness and the remains of Seattle to keep what is left of her family alive. She has seen the savage side of human nature and found they are not much different from the aliens who conquered the Earth.

Hunter belongs to a unit of Trivators who specialize in quelling violent uprisings. His ability to track and capture is renowned, but he finds the tables turned when he is the one captured by a group of ruthless humans.

Hunter is shocked when a strange human female risks her life to help him escape, only to disappear into the ruins of the city! He now has a new mission: finding the female who saved his life.

Can he convince Jesse that he can give her and her younger sisters a better life on his world? Or will fear keep her from accepting what he has to offer?

If you loved this story by me (Susan aka S.E. Smith) please leave a review! My websites are https://sesmithfl.com and https://sesmithya.com. Be sure to sign up for my newsletter to hear about new releases. Find your favorite way to keep in touch here: https://sesmithfl.com/contact-me/

Recommended Reading Order Lists:

https://sesmithfl.com/reading-list-by-events/

https://sesmithfl.com/reading-list-by-series/

My Genres:

Contemporary / Romance

Girls from the Street

She was born on the streets; he was born to rule.

Science Fiction / Romance

Dragon Lords of Valdier

It all started with a king who crashed on Earth, desperately hurt. He inadvertently discovered a species that would save his own.

Curizan Warrior

The Curizans have a secret, kept even from their closest allies, but even they are not immune to the draw of a little known species from an isolated planet called Earth.

Marastin Dow Warriors

The Marastin Dow are reviled and feared for their ruthlessness, but not all want to live a life of murder. Some wait for just the right time to escape....

Sarafin Warriors

A hilariously ridiculous human family who happen to be quite formidable... and a secret hidden on Earth. The origin of the Sarafin species is more than it seems. Those cat-shifting aliens won't know what hit them!

Dragonlings of Valdier Novellas

The Valdier, Sarafin, and Curizan Lords had children who just cannot stop getting into trouble! There is nothing as cute or funny as magical, shapeshifting kids, and nothing as heartwarming as family.

Cosmos' Gateway

Cosmos created a portal between his lab and the warriors of Prime. Discover new worlds, new species, and outrageous adventures as secrets are unraveled and bridges are crossed.

The Alliance

When Earth received its first visitors from space, the planet was thrown into a panicked chaos. The Trivators came to bring Earth into the Alliance of Star Systems, but now they must take control to prevent the humans from destroying themselves. No one was prepared for how the humans will affect the Trivators, though, starting with a family of three sisters....

Lords of Kassis

It began with a random abduction and a stowaway, and yet, somehow, the Kassisans knew the humans were coming long before now. The fate of more than one world hangs in the balance, and time is not always linear....

Zion Warriors

Time travel, epic heroics, and love beyond measure. Sci-fi adventures with heart and soul, laughter, and awe-inspiring discovery...

Rings of Power

A powerful mage princess and her beloved stone dragon use her father's Rings of Power to explore new worlds—and find a safe haven when danger threatens their existence.

Paranormal / Fantasy / Romance

Magic, New Mexico

Within New Mexico is a small town named Magic, an... <u>unusual</u> town, to say the least. With no beginning and no end, spanning genres, authors, and universes, hilarity and drama combine to keep you on the edge of your seat!

Spirit Pass

There is a physical connection between two times. Follow the stories of those who *travel back and forth. These westerns are as wild as they come!*

Second Chance

Stand-alone worlds featuring a woman who remembers her own death. Fiery and mysterious, these books will steal your heart.

More Than Human

Long ago there was a war on Earth between shifters and humans. Humans lost, and today they know they will become extinct if something is not done....

The Fairy Tale Series

A twist on your favorite fairy tales!

A Seven Kingdoms Tale

Long ago, a strange entity came to the Seven Kingdoms to conquer and feed on their life force. It found a host, and she battled it within her body for centuries while destruction and devastation surrounded her. Our story begins when the end is near, and a portal is opened....

Epic Science Fiction / Action Thrillers

Project Gliese 581G

An international team leave Earth to investigate a mysterious object in our solar system that was clearly made by <u>someone</u>, someone who isn't from Earth. Discover new worlds and conflicts in a sci-fi adventure sure to become your favorite!

New Adult / Young Adult

Breaking Free

A journey that will challenge everything she has ever believed about herself as danger reveals itself in sudden, heart-stopping moments.

The Dust Series

Fragments of a comet hit Earth, and Dust wakes to discover the world as he knew it is gone. It isn't the only thing that has changed, though, so has Dust...

CAST OF CHARACTERS

Jarmen D'ju (Unit 482) destined to be with Jane Doe
Jazin Ja Kel Coradon mated to Star Strauss
Ajaska Ja Kel Coradon – Ambassador to the Alliance; father to Torak, Manota, and Jazin
Torak Ja Kel Coradon mated to River Knight
Manota Ja Kel Coradon mated to Jo Strauss
Jazin Ja Kel Coradon mated to Star Strauss
Gril Tal Mod mated to Madas Tralang
Trolis – Tearnat Warrior/traitor; Gril's son/Madas's stepson; killed by River
Progit – Tearnat Warrior/traitor; killed by River Knight
Armet – Jazin's Captain of the Guard
Shavic – Healer on Torak's warship
Councilman Rai Marc
Councilman Grif Tai Tek – traitor, working with the rebellion
Kev Mul Kar – Torak's Captain of the Guard
Dakar – real name Adron, Kev Mul Kar's brother, spy working undercover as Tai Tek's Captain of the Guard
Ristéard Roald mated to Ricki
Joren Tralang – Madas's younger brother

HUMANS/CIRCUS MEMBERS

Jane Doe
River Knight
Star Strauss
Jo Strauss
Walter Bailey
Nema Bailey
Suzy
Curly
Marvin (alien disguising as a human; Kor d'Lur)
Martin (alien disguising as a human; Kor d'Lur)
Ricki Bailey-Roald
Stan: Computer guru for the circus
Marcus the Magnificent
Jon Paul
Luc
Vivian Davidson
Samuel Davidson

THE HOUSES OF KASSIS

North House – Lead House, ruled by Torak. The Lead House houses the next leader of the House of Kassis and is Torak's primary residence now even though his father is still alive and the leader of Kassis

South House – conference rooms, dining rooms, a medical wing, additional guest rooms for visiting dignitaries, and rooms for entertaining guests

East House – East House ruled by Manota and is known as the Second House of Kassis. It was built almost identical to the North House with only the few modifications requested by Manota.

West House– also known as the Third House of Kassis and ruled by Jazin

TERMINOLOGY

Old Kassisan
"Kil mai ta eff mauway!: *Stop and identify yourself!*
"Ki taka makki: *I come in peace.*

Latin:
dic nomen tuum: Say your name.

HISTORY OF KASSIS

The ancient scripts tell of a time when the people of Kassis were almost made extinct when their world was attacked by a cruel race of aliens who wanted to strip their world of everything that lived.

Zephren, the God of War, his two sons, and three daughters arrived at the Kassisan world thousands of years ago on the night the twin moons of Kassis aligned with one another to appear as one moon. It was said to only happen once every two thousand years. The skies turned a dark purple from the fierce storm that raged in the heavens. Out of the storm, five great ships appeared in the skies over the last remaining cities of Kassis, each commanded by one of the Great Gods and the Goddesses.

It is said that is how the Four Houses of Kassis were formed. It was intended to make the Kassis world stronger.

ELPIDIOS

Ristéard Roald mated to Ricki Bailey – Grand Ruler of Elpidios
Commander Mena Rue – Ajaska's former lover

DRAKA

Unit 626 — Genetically modified assassin for the Draka, Renamed Charon by Luc

General Palatine Namla — Draka Commander

Doctor Seanna Labyrinth — Doctor in charge of Draka research

Lieutenant Hast — Assistant to General Namla

Commander Cerberus Teivel – Commander of the research lab on the moon of Ala'mont; Seanna Labyrinth's father.

ABOUT THE AUTHOR

S.E. Smith is an *internationally acclaimed, New York Times* **and** *USA TODAY Bestselling* author of science fiction, romance, fantasy, paranormal, and contemporary works for adults, young adults, and children. She enjoys writing a wide variety of genres that pull her readers into worlds that take them away.

Printed in Great Britain
by Amazon

21495193R10153